Other books by E. R. Wytrykus:

Novels:
The King of Coins
The Money Run
A Stone To Roll
The Girls of His Dreams
A Road Of Your Own

Short Stories:
By The Short Hairs
The 9th Inning and Other Stories

Screenplay:
The Money Run

"FAMILY TIES"

a novel by

E.R. WYTRYKUS

"FAMILY TIES"

Wheat Field Publications
109 Kiwi Court.
Lincoln, CA. 95648
NDWY2@aol.com

ISBN: **978-0-9839338-1-6**

This book is a work of fiction. Names, characters, places, and incidents are either products of the author's imagination or are used fictitiously. Any resemblance to actual events or locales or persons living or dead, is entirely coincidental.

To my wonderful Family, both near and far

PROLOGUE:

August, 2001

I stood there looking at her, dumbfounded, my face scratched and my hands bloody from clawing at the wall.

The very tall, very pretty blonde smiled at me as if I were her long-lost lover, her tiny dimples, one on each cheek, giving her the slightest cutesy look, a sweet, girlish appeal. Her long hair swept down ending somewhere towards where her back met the curve of her backside. Her legs began way up here and ended way down there.

I'd met her, briefly, and had exchanged polite greetings—'Hello, having a good time?' or, 'How are you today?', and that was about all, although more than once I had the feeling the casual sound bites between us were the prelude to a more significant acquaintance. She had smiled those times, too, her mouth wide and full of teeth almost blinding in their brilliance.

The second day on the river, when the sun appeared on a cloudless day and many of the passengers took to the top deck to tan and warm their old bones—some of them had severely old bones—I saw her stretched out on a lounge chair, wearing a bikini that was probably illegal in several States. She and I were among the handful of passengers that kept the average age below seventy.

Those old fogies kept finding excuses to walk past her, back and forth, getting their exercise, I guess, the first time in years any of them had decided to take up walking as a hobby. Their wives kept calling them back to sit down or take a nap. I only stepped on my tongue once, so I was doing pretty well, I thought, in containing my admiration for Miss Longlegs.

Now I was quite surprised to meet her along the deserted streets of the village of Viviers at a time when most of the cruise ship's passengers were back on board, showering and changing clothes, or having a drink, relaxing and unwinding from a day of traversing the streets of Viviers.

Besides being taller than me she was standing up hill and looked down with a grin that was a combination of Mona Lisa's and Cruella Deville's

"So what are you doing here, Mr. Hardin?" she asked, pleasantly. (She knew my name?!)

My eyes were level with her breasts; if she took another step forward I was afraid she'd poke me in the eyes.

"I, ah, was just admiring... the view," I said, and looked up her. Her smiled widened. She stepped forward and I stepped back, stumbling on the uneven pavement, bricks laid decades ago. I caught my balance by bracing one hand against the wall.

"You should go home, Mr. Hardin," the lady said, "before you get hurt."

Her right hand emerged slowly from the pocket of the thick, woolen sweater she was wearing, a striking off-white and soft tan combination, and when it was out of the pocket it held the gun she had just used. I'm sure it was still warm and still loaded.

ONE: Colonel von der Dusenberger, near Geissen, Germany, March, 1945

The sergeant halted as he neared the colonel's tent, brushed a speck of dirt off his uniform blouse, and reached up to assure that his helmet was on exactly right. To his left, at the edge of the entrance to the tent, a stream of gray smoke twirled upwards from a dented and rusty metal container. As the sergeant glanced down at the smoking can the colonel appeared with a stack of papers in his hand. He nodded to the sergeant, and dumped the papers into the can, feeding the flames.

"Ah, Heinz, come in."

Before he entered, the sergeant scanned the other tents, the makeshift field headquarters that had been hastily abandoned. Most of them were collapsed. On the road a quarter mile away he could see a line of troops double-timing away from the camp.

The sergeant followed the colonel inside, where he stopped, clicked his heels, came to attention and saluted smartly. Even with his mud-stained uniform and a face spotted with grayish pocks from where dirt had become so engrained it wouldn't wash out, the career soldier stood with pride and enthusiasm, always ready and eager to do his duty. The fact that his world was crumbling around him distressed him but it did not allow him to slip in his behavior patterns. It would be difficult for him to adjust to civilian life. Without the military he had no other interests, no place to go. The world might as well go to hell.

"Excuse me, *Oberst*, I am at your service."

"Yes, Heinz, good to see you. Be at ease."

Colonel Wolfgang von der Dusenberger, himself a career soldier, was more casual in dress, somewhat a surprise to the sergeant. His coat was unbuttoned and his hair was mussed. He sensed the sergeant's disapproval and ran fingers through his hair, combing it as best he could.

The sergeant remained rigid out of habit and training as he faced his commanding officer. The air outside the tent was filled with the sounds of the battle closing in on them and Heinz expected to receive his orders soon, if the colonel's plans had any chance of success.

"The staff, sir?" the sergeant asked.

"They have their orders. Lieutenant Holder is to reorganize near the river, as previously planned, and I instructed him that if he hasn't heard from me in two hours, to adjust to the current situation as best he can, and that his orders would be supported by me."

Sergeant Heinz Zimmer stiffened.

The colonel looked at him and frowned. "Don't judge me, Heinz. You think this is easy?"

"No…no, sir, of course not. I…"

"I know what the orders from those bombastic fools in Berlin are, but I also have an obligation to do what is best for my men, else how can I do what is best for my country?"

"Yes, sir, I understand."

"Be at ease, Heinz, please. Our war is nearly over."

Still standing at attention, the sergeant remembered what he had come to tell the colonel.

"Sir, we've received word that the Americans have captured a bridge near Remagen."

The colonel shook his head and frowned. "Fools, Heinz, fools."

"Excuse me, sir? With all respect, you can hardly call the Americans fools for capturing an intact bridge on the Rhine. It will allow them to swarm into…"

Colonel von der Dusenberger looked at the sergeant with a mix of surprise and doubt. Tall and thin, his face was almost gaunt from lack of proper food—not that food wasn't available for officers, but he hadn't had much time to eat or an appetite for weeks. The colonel smiled thinly and gripped Heinz on the shoulder. His aide took everything too seriously and literally. Like many of the soldiers who followed orders and believed the hierarchy, the sergeant believed the Third Reich still had a chance of winning this foolish war. As someone who had followed the progress of the war closely since it began, the colonel had never maintained that belief, other than maybe early on, when victories were easy and often. Even then, he felt the best Germany could hope for was to regain the honor it had lost in the Great War, and take its place among the powers of the world. Defeat the Russians and make peace with the Americans and British, was the best outcome he and most of his fellow officer's hoped for. But now, he knew, his worst fears were being realized.

"No, Heinz, I mean us, our leaders, all of us, for thinking we can still win this…this debacle." He waved his arm outward encompassing everything for as far as they could see or hear through the dirt and dust raised by battle, and in fact, what they could not see

11

from their position just east of the Rhine all the way to the Normandy beaches.

"To think we ever could have won."

"Sir? The Fuehrer is still…"

The colonel cut him off. "Are you still with me, Heinz?"

"Of course, *Oberst*, if you still wish me to be."

"Without a doubt. And soon you won't have to come to attention and salute. We will be equals, Heinz, as soon as we are ou of these uniforms."

"The plane is ready for whenever you are, sir. I, ah…don't understand…"

"Don't understand what, how we'll get away with this?"

"Yes, sir. You do have orders to move east and report to General…"

"Bah!" Von der Dusenberger slapped the air in disgust. "M big mouth, my opinions, they always have gotten me in trouble, haven't they?"

The colonel laughed, a tentative laugh meant more to show disgust with the people he had to take orders from, not at anything particularly funny. Heinz allowed the faintest of smiles to grow on his rugged features and nodded in agreement. As recently as a week ago he would never have indicated agreement with something that everyone knew, the colonel's penchant for saying what he thought, often to the wrong people, but his relationship to the man who had been his commander for over four years was changing quickly. He relaxed slightly from his formal stance.

"Do you know what will happen to us if we have to fight on the Russian front, Heinz?"

The sergeant was quite aware of what the likely result would be but he remained silent.

Colonel von der Dusenberger nodded as he answered himself.

"We will die, Heinz, we will die! Either from a Russian bullet or in one of their prison work camps. You probably before me, as they'll put you to the task of rebuilding the roads we destroyed, working you from before sunrise until after sunset, until you die of exhaustion. Then some other starving prisoner will be pushed into your place until he, too, collapses and is smashed into the mud."

The noise of artillery became louder and more frequent, the sounds drawing nearer by the minute, an indication as to how quickly we are losing the war, Heinz realized. The squeal of a low-flying airplane momentarily drowned out the colonel's voice.

"You..." The colonel stopped, as both he and the sergeant held their breath, waiting for an explosion that might put a quick end to any plans they had. The plane soared away and they heard a thump—possibly a dud. The colonel took a breath and continued.

"You have destroyed all the other papers, I trust," he asked, "besides what I had here?"

"Yes, sir, I've done everything as you instructed," replied Heinz, a bit disappointed that the colonel would even need to ask.

The colonel reached under the desk and came up with a crystal carafe. The bottom half inch of the carafe contained an amber liquid. He reached down again and retrieved two brandy snifters. He poured the liquid into the glasses, just enough for a taste for each of the two men. The colonel handed a glass to the sergeant.

"To us, Heinz, and the future."

The sergeant clinked his glass against the colonel's and drank the brandy, as did the colonel. They put their glasses on the desk next to the carafe.

"I'll leave these as a gift to whomever captures this tent, ha!"

"Let us be on our way, Heinz. By the time anyone realizes that I…we, have not reported, and by the time they realize our bodies haven't been found, and by the time they realize the allies haven't taken us prisoner, the war will be lost and we will thousands of miles away, far from this idiotic war. It is going to be chaos compounded by panic in the next few days, Heinz. You are lucky at this time in your life not to have any family. It will make it easier for you."

The sergeant was taken aback for a moment by the colonel's mention of 'thousands of miles'…he thought they were going to Switzerland.

"Yes, sir. And Frau von der Dusenberger?" It was a daring question for a subordinate to ask. If the colonel was serious about their eventual equality in status with each other, he would show it now.

The colonel looked sharply at the sergeant as they walked towards the car. Above them the aqua sky's beauty was antithetical to the dull booms of distant explosions and occasional sharp blasts of the nearer artillery shells that shook the air and reverberated in the sky. Birds flew in confusion or tried to hide in trees that too often were blown apart by a direct hit. The lives lost in this fury were not only human ones.

Colonel von der Dusenberger hated being reminded of Ruth and their young son, Maximilian. Even now he wasn't sure exactly how things would work out. He honestly believed it was safer for Ruth to not know anything about his plans, in case she was interrogated. Later, much later, he'd try to get them out, her and the boy. But with his past history with the Nazis, it would never be safe for him in Germany, or anywhere in Europe. Who knows, his family could even now be dead, buried under the bricks of pulverized buildings.

"Frau von der Dusenberger…I'll need time to arrange for her and the boy. I may need your help, Heinz."

"Of course, sir, always at your service."

The colonel stopped as they reached the car. He looked at the empty driver's seat.

"You dismissed him?" he asked the sergeant.

"Yes, sir. I thought it better to do it earlier."

The colonel nodded approval. "Good thinking. The clothes?"

"In the car, sir."

"And…?"

The sergeant stared at his colonel, respectful of him, as he had been all these years of war, but still fearful.

"The gol…it is all packed in the plane, and the plane is guarded by someone I trust. He does not know what's in there."

Colonel von der Dusenberger nodded and smiled, and patted the sergeant firmly on the shoulder, and holding it for a moment, a rare show of warmth.

"Well done, Heinz, well done. Let us go then, to Zurich, and our freedom."

The sergeant got into the driver's seat and the colonel in the rear, where he began to take off his uniform. Next to him on the seat were civilian clothes: a suit, shirt, tie, everything to make him look like a respectable businessman. He began to change clothes.

"Your French is still manageable, Heinz?" the colonel asked

Heinz nodded. "Yes, sir. I had opportunity to speak French frequently in recent years. I am capable in Italian, also, sir."

The colonel laughed lightly. "Yes, yes. Life was good while we were in Paris; those were excellent days, yes, over all too soon. We were spoiled by all the wonderful French wines, no?"

The sergeant started the car as the clamor of the war came closer every second. The roar of the explosions drummed in Heinz's ears and overwhelmed the sound of the engine as the two men drove off. Trusted though he was by the colonel, the sergeant had not yet been told that the trip would not end in Zurich, but if successful, would find them in South America, where they would have the opportunity to begin new lives with new identities.

As Heinz maneuvered along the muddy road, a road in name only, one not on most maps and not likely to attract the attention of Allied dive-bombers, Colonel von der Dusenberger suffered slivers of doubt.

He'd been a loyal soldier, a loyal husband (even with all the distractions and attractions an officer is exposed to), and a loving father. He thought of the boy and promised himself that he would find a way to see that his son was taken care of. He thought of Ruth, a fine wife who had always come second in his life to his career. She had known how it would be and while he said repeatedly that he would find more time for themselves, once the war came the colonel knew it was a promise he couldn't possibly keep. Now, it was either the Russian front and sure death or imprisonment, or escape and trus that his family would survive until he could send for them. Capture by the Americans would be better than a Russian gulag, but with his record, his fate would surely be prison, or worse. It was hard to tell what the allies would do, how angry they would be and what revenge they would extract.

And amid these ruminations his instincts told him that he never would send for his wife and son. It would be years before it would be safe to even try and by then he would have been given up for dead and Ruth would be with someone else. Maybe the boy would have a new father. Later, perhaps he could find a way to help…perhaps.

A jolt thrashed his daydreams and bounced the colonel so hard his head hit the roof of the car.

"Sorry, sir, a hole I couldn't avoid in time."

Von der Dusenberger didn't say anything. He was relieved it had only been a pothole and not a bomb. For an instant he pondered that maybe it would be better if a bomb did hit the car, then he would be truly dead and not a traitor and a coward. Ah, but I'm already in civilian clothes—they'd know I was running away.

"How much farther?"

"Just a minute more, colonel. I can see the plane from here."

"When we get to the plane, Heinz, dismiss the guard. I don't want him to see me out of uniform."

"Yes, sir."

"And you, Heinz, you have clothes for yourself?"

"Yes, on the plane."

"Good, good, Heinz. You have been a good aide. I could not have asked for anyone better. I trust we will have many more years working together."

"As you wish, colonel."

The colonel had changed from his uniform while bumping along as Heinz drove. For a man who had spent more time in uniform than out, it was like changing his skin, the way a snake throws off the old to prepare for the new. But the snake is what it has always been, a snake, and it can't change what it is and wouldn't want to. For the colonel, though he was sure he was doing what was best for he and his family, he felt a bit like a snake, no longer like a loyal soldier.

As with many soldiers who had worked for and obeyed officers without question for years until it became routine, Heinz could not conceive of a time where he and the colonel would be on an equal footing, without him having to salute and jump at the colonel's commands. Doing his officer's biding did not bother him. It was the life he was used to and the life he wanted. He wasn't sure he could function outside the military. What Heinz wondered was what would happen when they reached the plane. Heinz could drive but he could not fly—the colonel could. So why did the colonel need Heinz? And did the colonel really think they could stay safe and hidden in Switzerland for very long? Surely people will come looking for them.

TWO: Max
Berlin, May, 1945

The boy shuffled his feet in the dust, kicking at rocks and bits of concrete, which were in fact, bits of buildings that had been bombed to rubble. His mother tugged on his arm, urging him to hurry.

"Mach schnell! Es wird dunkel!

It was late in the afternoon and between the cloud cover and the dust that hovered overhead like a dirty blanket, the light was dissipating quickly. The mother and child, a boy of about eleven or twelve years of age, needed to find shelter for the night. They hurried along, their movements kicking up even more dust. Ash and harsh concrete dust drifted down as another tottering wall, a relic of a building that once was, fell to the ground. Then, often before they settled, the particles were churned upward and in spirals by vehicles and foot traffic. The ash muddied puddles of water, the residue of the useless effort by firemen trying to fight the flames that had engulfed so much of the city, and it caused the skin to itch and the eyes to water.

Home these days was in whatever ruins the woman and the boy could find a safe nook—safe from the elements but even more important, from other homeless and starving people who wouldn't hesitate to take from a skinny woman and a scared child. It wasn't long ago that the woman and her boy lived in one of the nicer homes in Berlin, along with her husband, who had been away for many months, fighting somewhere. Day by day the woman and the boy were working their way back to whatever remained of their house.

On February 3, 1945, hundreds of bombers of the Eighth Air Force attacked the Berlin railway system to prevent the German Sixth Panzer Army from moving by train to the Eastern Front. Several districts were severely damaged. The intense bombing caused a conflagration that was spread by the wind and lasted for days.

Three weeks later another raid destroyed thousands of homes. The neighborhood in which the von der Dusenberger family lived was virtually pulverized by the endless stream of bombs, tons and tons of flying destruction. Most of the bombs were meant for a munitions factory several miles away. Sadly, strategic bombing was not nearly as accurate as the planners would like people to believe. I was by God's hand or shear good luck that the woman and the boy had escaped with their lives. The only thing they saved as they dashed from their home were the clothes they were wearing. Ruth still could see in her mind's eye the flames erupting all around the house as she dragged the boy to safety.

It wasn't as bad now as it had been a week ago, before the Americans rolled into Berlin. The fighting had ended, for the most part. Occasionally a fanatic sniper who wouldn't give up took shots at the Americans, but he was soon killed. The victors could be both merciful and brutal, sometimes both within the time it took to turn one's head. The conquerors brought food and water and clothes, not enough yet for everyone, but they had no patience with snipers. No more prisoners were taken. Snipers and looters were treated as common criminals and shot on sight.

Some days the mother could get food from the soldiers at distribution centers, and it would last her and her son for a day, or two if she ate little herself. She was afraid to stay overnight at shelters because she'd heard terrifying stories of the soldiers taking the boys and shooting them, lest they grow up to be another Hitler. It was a ridiculous suggestion, yet, she was afraid to take the chance. She also feared what the soldiers might do to her. She'd heard horrible stories from people moving away from the eastern front, from where the Russians were advancing. She didn't think the Americans and British would act like monsters, but no one could be sure how angry they would be over this war. She'd lost her husband and all she had now was the boy, Max, and all he had was her.

It was late in May when they returned to the ruins of their neighborhood. Looking at it now, in the light of a day without bombs dropping and without a constant cloud of dust blocking the sun, their house looked to be in relatively good shape compared to the rest of the neighborhood. She saw shadows slitter among the brick walls and charred boards that represented the sad remains of many of the formerly beautiful homes, sentinels proclaiming the near total destruction wrought by thousands of bombs. The dark shadows might be the original residents or squatters who took shelter wherever they could find it. She wished she had a gun for protection.

Ruth was equally amazed to find that a few houses had survived virtually intact, including hers, almost like a solitary palm tree on a sandy beach that had outlasted the hurricane winds while all the other trees were uprooted and ripped apart. Possibly the reason no one had moved into the house was because people in the area knew it belonged to a high-ranking officer and his family, and they might return any day.

The door was unlocked, just as she had left it when she and Max had run for their lives that terrifying night several weeks ago, when the deafening blasts of the bombs and the heat of the flames engulfed dozens of city blocks of homes. She and the boy had fled wildly and even now she wondered how they had stayed alive under the rain of bombs.

Ruth stepped quietly into the house, after telling Max to wait outside. She called out, lest someone be lying in wait. And if there was someone, would they believe that this was her house? If only Wolfgang were here. Most of the windows were shattered, the floors were covered with dirt and debris that had blown in, and the fireplace was as cold as the brick floor. There was food in the pantry, cans of beans and packages of pasta and dried fruit, enough to keep the two of them fed for months. There was no electricity and no heat and no running water, but the roof appeared to be intact, unlike most of the nearby houses.

The first thing the mother did was to package up some food in her shawl and set it by the door, in case they had to leave in a hurry. Next she went for water, to the old well in the backyard. It was a relic from before the neighborhood had modern plumbing and was more of a conversation topic than anything else. She feared it would be destroyed but except for a few bricks that had been blasted loose, it was serviceable. She and the boy brought the bucket up several times and filled containers they found in the kitchen with the well water. There was debris in the water but nothing they couldn't deal with. Next she looked for wood and matches, to get a fire going.

By the time night fell Ruth had been able to make soup, which was the first hot food she and her son had eaten in many days. The boy even smiled as he ate his dinner. Tomorrow we will clean the house and ourselves, the mother told the boy.

In the bathroom Ruth stared into the mirror. Two long cracks ran from top to bottom and she was amazed that the entire piece of glass had not fallen out of its casing. She looked at a face she hardly recognized. It was thin to the point of sickness, her skin gray, her eyes dull, almost lifeless, her hair tangled with dirt. She began to sob, but her body was so tired it couldn't even produce tears. She coughed from the itch in her throat, a common ailment lately as the air was always filled with dust from crashing buildings or from the dirt kicked up by passing vehicles.

In the following weeks activity around the neighborhood increased. People were returning and beginning to clear the rubble, which included knocking down whatever teetering walls had not yet collapsed, to prepare to rebuild. The Americans came with more food and clothing. Traffic, mostly American Army vehicles, became regular sights and sounds. It had become assumed that Frau von der Dusenberger and her son belonged there and no one questioned them. Still, the woman worried that some day the Americans would order them to leave.

And sure enough, one day two American soldiers came by. The boy was playing outside, whacking a stick against the fence and hitting stones with the stick, simple games, since he had no toys. His mother was inside the house, cooking. The soldiers came into the front yard and the boy stopped his play and stepped back in fear.

They carried rifles slung on their shoulders and both were tall and towered over the boy. Unlike some of the other soldiers the boy had seen, whose uniforms were dirty and who looked like they hadn't shaved or bathed in weeks, these two were clean-shaven and their uniforms were crisp and clean.

"What's your name, son?" one of the soldiers asked. The boy didn't understand him.

"Name," he said, giving a German accent to the word. He pointed to himself and said, "My name is John." The boy repeated, "John", and looked at the strip on the soldier's uniform shirt which spelled out the soldier's last name.

"My name is Bill," the other soldier said.

The boy understood and pointed to himself, "Maximilian," he said with a grin.

"Okay, Maximilian, now we are your friends. Ah, freunde, friends?"

The boy nodded his head but still kept his distance.

"General?" the boy asked, the word coming out like 'Zeneral?'

"What's that? Oh, no, no, I'm a lowly lieutenant, the soldier named Bill said.

"And this lug, he's even worse; he's a mere sergeant," he added, pointing to the soldier named Schneider.

"Do you live here, Maximilian?" The lieutenant asked, pointing to the house. The boy looked back at the house, then nodded. He pointed to the house and said, "*Mutter.*"

"Your mother?" asked the sergeant, also pointing to the house.

Just then the door opened and Frau von der Dusenberger came running out. She ran to Max and pulled him towards her, hugging him with both arms. She was scared and her heart beat fast as she spoke, afraid they were either bringing her bad news about her husband, or telling her she and her son had to leave the house.

"*Was wollen Sie?*" The soldiers didn't understand, but they both politely took off their helmets.

"*Guten Morgen, Frau,*" the lieutenant said, trying his best to use the spattering of German he'd learned in a crash course and had otherwise picked up in the weeks he'd been in Berlin.

With bombing raids at an end, and the house cleaned, Frau von der Dusenberger had had the opportunity to clean the dirt out of her hair, to bathe, and had eaten regularly, stout foods and fresh bread. She had been quite pretty before the war and with regular food she was again an attractive woman, still a bit skinny but with a healthy glow on her face. The soldiers were both taken by her good looks, and when she smiled in an attempt to show that she was wasn't afraid of them, they returned the smile.

"Ah, is there anything you need? Food, clothes?" When the woman didn't answer, the sergeant opened his mouth and moved his hand towards it, saying, "food?" then he tugged at his shirtsleeve and said, "clothes?"

Frau von der Dusenberger shook her head and said, "*Willkommen,*" and gestured with her hand for them to come into the house.

"Thank you," they said in unison. "*Danke.*"

As they moved to enter the house the boy looked at them and pointed to each in turn. "John," he said, then, "Bill".

The men laughed. "Yes, that's right, Max."

"*Geh draußen und spiel*, Maximilian," the mother ordered the boy. "*Wenn du laute Geräusche oder Schreien hören, Hilfe suchen.*"

The boy obeyed and went outside. The mother was still a bi apprehensive about the two soldiers and wanted Max to be ready to run for help if she needed it. She'd heard that the American soldiers were looking for women to take to bed, and that some women did grant sexual favors in exchange for food or clothing. She could hardly blame them; were she and Max still living from day to day in the ruins of bombed-out buildings, she would have done whatever she needed to do in order to keep Max alive.

Inside, the house was cleaned and organized, and what furnishings remained looked to be of high quality. The MPs were sure they had come upon the wife of the German officer they were looking for, and maybe she knew where he was. Likely, though, any high-ranking Kraut soldier who'd been on the Eastern Front was stil being held prisoner by the Russians, or was long dead.

"Your husband?" the lieutenant said. "*Mann?*"

The woman considered saying that her husband would be home soon. Outside she could hear vehicles passing by, jeeps and trucks, and she heard the voices of people and she decided there was no chance these men would try to take advantage of her with so much activity around. Still, they might come back at night.

"*Mein Mann? Ah, ich glaube daß er tot ist.*"

"I think she said he's dead," said the Sergeant Schneider.

"Sorry, ma'am, ah, Frau."

They were all still standing, the men unsure what to do and the woman unsure if they intended to stay or what they really wanted. What they did know is that they were two tired young men who at this point were just elated to be in the company of a young, pretty woman, whether she spoke German, broken English, or pig Latin.

The sergeant stepped forward and offered his hand. "John," he said. The lieutenant did the same and gave his name, "Bill." The woman shook their hands tentatively, her fingers swallowed in the callused hands of the soldiers. "Ruth," she said as she nodded to each man.

"*Setzen Sie sich bitte hin,*" Ruth offered, indicating a dark green sofa whose cushions looked like they'd been used for shotgun target practice, but they were clean. The men sat, not that they worried how clean the sofa was, having spent several months sleeping in mud.

"*Ich bereite Tee zu,*" Ruth said. The men weren't sure what she meant so they waited quietly while she disappeared into an adjoining room, which they could see into and determined was the kitchen. They heard the rattle of dishes and soon the whistle of a teapot.

"Tea," said Bill, "I think she said she'd make tea."

"I'd rather have a beer," said John.

"It's nice, though, sitting here, isn't it?"

The sergeant nodded. Both men rose when Ruth returned with a tray holding the teapot, three sets of cups and saucers, and a plate of cookies.

"Here, let me help you with that," Bill said. He took the tray from her and put it on a table that set in front of the sofa.

"*Danke.*" Ruth poured tea and sat down in a chair opposite the men.

The three sat quietly, sipping their tea, not sure what to say, all feeling the incongruity of the situation, two soldiers who only weeks before had been killing Germans, maybe even had killed this woman's husband, and now they were sitting in the living room of a frau, (or was it fraulein? Bill wondered), sipping tea. They felt slightly ashamed that they were actually looking for this woman's husband, if he was till alive, in order to arrest him. But at this moment, they didn't want to find him.

"The guys could see us now!" said the lieutenant, laughing. Sergeant Schneider also laughed and Ruth smiled broadly, not sure if they were making fun of her, or talking about what they'd like to do to her—with her—rather than sip tea.

The door banged open and the boy stomped in. He stopped and looked at the adults. It had become quiet inside and he had begun to worry.

"*Alles in Ordnung?*" he asked. His mother nodded. "*Ja. Möchtest du etwas Tee?*"

Max nodded and his mother went into the kitchen, returning shortly with a cup into which she poured tea. The boy took the cup and sipped his tea, enjoying the opportunity to copy the adults.

"*Haben Sie meinen Vater umgebracht?*" the boy asked, looking at the soldiers.

"Maximilian!" his mother cried. "*Das ist sehr unhöflich! Entschuldigst du sich bei ihnen!*"

The boy frowned and lowered his head. He hated to be scolded by his mother, sorry to have said anything wrong, but he thought the soldiers were here with news about his father.

"*Entschüldigen Sie mir, bitte,*" Max said, meekly. He put down his cup and went back outside.

"What was that all about?" asked the lieutenant.

"*Sein Vater,*" said Ruth.

"*Vater?*" repeated John. Ruth nodded.

"The kid thought we had news about his father, is what I think," John said.

"Maybe he thinks we killed him," said the lieutenant.

The sergeant looked at him, said, "Maybe we did, who knows. I think we should go." He rose and turned to speak to Ruth.

"*Danke,* ah, for the tea." The lieutenant bowed slightly. "Ah, may we visit again? Ah, what am I trying to say, John?"

"Tell her you got the hots for her, Bill!"

Bill slapped John on the arm, which startled Ruth.

"Oh, sorry." He laughed, as did his pal. "We're just funnin'."

The men made to leave and Ruth walked them to the door.

"*Sie sind willkommen, wieder zu besuchen,*" she said.

The men backed out and put their helmets on, passing the boy as they left the yard.

"What'd she say there at the end?"

"I think she said we could come again," said Sergeant Schneider. "Me, anyway!"

"Forget it, dreamer! She was looking at me the whole time!"

Ruth von der Dusenberger was indeed the wife of a German Army officer, Colonel Wolfgang von der Dusenberger. Her husband was fairly wealthy in his own right in the sense that he had inherited wealth and a military family history. It was also widely rumored that he had accumulated vast quantities of booty from France and Belgium, when the German armies had overrun those countries. Along with the fate of Colonel von der Dusenberger, the disposition of his rumored wealth was unknown as the war wound down and the Allied armies took control of Germany.

With the fighting over, Ruth desperately wished to hear from, or about, her husband. Had he survived? Was he a prisoner? Should she wait for him? What to tell the boy?

She made inquires to the Allied authorities regarding prisoners-of-war, but there was no record of her husband, nor a record of his death with either the Americans or the Germans. He had simply disappeared, probably shot dead and trampled in the mud of the Russian plains. Or possibly a worse fate, slaving away in a beastly Russian prison camp. She shook her head vigorously whenever such images entered her mind. All she could do was take care of her boy, and to that end she worked helping to clear rubble so rebuilding could begin. The boy worked along side her.

The trouble is, even when the rubble was cleared from the streets, it simply made for larger piles of concrete, burned wood, glass, and metal twisted like so many pretzels. There was no money to actually build new homes or stores, little food, and a lack of men to do the heavy work.

The victorious soldiers helped to some extent, but like with every Army, there were good soldiers and bad ones. Luckily for

Ruth and Max they were taken under the wing of two soldiers who were not using the end of the war to take advantage of helpless women.

Not to say they weren't looking for a bit of fun and relaxation after a year of crawling their way from the Normandy beaches to this formerly great city. There was something, however, about the woman and the boy that confused them. It must have been the idea that in this war there were people who you thought of as the enemy, who really weren't so awful once you met them. And, how can you blame the boy, even if you blame the adults? He didn't start the damn war!

The lieutenant and the sergeant continued to visit Ruth von der Dusenberger on the pretense that they were searching for her husband, which, truth be known, they were, though not as diligently as they should have been. Colonel von der Dusenberger was known to be a member of the National Socialist Party, a Nazi, and was wanted for questioning regarding war crimes, specifically the murder of prisoners of war, and the looting of national treasures. Ruth, in turn, wanted news of her husband, but also realized that if he was found alive, the Allied Army would surely arrest him.

The weeks passed swiftly and the Americans soldiers visited often, using their search for German officers wanted for questioning as their excuse, but also on their free time. They politely sipped tea, practiced their language skills and taught Ruth some English, played with Max, and helped repair the house. Both men were attracted to Ruth, and she to them. After a while she began to accept that her husband wasn't returning, but even if he did someday…

Eventually, she made her choice, or at least she came to a realization, a mere gesture of affection… an affectionate kiss for the one while holding his hand for longer than was necessary, and a mere hug for the other. Eventually, the lieutenant began to visit without the sergeant.

Most of the American soldiers were eager to get home by Christmas, especially once the war in the Pacific was over and they knew they weren't going to have to invade Japan. However, John and Bill weren't in a rush. Both were orphans and had no one special waiting for them back home. Bill had another reason, and soon he was considering how he could arrange to marry a German woman, and bring her and her son home with him. Among the problems, though, was that he wasn't sure yet whether the woman was a widow, nor was she sure. And he was supposed to have been looking to arrest the woman's husband, a task he had mixed feelings about.

If he found that Colonel von der Dusenberger had been killed, Ruth would be free. If he didn't find the colonel, Ruth might feel she had to wait to see if he would return from wherever he was, probably a Russian prison camp. And who knew if would survive, or when the Russians might release him. To herself, Ruth wondered if Wolfgang had made an escape, and any day he would contact her and make arrangements for she and Max to come to him.

Posing a hypothetical question to his superior, the lieutenant was told by his major, 'in no uncertain terms' was anyone going to marry this woman anytime in the near future, not with her husband still at bay. Tell your hypothetical friend to forget the woman. The lieutenant then considered the possibility of returning to Germany once he was mustered out of the army.

Wolfgang thought she was ignorant, but Ruth knew her husband had supported the Nazi party, and she recalled him speaking of the treasures being looted in the conquered cities as the German army advanced across western Europe. She never paid serious attention to her husband's business, figuring it was either political or military, and none of her concern. She knew, too, that he had financial resources he had wisely kept in Switzerland, and if he had managed to get there, soon he would send for her. In the mean time, well, if he is dead, the American was pleasant company and would make a good father for Max. And as the weeks went by more and more aid from the victorious armies was coming to help the people. It was a surprise as most of the German people did not expect any sympathy or help from the allied forces that had defeated them.

As the weeks went by without word about her husband's fate, the more Ruth began to think in practical terms about how she was going to care for her son. Especially because of her condition.

One day Ruth realized it had been a week since Bill had come to visit. She became worried. What if he, too, abandoned her and Max? She had the house, but little money. She'd have to find work, and she'd never had to hold a job while she was married to Wolfgang. There had always been plenty of money when her husband was around. For all she knew there might be assets available to her but she had no idea how to access them.

Ruth touched her stomach. She had planned to tell Bill the next time he came to visit. He was a good man and she was sure that when she told him she was pregnant, he would stay with her, or maybe arrange to take her and Max to America.

It was the other one, Bill's friend, Sergeant John Schneider, who came to the house. Her first thought was that Bill had been hurt by one of the old bombs that were frequently exploding in the wreckage of the cities

"Ruth, I'm sorry, but we are being sent home. I mean, I'm not sorry to go home…the orders came suddenly. Bill has an assignment and can't get here. He sent me to tell you that he'd come for you as soon as he was out of the Army."

"Why couldn't he come himself?" Ruth asked in her primitive English.

"It's just…it's the way things sometimes happen in the Army…he has orders to go to Brussels and he didn't get ten minutes to get ready. From there he has to go to London. I expect to meet him there, so I can take a message if you…have one."

Ruth nodded, the sadness in her rising to permeate the room. She ran a hand over her stomach and considered telling John about the baby, but she was afraid it might scare Bill off, if it wasn't too late for that already.

She slumped down into a chair, and forced a smile. She reached out to John who returned her touch, a gesture of friendship that they both suspected was a final goodbye. He wished he was the one she wanted.

"Tell Bill…I will wait for him. I'll be here."

Having the American soldiers look after her had given Ruth a sense of safety. Now, she was worried how she and the boy would manage. She couldn't even be sure she'd be here if Bill did return. She couldn't be sure if her husband might show up, or if she'd have to find another place to live depending on what work she found.

Why would Bill return, once he goes back to America? He probably has a girl there and will quickly forget about me. Ruth wasn't sure of anything. She hoped the end of the war would bring calm and steadiness to her life, but instead it was still full of worry and uncertainty. She stood up and walked John to the door.

"I…I have been fortunate to have met such fine young men as you two. I'm sorry it had to end so suddenly."

John smiled at Ruth. A quick thought passed through his mind that there must have been thousands of relationships that had developed during this insane war that obviously couldn't have happened without the war. Bill and Ruth weren't unique.

"The war wasn't your fault, Ruth."

"Sometimes I feel like it was."

Bill kept his promise. A civilian now, he did return to Berlin, although it took him nearly a year to manage it. He'd written twice to Ruth but had never heard anything from her. When he found the house it was empty. It took him the better part of two days to find someone he could converse with well enough to find out what had happened to Ruth. He assumed her husband had returned and they had moved away, but he needed to know.

The story he heard was chilling. Ruth had become pregnant, a gray-haired neighbor woman explained to Bill. As she told him this she eyed him as if she was accusing him, not merely explaining. She assumed no American would have come back here months after the war for a woman unless he'd already known her intimately.

"What is your interest in this woman?" the lady asked. "You are the second man who has come looking for her."

"Was her husband here?" Bill asked, assuming that's who the lady meant. Between the language skills he picked up while he'd been in Germany, especially from conversations with Ruth, and the woman's bits of English, they managed to converse.

"No, someone else, I think he was military."

"In uniform? German army or American?"

"No, not in uniform, but he had that stern, military look. He said his name was Heinz. When I told him what happened to the woman he asked about the boy. You should have come sooner, you might have saved her," she said, pointedly letting Bill know the burden of guilt lay on him.

"What do you mean, save her? Was she hurt?"

The old woman shrugged. She struggled for the words, mixing English and German. Bill stumbled along with her, trying to understand what she was telling him. Eventually she directed him to a hospital, and it took another several hours before he could obtain the story. After all, who was he to ask about a German woman who had come to the hospital in an ambulance, bleeding and screaming, ready to give birth?

Apparently she had fallen down the stairs to the cellar. Maybe she had tripped on a broken riser, one that had been weakened by bombings. Besides internal injuries she suffered a broken leg. The boy, Max, was outside playing and Ruth called for him for nearly an hour before he came inside looking for her.

The baby survived, Bill learned, but Ruth had not. The baby a boy, had been sent to an orphanage but the hospital staff would not tell Bill the name or location. Only family, he was told. But I'm the father, he insisted. No one believed him, or if they did, didn't think he deserved to know.

What about the older son, Maximilian, he inquired. No one knew. The long and short of it was that Bill spent two weeks in Berlin, and could learn nothing about the whereabouts of young Maximilian, or the baby, his son, or about a Colonel von der Dusenberger. He visited the grave of Ruth, and said goodbye to Berlin.

THREE: Charles
Los Angeles, 2001

My intended sister-in-law to-be, Mary Jo, had married an eccentric, grizzled, wealthy German real estate investor who was more than twice her age. His name is Maximilian von der Dusenberger and he's worth upwards of five hundred million dollar give or take an office building or two. Maximilian wasn't my boss a the time, but soon after his marriage he hired me.

Mary Jo, who had worked in real estate in partnership with her sister, Mary Grace, wasn't my sister-in-law yet because Mary Grace and I weren't in a hurry, at least I wasn't, our engagement being a sort of an opened-ended one. Mary Jo, with little subtlety, urged us to set the date, but Mary Grace and I were having fun dating, while maintaining a certain level of independence, so why rush. It's fortunate we both procrastinated on setting a date, because had Mary Grace been pushy I would have been outta here.

Tell the truth, it was mostly me keeping the reins in check and I think Mary Grace recognized my reluctance to move the relationship too far too fast, so she was biding her time rather than risk chasing me away. I run away easily.

For all my life I've been pretty much of a bastard. My male friends didn't think so, because I did an excellent job of concealing my Mr. Hyde personality. I blame it on my not having a father, but more of that later.

In retrospect I freely admit that the day I met Mary Grace was one of the luckiest days of my life. Actually, the day I first saw her, I should say, because I didn't actually meet her until several days later.

It was a Monday morning and I showed up at the office looking like I'd slept in my clothes all weekend and had forgotten to shave. That might have been the case, I don't remember. I think I'd had a night that started out as a pleasant date and ended badly because I did or said something stupid. I always felt bad after those episodes but I knew it was my way of avoiding a relationship from developing complicated entanglements. So, third, fourth date, got to ruin it.

She, this new woman, was walking down the hallway, an unfamiliar face in the building, and our eyes locked. Suddenly I felt foolish, like a slob. Had it been a sports event and I was the team and she the fans, she would have booed me.

I watched her continue down the hallway, ignoring me as my head swiveled to follow her. Then I rushed to the restroom and looked at myself in the mirror. It wasn't as bad as I'd feared. I didn't look quite like Yasser Arafat, who somehow always managed to look as if he hadn't shaved in three days, yet neither did I resemble one of those GQ hunks who manage to make a two-day old beard look sexy. My tie was straight and my hair was only slightly mussed, sort of a casual combed do. I stared into the mirror and tried to be objective about my looks. I wasn't Clark Gable, but I wasn't Quasimodo, either.

I splashed water in my face and rubbed a finger across my teeth. I'd forgotten to brush before I left home and the taste in my mouth was yucky. Fortunately, the likelihood of kissing anybody anytime soon was slim. My eyes looked tired and I vowed to get a good night's sleep. I hope she hadn't thought of me as a rummy. I couldn't remember the last time I'd preened for a woman I hadn't even talked to yet.

I returned to the main work area and searched for her. Something had flashed between us in a way I couldn't explain. It wasn't that she was beautiful (she was, and is, but that's not the point). She resonated a glow of self-content, a vibe of happiness but not of arrogance, of satisfaction with herself and confidence in her abilities and her place in life. Sort of like a tall woman who wears high heels. The fact that her eyes glistened with interest, just a smidgen, though she has always denied it, told me that she was a tiny bit attracted to me, too, maybe one-thousandth as much as I was to her. Me, the guy who is figuring out how to dump a new girl before the first date is over.

Actually, to go back further, the previous luckiest day of my life, other than the actual day I was born, would have to be the day Maximilian hired me, else I never would have met Mary Grace, much less landed the lucrative job Maximilian gave me. On the other hand, knowing Maximilian almost got me killed. More of that later, also.

Since I was usually worked outside the office it was several days before I ran into Mary Grace again, and to tell the truth, I was in the office mainly, solely, to try to meet her. I did, she acknowledged my existence, she let me buy her coffee, and later she maneuvered me into buying her lunch. The next day she wrangled a dinner out of me while I thought we were going for a drink. She was so infatuated with me I would have gone broke from her letting me buy her meals if I hadn't cooled things down before they went overboard too quickly.

I must admit I didn't mind at first. My usual resolve, as it had been ever since I was six years old and had my ego destroyed by Tammy Willson, is to never get emotionally involved. Leave 'em before you love 'em, was my motto. My excuse, when I do my self-analysis, is that I'll do like my father did and abandoned my wife, so why marry in the first place. It's not fair to my father, whoever he was, since he apparently had no choice. Except, the older I get the more I wonder about the truth of my father's demise.

I'd done a good job of keeping my emotions in check, mostly by vanishing like a wisp from a woman's life if I felt either one of us was getting serious. I'd hurt one or two ladies, I'm sure, but I also had hurt myself. This time I was adamant that I would let nature take its course, and its own sweet time. Selfishly, I knew part of my reasoning was because I was having so much damn fun with Mary Grace and her sister and her husband, who by now was my boss.

The sisters, the Marys, first encountered Maximilian at some shindig where they give out awards for selling the most overpriced property, or something of that sort. The Wolfe sisters had been on a team that handled a very big deal involving an office-building complex, and unbeknownst to them, the money behind the purchase was the wealthy and somewhat reclusive gentleman with the preposterous name. They assumed their meeting Maximilian was serendipitous.

I don't recall the exact timeline but a few months later the wealthy geezer Maximilian von der Dusenberger married the young and lovely Mary Jo Wolfe. And a few months later I was working for Maximilian, which is how I met Mary Jo, which is how I met her sister, who everyone who knew either of us expected me to marry, not to repeat myself, which is how Mary Jo would become my sister in-law, and Maximilian my elderly, and splendidly wealthy, brother in-law. At the time I first started making goo-goo eyes at Mary Grace, I didn't know she was the boss' sister-in-law. Had I known it I most likely would have backed off.

My name is Charles. Charles Oliver Hardin. I don't like the name Charles. It sounds too sophisticated, or I should say, pseudo-sophisticated. Obviously my mother liked it because that's what she named me, and that's what she called me. Almost as bad as Maximilian.

"Charles, eat your cereal like a good boy." "Charles, don't be late for school." "Charles, don't get dirty playing outside." "Charles, why don't you sit down for awhile and keep quiet."

My mother said I was actually Charles Oliver Hardin the *Second,* I'll have you know, named after my father, who died in Vietnam three months after I was born. When I got old enough to ask her about him she'd start to cry. She said it hurt too much to talk about him and she'd go to her bedroom and close the door. When she came out she'd pour herself a drink and pout the rest of the day. When I asked if she had saved any of his things she said, no, it was too painful to have his things around so she'd gotten rid of everything, even pictures. I took her at face value; why wouldn't I?

My boyhood friends usually called me Charley, which isn't so bad for a kid. But as you get older, it's like, "Hey there he goes, good-time Charley, the town drunk." Reminds of a W.C. Fields look-alike with a bulbous nose as bright as a stop light and veined cheeks that look like maps, left side, west of the Mississippi, right side, east of the great river.

Then there's the nickname Chuck, which reminds me of a piece of beefsteak, so I never cared for that either. Some guys started calling me Chip, as if I was their golfing buddy or fraternity pal. Made me want to wear a sweater vest and argyle socks. I considered encouraging people to call me 'Buddy', you know, being my name *is* Charles Hardin and…well, if you're not into early rock 'n' roll you don't get it.

I considered going by my initials, C.O. (can you believe it…Charles wasn't bad enough my mother had to tack on Oliver!). I can't blame my father because I never knew him. In fact, I was five years old before I knew I was supposed to have a father, but that's a whole 'nother story. I had business cards made up that identified me as 'C. Oliver Hardin', which was really high-falutin'.

But what goes around comes around, doesn't it? In college the guys called me Chuck, and now it sounded kind of manly, so I accepted it. And some of the cute co-eds called me Charlie! Not Charley as in the town drunk, but *Char-lie,* as in, "*Char-lie*, can you walk me to the bookstore?" Or, "*Char-lie*, can you help me study tonight?" Absolutely! Now, if anyone called me Chip, or Chick, I played deaf.

So eventually I decided Charles wasn't so bad after all, especially when I went into business and wanted to appear as someone sophisticated, intelligent and successful. I can't say much for the first two, but I fooled enough people so that I did become moderately successful.

As Maximilian told me later he truly did fall in love with Mary Jo, though she was young enough to be his granddaughter. She was 27, and he was a crisp 67 when they were married.

When I knew Mary Grace better, in fact, after we'd been dating a few months, I dared suggest that her dear sister had married for money.

"Shush!" Mary Grace admonished me. "Don't say such things! They love each other and his money had nothing to do with it."

Big chance to inherit big bucks, was my thought; real romantic, aren't I? But that's me, so afraid of a permanent hitching that I assume reasons for doing so must be predatory. Actually, the sisters came from a family that wasn't exactly destitute, and both stood to inherit more than loose change in the future. Not that it would matter to Maximilian, with his millions, but it might make a difference to my and Mary Grace's financial planning, were we ever to advance to the joint checking account stage.

Sometimes I think Maximilian was telling the truth when he told Mary Jo he loved her. When I knew him better, more as 'family' than as a boss, he explained to me that though marriage wasn't exactly what he had originally planned, even for someone like him, who planned everything to a T, quirks can develop when you least expect them. As if getting married was a mere quirk of fate!

"There are plans," he would say, "and then there are the events that occur while you're trying to implement your plans". Sor of like, 'stuff happens,' but Maximilian put finesse into his speech. (And he didn't abide swearing in front of him; he'd been known to fire people who said 'goddamn.')

Actually, Maximilian was none too thrilled when Mary Grace and I began seeing each other. The cold shoulder he gave me made it clear he disapproved of Mary Grace and I dating. I got the impression it was another one of those quirks he hadn't counted on, and Maximilian hated to be out of control of events. Maybe it was the idea of two employees getting romantically involved that he didn't like. No frolicking in the office. As it turns out—a slight twist in Maximilian's plans, but it worked nicely—he had married Mary Jo so it was difficult to pass an edict against inter-office romances. Which worked out nicely once I met Mary Grace, as I've explained. We hit it off like Romeo and Juliet—without the family feud problems. After a while Maximilian accepted us as a pair and eased off his unspoken disapproval.

In fact, the four of us had something in common—practically no relatives. I was an only child, my mother had been an only child—who knows about my father—Mary Grace and Mary Jo had each other, but their parents only had one sibling between them, he a bachelor near-hermit who lived somewhere in a cabin in Montana and hadn't been in contact with his relatives since the Nixon Administration.

This meant that except for my mother and the girls' parents, we didn't have to spend boring holidays with obnoxious relatives, nor be invited to a slew of weddings of second and third cousins, the parents of whom we hadn't seen since we were children, nor feel obligated to send gifts to weddings we wouldn't have to attend, had we had relatives.

I, too, worked in real estate. I did well enough to make a good living, but I wasn't driving a Lexus or a Mercedes when I got the call from Maximilian. I had decided to move on to commercial realty and see if I could increase my income enough to start a 401K. I did okay, and became fairly well known in the local industry, until the market went stale, allowing me too many free afternoons to play golf.

One day I got a call from someone who identified himself as the executive secretary to Maximilian von der Dusenberger. I thought it was a gag and I strained to place the voice among my weird friends.

"Is that an automobile or a Nazi General?" I asked. Actually I knew who von der Dusenberger was, I was just being a smart-mouth. I had no reason to think it was truly the wealthy real estate magnate calling lowly me.

Silence, then: "Mr. von der Dusenberger would like to talk to you about a position of employment, sir."

"What kind of position?"

"You'll have to talk to Mr. von der Dusenberger," he replied his voice maintaining an even tone despite my obvious lack of appreciation for his call.

"Does he have a nickname?" I really didn't want to have to say, 'Mr. von der Dusenberger' every time I spoke to him, if I ever did, which might not happen if I didn't quit my smart mouth remarks. I still thought it was one of my buddies from my pre-real estate days, maybe a wise-ass from college I hadn't seen since graduation.

"No, sir." His voice was deep and solid, as if he was projecting to make certain that no one thought odd of him, ahem, you know, he being a *secretary*, albeit an executive one.

I've always been sort of a smart-ass, a way to compensate, I believe, in my righteous self-analysis for perceived inadequacies, spawned by certain parental, or more like it, non-parental, factors in my upbringing.

It wasn't as bad as I'd feared; Maximilian did insist on being addressed as Mr. von der Dusenberger by people who didn't know him well, and later, Maximilian was acceptable, but no short cuts like Max, or Maxie; it had to be the whole five syllables. It could have been worse had I known at the time that he considered himself a Count, and then I'd have had to call him Count Maximilian von der Dusenberger! My tongue gets twisted just thinking about it.

Maximilian said he heard of me because it's his business to know what's going on in the commercial real estate market, and I accepted his explanation. What he wanted me to do, was to be vice-president in charge of 'Special Market Research & Acquisitions'. No, seriously, that is the title on my business cards. My job would be to nose around for properties which had high potential that wasn't clearly visible to others, and could be had for prices way below market. Also I was to learn who else might be interested in those properties so Maximilian could plan his strategy. When the economy stumbles, an alert and optimistic buyer with cash to spare can pick up properties cheaply from owners who are panicked and/or desperately need to get out from under crushing loans. Maximilian wasn't a young man by the time I met him, but some of these rich old farts think they are going to live forever. It's a hobby for them; instead of retiring like normal people and playing with their electric train or draining gin and tonics at the 19th hole, they keep working and make more money than they can ever spend. Reminds me of o Uncle Scrooge in the Disney comic books, frolicking in his vault fu of money. What did I care? Maximilian was going to pay me a retainer that was more than I'd ever made in my best years as an agent and broker. So I took the job. I assumed Maximilian hearing about me and wanting to hire me was serendipitous.

Despite being older than us, Maximilian fit into our cozy circle quite well. Or I should say, I fit into theirs, Maximilian and Mary Jo's, since they were a family while Mary Grace and I were still only a potential one, biological clock clicking away, I know. Whatever, the four of us came to spend a lot of time together, both work and outside the office, even before Mary Grace and I were unofficially engaged. We benefited from Maximilian's wealth to th point I began to feel we were taking advantage of him. Fool that I am, he didn't think so, and in fact, if anything, it was the other way around. But I had met Mary Grace, so how it happened or why it happened, I didn't care then, and I don't now, despite the subseque events, which after all, to be truthful, put some spice into my life ar set it spinning in a direction I never imagined. A lot of spice! You never know for sure how things are going to work out.

The first time Maximilian told me the story of his childhood he said he had no known relatives, his family having all died in World War Two. He neglected to mention that his mother had survived the war, but later when I knew him better he revived the story and I didn't blame him for not wanting to talk about it to people he didn't know well.

He had grown up as an orphan in the cratered streets of Berlin, he claimed in his first version, fighting other homeless kids for scraps of food and a place to sleep. For months he lived in collapsed buildings, moving from one to another as work crews bulldozed the ruins. Maximilian did tend to exaggerate, not that I mean to make fun of starving kids scraping for morsels of food.

Eventually, and obviously there's a big hole in the story, which I figured he would fill in as Maximilian and I developed our camaraderie, he came to America, via Canada, when he was a young man. He ended up in the Houston area working in the construction business (I guess his experiences moving busted concrete in Berlin helped his resume), and began to buy up real estate. As Houston boomed, so did Maximilian. You wouldn't of thought he'd have made so much money that he could invest in real estate, young man that he was, a good-looking one who you'd think would spend all his salary on girls and cars. But he had another source of funds, it turns out.

We all thought our meeting and getting to know one another was providence and Maximilian chuckled along whenever anyone suggested that the Fates of Greek mythology must consider us special. As we would find out eventually, while Maximilian believed in fate and coincidence, he wasn't opposed to nudging the Fates to keep things moving in the direction he desired.

Maximilian and I were enjoying hot tea in front of the fireplace in the family room of a condominium he owned in Mammoth Lakes. Mammoth is a mountain resort a little south of Yosemite National Park and a bit north of Death Valley. It also sits atop several earthquake fault lines, but if you grew up in southern California the shaking of the ground isn't something you think about on a daily basis. It just happens, often enough to take with a wary grin, at least after the first few seconds pass, when any normal person shudders a bit waiting to see if the roof will collapse on them. The faults are there, pretty much everywhere you go in California, and the betting is they won't move significantly for the next thousand years, or at least until after everyone who's around now isn't around anymore to worry about them. Then it'll be someone else's turn to worry.

It was late afternoon and dusk was near upon us. It was almost time to toss the tea for something more invigorating. The sisters were still skiing, one last run or two. Maximilian had given up skiing when he passed 65 years of age, and while I still took part, I had fallen enough times today. I couldn't keep up with the Marys anyway, so why embarrass myself?

Maximilian wanted to talk, and it was then that he told me he hadn't exactly been an orphan during World War Two. He had become one shortly after, when his mother died in 1946, when the allies occupied Germany and the rebuilding of Berlin was slowly under way. I was so lucky, he said, that we were in the zone that the Americans controlled. On the other hand, maybe mama wouldn't have died, so… He faded then, his weary eyes seeing a past that I knew nothing about.

"Time for a drink," he suggested, and he bounced up to do the honors. When it came time to fix a drink, Maximilian was a bundle of energy.

I remained sitting and looked out the window at the mountains, beautiful in the diming light, the sun still bright as it rolled inexorably lower, soon to pass behind the mountains and a few minutes later, below the horizon. The snow was taking on a variety of shades of golds and yellows and oranges. The sky was as bright a blue as God ever made. There were no clouds, and no sign of additional snow, but it would be biting cold soon and throughout the night.

"I hope the girls don't stay too late," I said.

"They'll be fine, I'm sure," offered Maximilian. "It looks darker from here as the sun drops below the mountain top, but where they are they still have an hour of light."

I had a sense Maximilian wanted to tell me things in the time we had before the girls returned that he didn't want them to hear. It made me apprehensive. Maximilian oozed an aura of mystery, whether he was working diligently on a multi-million dollar real estate deal, playing a friendly game of poker, or discussing the ramifications of the latest tax law changes and financial regulatory proposals. He always seemed to know more than he was revealing, as if holding something back gave him power over others. Probably so; they say knowledge is power, or is it, the appearance of knowledge is power?

I wondered if he wanted to talk about his Foundation, which he'd set up a few years ago with a grant of twenty-five million dollars of his own money. He sponsors a number of fund-raising events, including a golf tournament, and the money raised goes to a variety of charitable causes. It's a wonderful venture and I speculated whether he might want me to run it, as the current manager had recently announced his retirement. Though Max originally funded the Foundation and his name is intimately connected to it, he likes to keep himself out of the limelight as much as possible. (He calls it the Dusenberger Foundation, afraid that the 'von der' portion of his name might sound 'too Prussian'). He avoid television interviews and even deplores getting his picture taken at the various events connected with the Foundation. I get the impression he feels a certain responsibility to spread his wealth, but doesn't feel the need to take credit for it. Well and good.

He brought drinks, scotch and soda for both of us, light on the soda. He sat down, we raised glasses in a silent toast to nothing in particular, and took sips of our drinks.

"I was twelve years old when the war ended. I've probably told you that before." I nodded, though I didn't particularly remember him telling me.

"My mother was still alive. My father, who knows? He was soldier and had to fight and the last we heard he was going to the Russian front. I was too young to understand that going to fight in the east against the advancing Russian army at that time in the war was virtually a death sentence. I remember a man in uniform came t speak to my mother and after the man left she told me Papa would b home soon, but I didn't know if that meant the war was over or because he was getting a leave. I know now she's was just trying to keep me from worrying. Papa didn't show up, and the war, of course, was rapidly coming to an end. Mama quit telling me he would be home soon and I quit asking."

This is when I thought to interrupt him because earlier he'd told me he'd been an orphan during the war, but I decided to keep quiet and let him speak and hear the 'director's cut' version.

"He was a colonel, the last I heard, and after mother's initial optimism that he would be home soon, the weeks went by, the bombs finally stopped falling, and I think she quit wishing her husband—my Papa—would return home and hoped he was dead rather than a captive of the Russians. Anyway…" Maximilian shrugged and was silent for a good thirty seconds.

"After that one bit of news we never heard from him or of him. What was left of the Army then was in total confusion and no one had any information. The soldiers knew the war was lost and didn't want to die uselessly. Many of them threw away their uniforms so they wouldn't be shot. Others simply dropped their weapons and surrendered to the Americans. No one wanted to be captured by the Russians. From what we'd heard, they were monsters. Of course, as a boy, I had no idea we Germans were monsters, too."

Maximilian talked on without me interrupting. I even got up once to refresh our drinks without him missing a beat, other than to nod a thank you when I returned his glass. He was condensing his history as a young man into a short story, leading up to what I could not imagine, but was curious to hear.

"One day two American soldiers came by our house. At first I couldn't keep their names straight. Maybe I did then, but I'd forgotten, or maybe it was the trauma of what happened. I did see their names on the identity strips of their uniforms. They also had big letters on the shoulders of their uniforms that I didn't understand at the time. 'MP', which I later learned meant the American Military Police. I believe they were looking for my father. At first both of them came together, and they'd always start the conversation by asking if my mother or I had heard from my father. Later, sometimes only one of them came by; always the same one and he didn't ask anymore about my father. I was only eleven or twelve years old, but already I knew there were things adults did with the door closed and the kids outside. So I know that at some point one of the men, for a long time I couldn't remember which one…came more often and stayed longer, and I was banished to the outside until my mother called me."

Maximilian looked at me as if embarrassed to be talking about his mother this way.

"You don't remember which soldier it was?" I interrupted. I don't know why it mattered, I just thought I should say something.

"Yes, years later the name popped into my head, like magic. I could see it as clearly as the first time I saw it on his uniform. It was the handsome one, the one who was very polite. Well, they were both polite, but this one, he had a pleasant face, a happy face."

"So what were their names?" I asked.

He stared hard at me, as if I was impertinent to interrupt him again. After a lengthy pause he said, "It's not important now for you to know their names." I felt chastised.

He continued his story. "By now we had moved back into our home that we had fled from during a bombing raid. We were surprised to find it virtually intact. True, there was severe damage and most of the windows were broken, but it was one of the few houses in the neighborhood that still had four walls and most of the roof was intact. The two soldiers helped to repair it so the rain and cold wouldn't seep in. I've always had a warm feeling towards the American soldiers, all of them, just because of what those two did for us.

"Then for a week or so they didn't come by, neither one. I asked my mother and she said they were busy doing soldier's duties. I sensed she was concerned, and a bit blue, as if she missed them, or at least, the one. I missed them too, because they often played with me, even let me touch their rifles, which they probably weren't supposed to do."

I needed a time frame so I interrupted him again. "When was this, Maximilian, what time of the year?"

"It was still winter, early in the year, right after New Year's. Most of the soldiers who had fought in the war had gone home, although others came for the occupation. I was surprised our two friends were still there, but I suppose they volunteered to stay on.

"Then one day the other one came by, the one that didn't come as often. He saw me outside and he looked sad. He didn't say anything and I followed him into the house, calling for my mother.

"She came out of the kitchen and I remember she smiled, then lost the smile when she saw who it was, then lit up again and gave the man a hug. I couldn't understand all that he said, but I gathered he was telling mother that his unit was leaving soon, and in fact his friend, the other soldier, the one I think loved my mother, had been suddenly transferred and had not been allowed time for a final visit. This one brought a message from his friend to tell my mother that he would try to see her again but didn't know when that would be.

"I remember my mother put her hand on her belly and a worried look came over her face, as if she had heard awful news, worried like she used to look when we were scrounging in the streets. I feared that after all this time without the protection of our two American soldiers we'd be thrown out of our house.

"The American didn't stay long. He patted me on the head as he was leaving, and told me to be a good boy, and we never saw either of the soldiers again."

Intimidating as Max could be at times, I still was perplexed by his reticence to mention the soldiers' names. So I asked again.

"I still don't get why you won't tell me their names, Maximilian. Is there some big secret?"

He looked at me and I know my face displayed puzzlement. We heard the door open, accompanied by the high-pitched voices of the girls, laughing and replaying their adventures on the slopes. We heard scuffling sounds as they stomped their feet, took off boots and gloves, giggling all the while, and piled skis in the corner of the downstairs entry.

"We'll talk more later, Charles."

I nodded and rose to greet the sisters Wolfe. I then went to the kitchen to put the teapot on; I knew the girls would want a cup of hot tea before a hot shower, and when warm and cozy they'd be ready for chilled Chardonnay. I would have to wait to find out where Maximilian was going with his story. I was one hundred percent positive he hadn't been talking just to update me on his family history.

INTERLUDE: Mary Grace

I was minding my own business when this guy ogling me crashed into a desk. I heard a bang and saw Mr. Hardin rubbing his shin. He had a pained look on his face, more, I suspect, from embarrassment than from physical discomfort. I smiled, yes, but I was laughing at his clumsiness. I realize that's not fair—I hadn't seen exactly what happened so I didn't know if he was a genuine klutz or was admiring my legs.

He kept coming into the office trying to find an excuse to bump into me, literally, bump into me. I knew who he was, but had yet to formally meet him, and couldn't believe he was one of Maximilian's most trusted assistants.

Eventually he got up the courage to speak to me. He was like a twelve-year-old, stumbling over the simplest words and gaping at me as if he'd never seen a woman before. I mean, the mirror doesn't crack when I look in it, but I'm no Liz Taylor, either. He fawned all over me until I let him buy me a cup of coffee, and he begged me to let him take me to lunch. When I declined an invitation to dinner I thought he was going to cry. (I could have gone, but I didn't want him to think I'd say 'yes' to everything he asked.)

The next day he practically crawled on his knees imploring me to go to dinner with him. This time I agreed and I must admit we had a good time and now that he was over his original nervousness he was pretty interesting. Before dinner was over I thought he was going to ask me to marry him.

Okay, truth is that once things began to get serious he seemed to back off a bit, but his recalcitrant behavior only lasted a day or two or three. By then we were more than casual dates, more even, than just friends, and he claimed (don't all men), that I was the first woman he could really talk to.

I was in no hurry to move the relationship up to the next level, whatever that level was, but content to take our time. My sister, Mary Jo was urging me to 'snag him', was the way she put it. He's handsome, makes good money, is polite, smart, you two are head over heels in love, and you're not getting any younger, sis, were her pros.

I'm not in a hurry to get married, (Charles seems a bit more so), I'm not sure I want to work at the same place as my husband, and I'm happy living alone, were the cons I gave Mary Jo in reply.

Yeah, yeah, well, you're twenty-seven, only a year younger than me, Mary Jo added, and if you're going to have a family it's time to give it serious consideration. You'll be getting gray hair soon, sis.

I'm of an independent mind, have a college degree, make good money on my own, enjoy my privacy, and like to go to movies by myself, and look who's talking, I retorted.

She then threw in what was really on her mind: 'I want to be an aunt,' a reminder to both of us that her choice of husbands, our boss, Maximilian von der Dusenberger, was closer to seventy years old than he was to sixty, and he was of no mind to become a father at such an advanced age, a matter that had conflicted with Mary Jo's feelings about marrying Maximilian in the first place. Mary Jo wanted me to have kids so she could enjoy them.

I'll have kids any time you want me to if you'll come over and change the kid's diapers and get up with him or her at three in the morning, I suggested. Mary Jo agreed, ha, ha.

So, to make a long story short, Charles (by now he was okay with me calling him Charlie, or, as he said far too often for it to be funny any more, I don't care what you call me, just call me), and we began to considered ourselves unofficially engaged but we haven't set the date, nor do I have an engagement ring, so I'm still not one hundred per cent sure that he's one hundred per cent sure. I'm not ready to nudge him because we're having a good time the way things are. But when he went to Europe, suddenly and by himself, and didn't have time for a decent goodbye hug, I was mad enough to either give him an ultimatum, or…I couldn't think of what else.

FOUR: Maximilian's Story

The sisters thought it amusing that they'd had a harrowing experience on the slopes. A skier had appeared seemingly out of nowhere, from behind a copse of trees situated far off the main ski run, and nearly crashed into them. Mary Jo had lost her balance and tumbled over, but was not hurt.

"What makes me mad is that he didn't even stop to see if we were alright. He turned around and saw I had fallen, but the S.O.B. kept on going."

"That's your second near accident in the past few days," Maximilian reminded his wife, his voice as solemn as a funeral director.

"Crazy jerks shouldn't be allowed on the slopes," Mary Grace said, as she took a tentative sip of her steamy tea.

"You should report him," I suggested. The ladies shrugged. glanced at Maximilian and his face looked ashen and far more disturbed than the event called for. Even Mary Jo and Mary Grace did not look as concerned as Maximilian did.

"Are you okay, dear?' asked Mary Jo. "You look pale."

Maximilian nodded, mumbled that he was fine, took a swig from his glass, glanced at me and when he caught my eye he immediately looked away, as if he hadn't wanted me to see the worry the girl's story caused him.

I'm no private eye, but it was easy to deduce that something was bothering Maximilian and that it was connected to the tale he'd been telling me before the ladies returned. I couldn't fathom what could be the cause of his concern.

It was about ten days later and Maximilian and I were at lunch, ostensibly to discuss a business matter we were working on. We were in a booth tucked away in a corner far from any other diners, perfect for discussing private matters. This was a posh, snobby, semi-private club. It wasn't officially a membership club, but you couldn't just drop in unannounced and unknown and expect to find a table, even if there were several that looked available. You had to be someone or be with someone who was someone. I wasn't enough of a someone, but Maximilian was.

The business issue was resolved quickly and when Maximilian developed a sullen look on his face I knew he was going to continue the conversation we'd been having at the condo. Though we'd been there for two more days, we never had the opportunity to return to it.

I should say, his conversation, my listening. For some reason that I couldn't explain, the thought made me nervous. Somewhere in all this Maximilian wanted something, and he was going about it in a peculiar way.

With Maximilian von der Dusenberger, he told you what he wanted and you either did it, or you didn't work for him any more. With friends, if he asked for something, and if he did it was always business related, they knew that he expected them to cooperate with him. If they didn't, he never dealt with them again, and past history had shown that Maximilian's friends made lots of money, while the ones who had failed Maximilian lost valuable opportunities.

I was in a unique situation. I was practically Maximilian's brother-in-law, and his wife liked me, and Mary Grace and I both made decent money even before we worked for Maximilian, and neither of us lusted for millions. Thousands maybe, but not millions. So I wasn't too concerned about not jumping every time Maximilian flicked his finger, but still, he had an intimidating way, and you found yourself feeling, maybe it's easier to agree with him, and pick a battle to win later, much later.

He surprised me again when our conversation went in a different direction. He asked me what I remembered about my father.

"I never knew him," I said. "I have no idea what it would have been like to have a father."

"What did your mother tell you, if anything?"

It was a subject I didn't often think about anymore. My mother is still very much alive, a spry fifty-five, working part-time. (I told her she didn't need to work anymore because I could afford to take care of her, but she wouldn't hear of it. She accepts lavish gifts from me, but never cash, and insists on working a part-time job. She won't work for Maximilian, though I'd often said I could get her a job, but she retorts it would be a distraction for me to have my mother as an employee, and she's probably right.)

She's happy, active with her friends, making up for all the years she never had time for fun because she had to work two jobs and raise me by herself. She lives alone and scolds me if I call too often, accusing me of checking up on her to see if she'd dropped dead overnight. Exactly the opposite of the cliché, wasn't it? Usually the way it goes is the mother expects her bachelor son to check on her every day, if not live with her. 'I'm fifty-five, not ninety-five,' she reminds me nearly every time I call. 'I'm in the prime of my life.' She dates, but isn't currently involved in a serious romantic relationship that I know of. I visit her fairly often, but we haven't talked about my father in years. And, as far as I could tell, her drinking was no longer a problem.

"My mother never cared to talk about him. She told me he'd been a career soldier who died in Vietnam, no more than a month after they'd met in Hawaii while he was on R&R. That was when I was conceived, she told me. Well, she didn't tell me when I was five years old, but later, when I had an inkling of what 'conceived' meant.

"I remember that I didn't ask her much at first. Later, I asked about pictures. She said she'd been so distraught she'd destroyed all of them. When I got a little older I asked about relatives, and she said my father was an only child and had no cousins, no aunts and uncles. It seemed sad to me, because all my friends had a father; even if their parents were divorced, they knew their father. And they would tell me about aunts and grandmas and cousins and all kinds of people, none of which I had in my family. Our family consisted of mother and me, that was it. My mother's parents had died when she was fairly young, so there wasn't even a grandmother's house to go to on Thanksgiving Day."

"And your father's parents?"

I shrugged. "Who knows? No father, no grandparents, I guess. Jesus, Maximilian, you're making me sad."

His eyes flickered, a faint acknowledgement of his transgression.

"After a while I quit asking and forgot about it. I never think of it anymore. So why do you ask, Maximilian?"

"Did you ever check the names on the Wall?"

"What are you talking about, Maximilian?"

"Please bear with me, Charles. The Vietnam Wall; surely you know about the Wall, where the names of all the Americans killed in Vietnam are engraved."

"Of course I do, but no, I never bothered to check for my father's name. I guess I wasn't interested in someone I never knew."

Actually, I had thought of it but I had never followed through, as if I was afraid of what I'd learn. I never have been able to shake the idea that my mother hadn't told me the whole truth and nothing but the truth.

Maximilian nodded, whether in understanding or pity I wasn't sure. "And you were named after your father?"

I was getting upset by this but I wasn't sure why. "Yes," I answered with unnecessary firmness. "My mother said she named me after my father, Colonel Charles Oliver Hardin."

Maximilian said nothing, as if waiting for me to finish a thought. I did. "Maybe that's why I never liked my name."

"There is no Charles Oliver Hardin on the Wall," Max said. "I checked; it's easy to do."

"What's the point, Maximilian?" Again, with more firmness in my voice than was required. It wasn't Maximilian's fault my father died in Vietnam, if he had. It wasn't his fault for the whole damn war, but where was he going with this? And why the hell would he check to see if my father's name was on the Wall? I started to ask...

"Eh, I find it interesting that both of us had military fathers and both died in a war, at least, we think they did," Maximilian said, before I could pose my question. "But there is no real evidence of what happened to either of them."

"What's that supposed to mean, 'we think'?" I said. I really didn't want to talk about this, but Maximilian was going to make it happen. He always gets his way.

"What I mean is my father was never found; no dead body, no record of being a prisoner-of-war. It was only a few years ago that the Russian World War Two records were made available. They show no record of my father having been taken prisoner by them or killed by them."

"Come on, Maximilian, the Russian's records of people they killed or parceled out to Siberia and were never heard of again, can hardly be considered absolute and irrefutable," I said, the skepticism in my voice virtually dripping down my chin. Maximilian was not generally a gullible person.

He nodded, a nice gesture actually, since usually when he thinks someone has said something dumb he stares at them with contemp.

"True, true. Still, my father was a high-ranking officer. It's likely they would have had a record of him if he'd been taken prisoner."

"Thousands of soldiers disappeared in World War Two and have never been found," I countered.

Still patient with me, he went off on another tangent.

"My father was a Nazi, Charles." He looked at me as if he made a particularly fantastic announcement. I thought, so? Yeah, a German officer a Nazi, so what? He sensed my confusion.

"Not all Germans were Nazis. Most soldiers weren't, in fact. My father, however, was an active member, and a wealthy one. We lived very well before the war. I'm not *exactly* sure what happened to the family wealth."

I wondered why he gave the word 'exactly' a slight emphasis, as if he didn't mean what he was saying, not usual for Maximilian.

"You seem to have done alright, Maximilian."

Maximilian then returned to his earlier story. He told me how his mother had become pregnant by one of the American soldiers. He related how he had found her in the cellar, bloody and hurt, having fallen down the stairs, and how he'd run out into the street screaming for help. And how his mother had been taken to the hospital and how a nurse had come to Maximilian and told him his mother had died, and asked where was his father was and did he have any other relatives and how he began to cry because he could not answer their questions.

The nurse had placed Maximilian in a waiting room and told him she'd get him something to eat. When he had the chance Maximilian slipped out of the room and left the hospital. He never looked back. He snuck under the tarp of a truck and fell asleep. When he awoke the truck was moving. He stayed there until the truck stopped.

Fortunately for him he was living in West Berlin. It was only dumb luck that no one had looked carefully under the tarp at the border between West Berlin and East Germany. Maximilian slipped from under the truck and at age twelve and a half went to look for work.

"So you didn't go to school?" I asked.

"Eventually, I did. You have read Dickens, Charles?"

I nodded. I wanted to get back to why he brought up the reference to my father. Maximilian treated me well, treated his wife well, and was respected in the community. But he could be a tyrant when he didn't get his way; he hadn't become the caricature of the Monopoly game tycoon by being easy-going. The point is, at times I didn't trust him, and this was one of them. He was circling the edges of danger, like a bullfighter teasing El Toro, leading me on, then cutting off the information just when he'd whetted my curiosity. He did it again.

"My story reminds me of a character from his books. A young boy on his own, hungry and without a home. But there was work, and I was street-smart by then.

"After a few years I was a young man, strong from working hard labor helping to repair the cities of Germany, and I had a little money to buy new clothes, and sometimes even a extra glass of beer.

"One day, the strangest thing happened; like I said, almost out of a Dickens' novel. A man came to see me and said I had been selected by a special committee set up by the Allied Command to help, what did they call them...displaced person, DPs, if you will."

Maximilian laughed at what would now be a politically incorrect usage of the term, 'DPs', but one that was accepted terminology shortly after the end of World War Two.

"This person…he was well-dressed, soft-spoken, very polite he gave me papers that said I was accepted at the university in Frankfurt, all expenses paid, plus a stipend for rent and food. It took me a bit of time to believe that this was true. So I went to Frankfurt why not?

"Then, when I did well, I received extra money, for spending as I saw fit. Even later I found that an account had been arranged for me, although I could not use the money until after I was twenty-five years old. I was becoming quite wealthy," he added with a slight chuckle.

"Much later the man came to see me again. It had been years and I'd almost forgotten what he looked like. He was older and grayer, but it was the same man. He called himself Heinz, no last name; I don't know if it was his true name. He came to me and told me I should go to the United States. He made arrangements for me get a passport and a visa, plane tickets, a job with a financial firm in New York, and an apartment with one year's rent paid in advance. Everything taken care of, but what was funny about it…"

Maximilian stopped now and stared at nothing, as if he was still perplexed by the events he was relating to me. The waiter came by and Maximilian waved him away. He lifted his head and looked at me.

"The way he talked to me, it was clear I could not refuse. I remember feeling a cold shiver, you know, like goose bumps on your arms. He had a determined cold look in his eyes, an icy stare. I scared me because it reminded me of a man who had once come to the house when I was a child, to talk to my father. The man was dressed in a black uniform and had these markings, I think of them as lightning bolts…"

"Gestapo," I interjected.

He nodded and went on. "Yes…but it was the look on his face, a frozen, frightening look that made me fear him. Like you've seen in movies. I couldn't understand why my father had business with this man who appeared to be so…so dangerous. The man Heinz had that same look."

It was the first time I'd ever seen Maximilian afraid, in the intimidated way he often made other people feel. He literally shook himself, as if the icy feeling he'd described had wrapped itself around him.

"Enough of that. The rest followed as if orchestrated. Money came to me, as did citizenship, good jobs, and connections to people who knew how to get things done. Finally one day I was visited by a lawyer who said he represented the party who had befriended me all these years, and that the party had died. He handed me check for over eight hundred thousand dollars, and told me the relationship was terminated.

"Can you imagine? The 'relationship is terminated', he said! What relationship, I wondered? Don't you think that's a strange story, Charles?"

"Very much so," I agreed. "The kind of story that when they make a TV movie out of it, sounds preposterous."

"You believe me, don't you?"

I shrugged, "Why not? Of course I do. Did you ever figure out who was sending you the money?"

"Not for certain, but I assumed it was my father. I figured he had escaped and this was how he was taking care of me. As I became more educated I realized what we, Germany, that is, had done to the world with the war. And I believed my father was not an innocent. If he escaped, maybe to Argentina or Paraguay, he would have feared returning to Europe lest he be imprisoned or executed. He may have learned that my mother, his wife, had died, and so there was nothing for him at home, except me, and I had run away. Somehow he found me and took care of me the only way he knew how. That is what I think."

"I appreciate you telling me this, Maximilian, but why now? Or why at all?"

"Don't you see?" He gave me that look I mentioned earlier, the one that said, 'You are so dumb!'

"My whole life, my businesses, my reputation, everything I have, was financed by Nazi money, by gold stolen from the Jews, or artwork stolen from the French. The money was tainted because of how it was obtained. When I was young, or even not so young anymore, I didn't think about it much. At first I even believed that silly story about how I had been selected for schooling by some committee. I didn't care; once I came to America, it was like heaven. Even if I suspected the money came from my father, I figured it was alright for me to take it and use it."

"You couldn't know, Maximilian, you still don't know for sure where the money came from."

Maximilian then showed me a letter he'd received at his home. I read it twice. When I was done he refolded the letter and put it in his coat pocket.

"Do you have any idea who it's from?" I asked, an obvious question, but I didn't know what else to say.

He sighed, deeply this time, indicating the disappointment in me that I hadn't figured it out. To him the answer was as obvious as the question. Who did he think I was, Sherlock Holmes?

"Charles, I told you about the American soldier who came to see my mother. And then later, after the American left, she had a child, and she died, but the child lived." He stopped talking, so my feeble brain would have time to catch up.

I stared at him, not that I was as stupid as he thought, but because the story was taking on a weirdness I wasn't grasping as quickly as he might like. Finally I caught on where he was going.

"Do you know for sure that the baby lived? You said you skipped out of the hospital." He nodded, and I believed he was convinced the baby had survived.

"Are you trying to tell me the boy, your step-brother, is trying to blackmail you? All these years later? C'mon Max, that's rather ridiculous."

Even I was surprised by what I'd said. Not only did he hate being called 'Max'—as much as I disliked my name, 'Charles', I don't think anybody had ever used the word 'ridiculous' in speaking to Maximilian and kept their job. I kept pushing the advantage of the near-kinship we shared because of the sisters that bound us together.

He laughed, a chuckle that grew into a hardy guffaw and went on for half a minute. I joined in the laughter.

"Well, *Maximilian,* it's too many syllables! I'm tired of calling you…that!"

"It's okay," he said, between his laughter. "I've wondered how long it would be before you got around to calling me 'Max'. Just please don't do it in front of the other employees."

I nodded. I picked up the letter and read it again. "I guess it is blackmail, but why not confront him? If he is your brother, give him a few bucks and have a drink to celebrate a reunion."

Max shook his head. "No, no, no. If he is who I think he is, he's not a person who would go away quietly. He would hold this"—he picked up the letter and waved it—"over me."

"So what? You can't be responsible for what your father was."

"You're being naïve, Charles. I have an impeccable reputation in my field. Through my Foundation I'm known as a generous contributor to many charities, including Jewish organizations. A wing of the art museum is named after me—they' probably take my name off! What would happen to my business if people knew I'd been funded by Nazi gold? Stolen gold? What would people think if they learned I had abandoned my infant brother?"

I wasn't sure I agreed, but it wasn't a point worth arguing. "You were twelve years old, Max."

He shrugged, a feeling-sorry-for-himself gesture.

"So what do you plan to do?"

He looked at me then in a way that frightened me as I hadn' been frightened since I first saw *The Exorcist*. His eyes told me he wanted me to do something, and it was going to be something I had no wish to do, friend, employee, in-law, or whatever.

It's hard to say how I knew he was going to tell me he wanted me to do something that was out of a bad made-for-television movie, a task I couldn't possibly undertake, no matter what was at stake. I guess there was always an undercurrent of danger about Maximilian. There was an edge to him, vibes that made those around him tread gently, lest they disturb him and earn his wrath. The fact that he was often lost in thought as he prowled the offices and ignored or grunted, at best, at those who greeted him, didn't help his reputation as a mean old bastard, to use the colloquial. So I actually wasn't terribly surprised when he told me what he was suggesting.

"Charles, I've watched you for several years. You are calm, precise, and exact about your work. You are honest and careful in your words and you never make a move without having factored in all the possibilities, all the consequences of your actions. You remind me of myself." I grimaced.

"Though a bit less serious," he added. "You are a man I can trust, and there aren't many of those."

I nodded in appreciation, but sipped my drink so I wouldn't have to say anything. Get on with it, Max.

"This man, he needs to be found and …ah, reasoned with, so he will no longer be a danger to me and you, and the Marys."

"Pardon me? What do you mean, *reasoned with*?" I was afraid to accept in my mind what I thought he was talking about; too many bad spy novels. He couldn't mean it, come on, really?

He waved me off. "Don't pretend you don't understand, Charles. What do you think I'm saying?"

I responded with a question of my own. "Why is he a danger to me, Max? Exactly."

"Because I'm going to make you the executor of my estate, as soon as you and Mary Grace are married, and because when I am gone Mary Jo, your sister-in-law, will inherit most of my fortune, and I will expect you to manage it for her. If this man is not removed as an irritant, than he will continue to be a problem, even after I'm gone."

"An irritant? Max, Maximilian, I can't believe this person could be a long-term problem, and anyway, I'm not your man. You want me to pay him off to go away, sure, I'll do that. But when you say *reasoned with*, I need clarification. Who do you think I am, James Bond? Or the Godfather? Jesus, Max, what do you want me to do? Do you mean, *eliminate* him? For God's sake, I couldn't do it."

"Even if he was a threat?"

"Go to the police, then, if he's trying to blackmail you."

Max waved my suggestion off as if it was worth no more than a gnat flitting around the room.

"No, no, the truth would still get out."

"That might not be as bad as you think."

He actually smiled at me then, and for a moment I wondered if this whole story was a charade for some bizarre reason I couldn't comprehend.

"I'm afraid I've mislead you, Charles, purposely. I was looking for a reaction. I apologize for testing you. I'm not asking you to do anything, well, you know what I mean, for that I have someone else, a professional. There are people in that sort of business. I've been in contact with someone who is searching for my stepbrother now, as we speak. A person who will do the job, get paid, and go away, with no risk to me or you or any of us. For once I'm having a difficult time explaining something because it is far more complicated than you might imagine."

"I think you're overreacting," I butted in. "You really have a hired assassin looking for him? To kill him?"

Ignoring me, he went on. "I wanted this done so that no one would know, other than you and me."

"Pardon my French, but you're crazy. And I still don't know what you want from me. You say you have someone looking for him? So you don't even know where he is, and then you say you want someone to reason with him. So which is it, talk or shoot? And why, for God's sake, are you telling me this? Some things I'd rather not know about."

He looked away, as if what I said was of no worth, downed his drink and motioned for the waiter. After we ordered food, Maximilian continued.

"Let me tell you a story about those two American soldiers."

"First, Max, tell me about this letter. When did it arrive, and how?"

He immediately reached into his coat pocket for the letter as if he was happy I was finally getting enthused.

FIVE: Max's Story Continues

Maximilian von der Dusenberger didn't get much mail delivered to his house, because only a handful of people knew his home address. Of course he got his share of junk mail and requests for contributions, types of mail that some folk might consider to be in the same category as junk mail. His manservant intercepted most of the junk, so when a letter came in the mail addressed to Maximilian and marked "Personal" in bright red ink, it was a curiosity piece, if nothing else.

Maximilian examined the envelope as he stood in his home office, as if he did so long enough he might discern the contents without having to actually open it. All his business mail came to his regular office. Hardly anybody wrote personal letters any more; who did, with e-mail coming into vogue? Most curious of all was that the postmark was Lyon, France.

Maximilian didn't like surprises so he wanted to know who the letter was from before he opened it, and thought that if he gave it enough time, he'd recognize the writing and know. Then, he'd have an idea what the letter was about. What he had realized almost immediately, was that there was only one person he could think of who might write to him from Lyon, France.

He set the envelope on his desk and before he sat down Maximilian poured himself a finger of Irish whiskey. He set the glass down on the desk then plopped heavily into the chair, slumping back and continuing to gaze at the envelope. Sighing, he opened it.

The paper was lined yellow paper, the kind a lawyer might use to record his notes. The handwriting was the same as that which had addressed the envelope. Maximilian began to read.

'My Dear Maximilian:

I hope you are surprised by this correspondence, or at least a little perplexed as to the source and reason for it. The source, well, it is I, and if you are confused then you will have to think about it for a while. I'm sure it'll come to you. It has taken me a long time to find you; shame on me for not searching worldwide sooner. So you don't think I'm a complete idiot I want you to know that I found you several years ago, I've just been waiting for the right time to contact you.

The reason? What else, money! You have lots of it, and I have considerably less. Of course, most people have less money than the great Maximilian von der Dusenberger, don't they?

Well, you earned it, didn't you? But how did you get your start, dear boy? Who funded you when you were young and stupid and lost? You can pretend you don't know, but you do, you always did, or, surely, you figured it out long before you made your first million.

It has taken me many years to find something that might encourage you to share the wealth with me. Now, I have it. So, if you don't want to, it's possible, just possible, that a bit of the history of the von der Dusenbergers might show up, in say, *People* magazine, in an expose of the renowned philanthropist. Even now, decades later, people cringe at the sight of the swastika, and how that ugly symbol fits in with the von der Dusenbergers would make interesting reading, wouldn't it? And it doesn't even matter if the story isn't all true! Nowadays, in this society of sound bites and disinformation, no one really stops to think about what is true and what isn't, not if it shows up on a talk show! I see there is a new electronic encyclopedia now available on the Internet, Maximilian. Just think what the Wikipedia entry for the Maximilian Dusenberge Foundation would look like if someone wanted to add a few scraps of information about the origin of its wealth. What would happen when someone linked together a search for the Nazi Colonel, Wolfgang von der Dusenberger with the former Argentinean ambassador to Peru, Frederick Dressen, and compared pictures and dug into Ambassador Dressen's background?

I know you value your reputation, Maximilian. And now, when you have become such a beloved philanthropist in the autumn of your days; even, more likely, the early winter, you wouldn't wan to spoil it, would you? What would your lovely young bride say? What would she do? She might not even stay with you, and once again you would have to face your nights alone in a cold bed, without the warmth of her sexy body. Speaking of which, just to convince you I am serious, do you know where your wife is at this moment?

You think about this, dear Maximilian; take your time, take ninety days—I know you wealthy people don't have bundles of cas lying around, so I will be generous with the time I grant you, trustir you will be generous in return. I'll be in contact again with the details of how you can transfer the funds. And I know you'll be wis enough to make a reasonable deal.

Be safe until then.'

Maximilian had reached for the phone on his desk instantly after he'd finished reading the letter, but it rang before he could pick it up. Maximilian could count on his fingers the number of people who had this number.

"Hello? Hello?" he said impatiently.

"It's me, dear, I'm okay."

"Mary Jo, what happened? Where are you? Are you hurt?" he spat out the questions rapidly, not giving his wife a chance to answer.

"Easy, Maximilian, take it easy. I had an accident, but I'm not hurt. But how did you know? Anyway, it seems like, well, it was like someone tried to run me off the road. Maximilian…?"

"Yes, yes…"

"I saw his face briefly; he was smiling."

***

"The fate of my father, and of my brother, always set there in the back of my mind. It never went away; for years, for decades, I always wondered about them, and if I could ever find out what really happened. Of course, as I said earlier, I suspected it was my father who had supported me; who else could it have been?"

"The American soldiers?" I suggested.

Max shrugged. "The thought occurred to me, yes, it was a real possibility it had been one of the soldiers. I wanted to know for sure, but I had no idea how to go about looking for the information I needed. Where to start? Who to ask? What records would exist, I didn't know. The end of the war...everything was so confusing. It seemed impossible.

"You can't just go the Yellow Pages under 'Detectives' and get someone who will do this kind of work. Work that may involve obtaining records locked away for decades, forgotten and buried, or possibly long since destroyed. Bribes and lies work better than court orders, especially since I didn't want anyone to know exactly what I was looking for. That made it difficult because I didn't trust anyone to have too much information about my family or me.

"Not to bore you, but I began to ask and soon I found what I needed, in Europe. Charles, it's amazing what you can buy if you have enough money. Not things, but information, services people are eager to do for you because they think some of your wealth will rub off on them. You can buy access, convenience, secrets; it's truly amazing."

"Happiness, Max? Does it buy you happiness?"

"You don't need to be sarcastic, Charles. Actually, I'm happier than I've ever been, and you're right, not because of money but because of Mary Jo. Did you know I'd never married before?"

I shook my head.

"I was always busy, working and making money. I never thought about whether I was happy. I just was...what I was. I knew women, but marriage didn't sound right for me. I kept putting it off, much as you appear to have done. Until Mary Jo. It's safe now because I'm too old to start a family."

"What do you mean, safe?"

"Safe because...I always felt inadequate to become a father; wouldn't know how to be one because I never had an example.

Rarely, anyway. My father wasn't around much even before he disappeared.

I think my subconscious avoided letting me get involved with someone at an age where I could become a father. And now I feel guilty for taking her away from a younger man."

"What younger man?"

"Oh, no one in particular. Just any man her age with whom she could share her life. Maybe someone she could have a family with. I'm too old to start a family."

"Well, she chose to marry you, so you shouldn't feel guilty."

"True, and when I'm gone she may still be young enough to marry again."

"You're not so old that you won't be around a long time yet, Max." He didn't respond so I said, "So tell me more about what money can buy, Max."

"I hired several people so that no one of them would learn too much. One was retired from Interpol, an expert on tracing people. Another was a German man formerly with the GSG 9, which is a special force created to combat organized crime and incidents of terrorism, extortion, and so forth. Another was a octogenarian who had spent his life hunting down former Nazis. None of the men knew the other or that I even had anyone else working for me.

"To one, I told the story about the two soldiers who came to visit my mother. I told him the soldiers had been kind to us and now that I had the financial resources I wanted to find them and reward them. I'm not sure he believed me but I don't think he cared, as long as I paid him. I wasn't asking him to commit a crime so he wasn't concerned why I wanted to find the two men."

81

"I thought you said you didn't remember the soldier's names until later?"

The look Max gave me was one I can only describe as sly. "I said you didn't need to know their names. Anyway, I already told you that later I did remember. I also remembered the insignia on their uniforms, the MP batch, which would help to narrow down their unit."

I should have been suspicious, but what difference would it have made?

"The second man I told about my mother giving birth, dying and the baby having disappeared. I knew the hospital where she'd been taken, and I told him how I, in a panic, fled the hospital and learned to fend for myself. I wanted to find out what happened to the baby. For all I knew, he hadn't survived, but I wanted to know.

"Finally, I told the old Nazi hunter about my father. Of course, I knew nothing about where he had been towards the end of the war, and didn't even know if he had survived. But I suspected that because of the money I received, my father had survived and prospered.

"I remember spending an evening with the old man. He was almost blind by now from decades of poring through papers trying to track down people like my father. He'd survived the death camps, he said, but had lost every other member of his family. The hate he felt for the Nazis still burned in him. You could see it in the wrinkles of his face, etched as they were into him like scars from the scenes of horror he had witnessed. He'd found quite a few of the people he'd hunted and was proud to have been responsible for the extradition and conviction of former Nazis. Supposed Nazis, anyway."

"What do you mean, supposed?"

Max looked off, staring at the wall. It seemed he was running a video of his meeting with the old man, re-creating the look of the frail eyes in the wrinkled face of a man who remained bitter because of what he had lived through and seen so many years ago.

"I got the impression that the hatred he felt for the Nazis had grown into a hatred of anything German. Any former German officer who had escaped was fair game to him, whether the man had in fact been responsible for atrocities, or had merely been a soldier who had never been involved with the death camps, or any war crimes. Who knows for sure? I doubt if he even listened to Beethoven's symphonies, more's the pity for him."

"Extremism in the defense of liberty is no vice," I muttered.

"What's that?"

"Oh, oh nothing; something someone said once. Go on, Max."

He sighed deeply, a bit of sadness slipping out from the austere manner Max worked constantly to maintain.

"At first nothing came of my inquiry. The old man ignored me for the better part of an hour while he dug through files and reports, mumbling in German as papers flew in the air and across the room. I didn't think my father had been so very important, but to him, it would be one more notch. He told me to go away and come back in a few days.

"I did, and he said he remembered the name, von der Dusenberger. It had never been confirmed for sure whether he—my father—had been guilty of any war crimes, the old man told me, but he'd been wanted. 'One of those slippery bastards we never caught,' he said. I couldn't help laughing a bit, in a small way pleased to hear that my father had been too clever to be captured."

"So you don't really know if your father was a good soldier doing his duty, or…"

"Yes, or no, I can't say with finality. The fact that he fled, if he survived, which I believe he did, and didn't return, suggests he was either guilty of war crimes, or simply afraid that the allies would be ruthless to the officers. Still, you'd think he would have come back for my mother and me. Maybe he learned of my mother's passing, I suppose… still, there was me."

"You felt abandoned?"

"At that age, then, I was frightened and terribly confused. I thought my father had died, and now my mother had died, so yes, I felt abandoned. But I managed."

"How did you do it, Max? I mean, at what, twelve years old?"

"Ha! At twelve years old, in post-war Germany, with every other building a pile of trash, with so many of the young men dead or taken prisoner by the barbaric Russians, twelve years old was a man. There was plenty of work to do, and I worked. The smartest thing I did was run from the hospital and hitch a ride on the truck that was going to West Germany. Of course I was lucky—I had no idea where the truck was going, or that I had to pass through the Russian Zone to get to safety."

Maximilian shrugged in a manner that said it was good luck but the kind of good luck he assumed was his birthright.

Again he stared off and I knew he was seeing himself, a scared kid, working in the ruins of a battered German city, alone and angry. He looked forlorn and dangerous simultaneously.

"Weren't you afraid of what this old Nazi hunter might find?" I asked. "You say you're worried about your reputation, so what if he had found your father and proved he'd been guilty of war crimes? Wouldn't that have defeated your purpose of trying to keep such information quiet?"

"He was a very old man, Charles, I didn't expect he'd live long."

"But if he had," I pursued.

Max looked at me and said, "He didn't find anything about my father and he didn't live much longer," and without turning away from me signaled for the waiter. I shivered and averted his eyes.

Max ordered refills of our drinks and a minute later our food arrived. No one spoke for several minutes as we ate. Max was taking a long time to tell his story and I was hoping if I didn't ask any more questions he might decide to end my education. No such luck.

"The other men had better results. I'm not sure how they did it, such as finding the hospital records from 1946. At first I wondered if they were just telling me what I wanted to hear. Of course I already knew about my mother's death. The baby, though, that's what I wondered about. Did I have a brother somewhere?"

I must admit it, I was regaining interest, but I still had an eerie feeling, one that was beginning to make my heart palpitate. I realize that I can be a cold-hearted no good bastard myself, a character flaw I was working hard to correct. So when Max broached the idea of whether I'd be interested in 'reasoning' with his stepbrother and hinted that he had already done so, or had it done, to a bitter and ancient, nearly blind Nazi-hunter, my mind began to drift to the idea of running away with Mary Grace, no turning back, no giving notice, just going. I had enough money for us to get by for a long time. I knew it was a foolish notion; Mary Grace was not going to leave her sister. I tried to refocus on Max's story.

"Killing is an awful thing, Charles. But if you have to...for food, for example."

"You killed for food?"

Max nodded. "When my mother and I were in the streets, working our way back to our home. It's not a nice story, but this young man, bigger than me, fifteen or sixteen years old, he tried to take from my mother what little food she had gathered one day."

"And you fought him?"

Max shrugged and looked away, at nothing in particular. "It wasn't much of a fight. I hit him with a piece of concrete, a bit of a destroyed building. I didn't expect to hurt him, I just wanted to chase him away."

"So did that incident make killing easier for you?" I asked, the cynicism unmistakable, I hoped.

Max looked at me with anger. I knew, as he stared me down, that this man who many people thought of as mean and unmoving, at least in business, could be dangerous in other ways.

"The man formerly of the GSG 9," Maximilian went on, his voice rising in volume, lowering in bass, "managed to find hospital records from 1946. Countless records were destroyed by the war, and when serious re-building began more were lost or accidentally destroyed. Fortunately a few dedicated hospital employees thought birth records were important to save. So they were shipped to a warehouse on the outskirts of Berlin, to an area that no one paid attention to for many years.

"Eventually someone was looking for birth records, probably a situation similar to mine, —someone who lost track of a relative during the chaos of the end of the war—and the records were located and moved to a more modern storage facility. The records that were salvageable were later transferred to microfilm. The man I hired, as I say, I'm not sure exactly how he operated, but a bribe here, a promise there, a smile, a persuading way, and he was able to convince the curator to let him have access to the records for the period of time I was interested in. Usually someone has to show a family relationship or a legal authority. He told me he had suggested to the curator that he was doing research on babies born to German women but sired by American soldiers, which was too close to the truth. I wasn't concerned about a lie here and there, after all, I felt I had a right to know what happened to my brother. The records for my mother were barely legible, having been damaged by water, but my investigator managed to procure them."

"The originals, or copies?" I asked.

Maximilian nodded knowingly. "The originals, of course. Not that the curator knew this is what my investigator was intending, and if he later noticed he'd have no way to recover the records. Since my man used a story about researching babies fathered by American soldiers, I instructed him to not leave any evidence for anyone else to follow-up on." Maximilian shrugged; again a movement that suggested it was an obvious and logical procedure for him to cover his tracks when involved in slightly less than one hundred per cent legal activities.

"Later my investigator admitted it was possible copies were stashed in another location. I'm sure he's right because later the trail was followed again by someone else."

I wasn't sure what Max meant but figured he would tell me eventually. After he didn't continue immediately I asked, "So? What did you learn?"

"What do you suppose? I thought it was obvious."

I nodded. As he said, it was obvious; why else would Maximilian be taking our time with this story, and having shown me the note he'd received, unless he'd learned that his stepbrother survived, and was the person who followed the same trail of old records as Max's investigator?

"Somehow my man was able to trace the boy. I know he had to grease some palms, certainly those were the 'miscellaneous expenses' he charged me. I've never seen such large amounts for miscellaneous, but I wasn't going to ask.

"The boy was raised in an orphanage, which sounds like an anachronism out of our friend Dickens. Somewhere he picked up the name 'Wilhelm', and he'd been given the surname of Dusenberger by the hospital. Certainly they identified my mother, but maybe they thought 'von der Dusenberger' was too long a name—or maybe it sounded too *Nazi*. My investigator found that the director of the orphanage had lost a son in the war named Wilhelm, so I assume that's how the name was chosen.

"From the orphanage's files he noted that Wilhelm was always in trouble, from the time he was a boy all through school, which was attached to the orphanage. It was a state institution, populated mostly by boys who had lost both parents in the war."

"Why did he get in trouble?"

Max shrugged. "It's difficult to say, but he was frequently disciplined for fighting, according to the records."

"Was he small for his age? If he was born early due to your mother's fall…"

Max nodded. "I don't know if that was the case or not. I have a copy of the birth record which will show his size and weight at birth, but I didn't pay attention to it when I first looked it over. Maybe he was a runt, and sometimes kids will pick on the runt for no other reason than that they can."

"Was your investigator able to trace Wilhelm's life after he became an adult?"

"For awhile. Through his own wiles, or bribes, he had gained access to the records of the institution where the boy lived, and found out when he'd left. He said the records gave a forwarding address but it no longer existed and it was impossible at that point to determine where Wilhelm had gone, or what kind of work he did. So I ended our contract, but soon after I hired another person to continue the work. This was my way of not letting any one person become too knowledgeable."

"His name? Did he keep the same name, Wilhelm Dusenberger?" Even a slow thinker like me could see that the obvious way to try to find the boy was through his name.

"Yes and no. Sometimes he used a shortened version, Berger, but still, in the aftermath of the war, even ten of fifteen years later, it was difficult to keep track of people if they didn't want to be kept track of. And the name is not uncommon."

"Didn't he stay in Berlin? I would think it would have been difficult to leave, being surrounded by East Germany."

"Yes, it would have been, and that's where the trail was lost in East Berlin."

"You mean he voluntarily moved to East Berlin?"

"It appears so. The trail becomes confusing for the next few years, until he manages to return to the West."

"And how did he manage to return?"

"I had hired another investigator to continue. It's a long story, but I have his reports which you can read later."

Suggesting I could read the reports should have warned me.

"And you think it's he, your stepbrother, who sent you the letter?"

He nodded again. "And, threatened the Marys. My Mary, and your Mary, too, Charles. That's why I said he is a threat."

"I still say go to the police. Your reputation will be fine. If they find him in this country chances are they'll put him on the next plane to Germany and you'll never hear from him again."

Max scrunched his face. "Don't be foolish. He didn't spend all his life trying to find me to be scared away the first time I said 'Boo!' If he's had as a tough a life as I suspect, this will be a fight to the finish for him. And for me."

"Max, you're making this sound like a TV melodrama. This is real life, not some silly thriller with spies creeping through alleys and computer hackers breaking into your bank account."

"You're the one who is naïve, Charles."

He was probably correct. About some things I wanted to be like the three monkeys—see no evil, etc.

"So you don't think he's dangerous, Charles?"

"I'm not convinced."

"Then I'll have to tell you more."

I was afraid of that. I saw the waiter looking at us, but I knew he'd never suggest we'd overstayed our welcome. This was Maximilian von der Dusenberger and he lunched here three or four times a week. We'd stay as long as Max wanted and the waiters could just twiddle their thumbs if they had nothing else to do.

"There were these two Americans, long–time friends…they'd served together in World War Two. One was named William and the other was John…"

INTERLUDE: An Investigator

The Investigator read again the copies of the diary that had been sent to him. Someone else, someone in the same trade as he, had obtained these from the diary of a woman in the United States, the woman whose name had shown up in a yellowing letter tucked away in a long-forgotten folder in a warehouse in Berlin. Why someone—someone with plenty of money and patience—is interested in what sounds so mundane, the woes and angst of a woman who long ago had her heart broken, he could not understand. But, his was not to reason why, as long as he was paid.

The diary told of a woman, an American named Gina, who had come to Europe with a group of friends in 1969. After a time she decided to split off from the others and she and one of her friends traveled alone. She came to Austria where she met a man with whom she had a brief affair. The girl probably fancied she had met Prince Charming, a magical adventure where a girl comes to a foreign land and meets the man of her dreams, sophisticated, wise, worldly, and great lover.

The Investigator had found it fairly easy to confirm the identity of the woman's fantasy. The 'Mozart on the Square' hotel (almost every other business in Salzburg had the name 'Mozart' in it), still existed. The Investigator visited late one night, after midnight, when the desk was manned by an underpaid, sleepy clerk who was the only person in sight. It didn't take much money to convince the clerk to let the Investigator into the basement, where years of old guest logs still resided, many of the logs long ago food for rats. Just as long as you're gone before five a.m., when the morning janitor arrives, the clerk had said.

The Investigator found the logs for 1969, luckily still intact, if dusty and faded, and quickly located the two-week period mentioned in the girl's diary, when she had stayed with her German paramour. And here it was, the name Wilhelm Berger, the same as written in the diary. To be thorough, the Investigator checked for the two weeks prior and after the dates given, and did not find any other persons named Wilhelm, or Berger, or similar to Berger, who had stayed at the hotel during that timeframe.

The Investigator had come full circle; it was not a simple task, but he was sure that the Wilhelm Berger born in Berlin in 1946, the one he had been tracking, was this same man. The initial research had actually been fairly easy. The old hospital records showed that a baby was born to a woman named Ruth von der Dusenberger, who had died in childbirth, apparently due to injuries from a fall, which had induced labor. The baby boy was given the name 'Baby Dusenberger' in the hospital records, the last name shortened either on purpose or by mistake. The woman was known to have been married to a high-ranking German army officer who had disappeared towards the end of the war, so the father of the boy was unknown, though it was hinted that it was an American soldier. Hmm, the Investigator chuckled to himself, I guess the woman decided we were now allies with the Americans so she would show them how friendly we could be to our conquerors.

The baby was later sent to a state orphanage and given the name, 'Wilhelm.' He continued to use the surname of Dusenberger, according to school records. The orphanage no longer existed but because of the German penchant for keeping good records of everything, other than the incriminating records from the war that had been destroyed (and even then, many such records of horrible excesses had been located), the school records still existed. It was merely a matter of paying the going price, in this case a small one. Ah, yes, bribes, big ones, small ones, it seems nothing gets done without a bribe. Of course, nowadays they are often called something else, like 'political contributions'.

The records showed a boy who was often in trouble, in fight with other boys, and in need of frequent discipline. The notes said that the boy was often teased because his mother's father had abandoned the family and that he was the son of a drunken American. How cruel children can be, long before they have reasons to be, the Investigator reflected.

At eighteen the boy left the orphanage and went to work for one of the construction firms in the city. Once again, digging, persistence, and marks, or dollars, in the right hands found the old records. The work permit showed the name he used was Wilhelm Dusenberger. Within six months he had been accused of associating with known drug dealers and reprimanded. He must have had good friends because he continued to work in the industry and for awhile it appears he stayed out of trouble, other than involvement in a couple of bar fights that resulted in mass arrests and minor fines.

By this time he had money and a house waiting for him. When his mother had died and Colonel von der Dusenberger was nc located, the house his mother and brother had lived in was rented out, with the money not used to maintain the house or pay taxes put into a trust in the name of Maximilian and Wilhelm von der

Dusenberger. When Wilhelm turned eighteen, and his stepbrother had not been located, the funds were paid to Wilhelm and the ownership of the house reverted to him.

In 1969, now twenty-three years old, his company sent him to work in Austria on a project, after which he was given time for a vacation. His file showed he was based at the 'Mozart on the Square', noted in the project file as the company was footing the bill. The project was completed on time and under budget and to the satisfaction of the customer and Wilhelm's supervisor recommended him for promotion.

A year later the company suspended Berger for suspicion of dealing with drugs. Soon after he was arrested by West Berlin police, but the case was dismissed for lack of evidence. Then he disappeared. Because of the Investigator's suspicions regarding the drug connection, he contacted a friend of his who had worked in East Germany for half a lifetime.

For his friend, at least, he was not an enemy, to look for the information the Investigator wanted was going to cost a significant amount more than the petty bribes that had purchased other information. He requested approval for such an expenditure and his contact, the lawyer for the interested party, gave the approval and the Investigator wondered briefly, who was the interested party, but again, as long as he was paid well, no matter.

The Investigator's contact in East Berlin found that in late 1970 a man calling himself Wilhelm von der Dusenberger had defected to East Germany and requested a work permit. It took several months to approve the request, the natural suspicion being that he was a spy, but eventually he was allowed to stay in East

Germany. However, he was required to serve in the army for three years.

Over the next two and a half years Wilhelm was reprimanded twice for associating with suspected drug dealers, and once he was questioned regarding the smuggling of prohibited goods from the West.

In 1973 he was arrested and convicted of drug dealing and sentenced to seven years hard labor. The charge of attempting to help a fellow soldier defect was suspended.

In 1978 the file for von der Dusenberger shows that the 'inmate cannot be located', (euphemism for 'escaped'), and is wanted and considered dangerous. Anyone attempting to capture him is authorized to 'shoot if the subject resists'.

Quite the resourceful man, the Investigator concluded, to escape an East German prison and, apparently, return to the West.

So now the trail was back in West Berlin, as it was the most logical place for the Investigator to start. He went back to his resource at the construction firm, an old man who had worked with his hands until his knuckles were so permanently swollen he could no longer make a fist, and now served as a night guard, more of an honorary position to give him something to do and add a bit of income in addition to his pension, to buy a stein or two at the neighborhood tavern, while he and his comrades shared lies about the war.

The old man dug out the records starting with 1978 and gave them to the Investigator. Take them, he said, no one here needs to see these anymore. They should have been burned long ago. It was

1991 and no one other than the Investigator was interested in decades old employment records.

How long have you worked here, the Investigator asked the guard. Since right after the war. There was so much work to do.

Do you remember some of the people who worked here, say twenty-five years ago? Like who, the old man said, I knew them all.

Like a man named Wilhelm Berger, did you know him? The old man ran his hand under his chin, scratching the stubble of whiskers, thinking, trying to place the name amongst the hundreds he had known who had worked here.

That was the colonel's son wasn't it, the man said after a spell. Then...no, the colonel's wife's son. Yes, that's the one they said was fathered by an American soldier. Von der Dusenberger! I remember now. The colonel disappeared, his wife became pregnant, and died giving birth. The guys used to tease Wilhelm that he had two fathers, but the story got all scrambled after a while.

What else did you know about him? Did he have any girlfriends? Oh, yes, like any of the other young men, but I don't think he ever married. He didn't talk about them much except for one, a girl he met in Austria. I remember because he said maybe he got her pregnant, and her child won't know its father, just like he doesn't know his. He thought that was so funny.

Did he mention the girl's name? Oh, maybe so, but I don't recall. Oh, wait a minute, here; let's dig some more. You know, he left us to go to the East. I think it was to get away from the girl.

You mean she found him? Well, she must have had an address because he got a letter from her and he seemed very upset. He was afraid she was going to come looking for him.

He must have been really desperate to hide from her if he defected to do so! The old man and the Investigator laughed heartily.

In a cardboard box half eaten away by mice the old employee files were found. There was a file for 'Dusenberger' and another for 'Berger'. But they were the same man, the old timer said, we all knew him.

In the 'Dusenberger' file Wilhelm had hid the letter from the girl. The envelope gave the name and return address of the woman in the United States. Why hadn't he destroyed the letter?

Sifting further through the records, now in the 'Berger' file, the Investigator found that in 1981 Wilhelm Berger (the 'von der' and the 'Dusen' were gone again) had applied for work at his old firm. He was hired back on a probationary basis. Within a year he was fired for selling drugs on a construction site but was not arrested.

The trail then dried up and the Investigator again had to pay excessive bribes to an acquaintance with the police who was willing to search old arrest records. He eventually found that Wilhelm Berger had been arrested multiple times during the period 1982 to 1989 for suspicion of drug dealing and once for attempting to bribe police officer. In all cases the charges were dismissed for lack of evidence. Since then, he'd had no arrest record.

Ah yes, the Investigator reflected, once again bribery rears its ugly and effective head. Berger must have made a decent living dealing in drugs, but payoffs were probably a major expense.

Current property records showed that Berger still owned and lived in the house in which his mother had lived at the time of Wilhelm's birth and his mother's death. The Investigator went to see the house. It was a good size house, especially for one person, and the neighborhood was clean with rows of trees lining the streets. All the houses had window boxes from which bright yellow and pink flowers grew. The Investigator remembered Wilhelm Berger's mother's husband had been a fairly prominent colonel who had the money to live in a nice neighborhood and keep the house well maintained.

No one appeared to be at home, which was fine with the Investigator, as he had no intention of trying to speak to Berger. Acting like a nosy government inspector he hovered in the neighborhood until he located someone who looked equally as nosy as he. An elderly woman, bent over, was sweeping the sidewalk in front of a house four down from Berger's, and was willing to chat as long as anyone would listen.

The woman claimed, and looked it, to be over eighty years old. She said she had lived in the neighborhood, on the same property, for over fifty years, more than half a century, she explained, in case the man didn't understand.

She'd lived there when the bombs had nearly destroyed the entire section of houses. Hers had been burned to the slab and she had barely escaped with her life. I still have the scars from the burns on my back and on my arms, she claimed, almost as a boast.

She had been hospitalized for four months, and had no idea at the time what had happened to the colonel's wife or anyone else from the neighborhood. I had my own troubles. The Americans had captured her husband and only by the grace of God had they found each other, several months after the end of the war. They returned to their neighborhood and began rebuilding.

The colonel's wife, Ruth, was back, too, along with her son. She had been more fortunate in that her house had fared better than most. She also had frequent visitors in the guise of two America soldiers. The gossip was that they were looking for the colonel, to arrest him, but later the rumors were that the two soldiers were both sleeping with her.

Eventually, only one of them kept coming to see Ruth. But shortly after New Year's, 1946, the soldier quit coming and by then it was obvious that Ruth was pregnant. No wonder he had skipped out on her, everyone grumbled. Some of the neighbors felt sorry for Ruth, others despised her for sleeping with the American.

And what happened to the colonel? It was rumored he had escaped to Switzerland or to South America, abandoning his wife and son.

And the boy? Who knows? It was said that when the boy learned his mother had died he ran away and hid, and no one has ever heard of him since.

By the time the Investigator had finished his conversation with the old lady he'd learned that as the orphaned child grew up he was frequently teased that even his own mother hadn't known who the boy's father was, that it could have been either of two American soldiers. They didn't want a German son so when they learned his mother was pregnant, they left her. One story was that his mother died from a beating shortly after giving birth, but it was only so much dirt.

The adult Berger was considered a good neighbor, quiet and friendly, though it was widely rumored he made his money in illega activities. He also learned that Berger had recently been spending a lot of time in Lyon, France, ostensibly on business.

The rest was easy. A trip to Lyon and a visit to a real estate firm and the Investigator soon found the small home Berger had purchased. And here the Investigator found the man himself. For several days he followed Berger, taking surreptitious pictures, and noting his activities. They seemed innocent, mostly visits to shops and cafes and short conversations with a variety of people. He seemed to know everyone, or at least was not shy about approaching people. The Investigator even saw him meet twice with policemen in dark cafes.

By the time he was finished the Investigator realized he had earned more money from this job than he had for jobs that involved much more dangerous activities. He would have loved to have done more work for this client but the lawyer told him the assignment was completed.

"Bill and John reconnected after the war was over. They'd learned that they lived less than thirty miles of each other in Orego and like a lot of soldiers who found themselves thousands of miles from home during the war, they promised they'd look each other u if they survived. Few wartime friends did find each other when the returned to America, until the reunions started, because they had their own lives to revive. But Bill and John did stay in touch and when they each got married, the two couples developed a tight friendship.

"Bill and his wife Abby had a son, David, and John and his wife Cassie had a daughter, named Beth. While they may or may n have planned it, or hoped it, their children fell in love, got married, and also made homes in Oregon for a time. They also had two children of their own.

"So the years passed and the families lived happily and prosperously. Bill worked in construction and John was in sales an eventually became a dealer of farm equipment. David and Beth we ambitious in there own way, he in law and she in marketing, advertising, something like that, and they moved to southern California. I suppose Bill and John and their wives weren't happy their kids moved away, but in a few years they had retired and now they had time to visit their children and grandkids."

I resisted yawning, though I did glance at my watch. Was I getting bored or what? The 'what' may have been the ticklish feelir in my gut that Max's story was leading to things I didn't want to know.

"Where are you going with this, Max? If you were trying to pitch this tale to a movie producer you'd have put everyone to sleep by now. You need a car chase, some explosions, and a good sex scene."

A faint snicker was what I got in replay. The story had been mildly interesting to a point, but it was becoming bland the more Max went on.

"Something exciting has got to happen soon, right, Max?"

He patted the table softly, a signal for me to be patient. I caught a waiter's eye and tipped my glass. He nodded and went to get me a refill; Max was paying.

"Charles, most people's lives are rather ordinary. Think about it; what happens to most people most days? They wake up and go to the bathroom. They have a cup of coffee and a piece of toast or stand in the kitchen eating yogurt corrupted with sweet fruit, because they haven't got time to sit down and have a decent breakfast. They tell their kids to have a good day at school, kids who aren't listening to them because they are listening to headphones attached to their ears, they give their spouse a peck on the cheek and off to work they go.

"They sit at a desk, drink lots of coffee, they stop for lunch, eat high-calorie fast food that gives you heartburn, or a sandwich laden with salt at one of those ubiquitous restaurant chains, and think they are having a healthy meal because they drink lo-cal soda. They return to work, and drink more coffee the rest of the afternoon to stay awake.

"They come home, go through the mail, most of which is junk, ask the kids how their day was but the kids are either on their cell phones or mindlessly playing a computer game, or aren't even at home because they are at a soccer game, which they hate but are there because the soccer Moms think that's what they are supposed to do..."

"Lots of people don't work in offices, Max, and they love their jobs, and..."

He waved me off. "Yes, yes, I'm exaggerating a bit, but the point is that most people live a mundane life most days."

I had to agree, once I thought about it. Made me want to get up and do something new and exciting. At the same time, there's nothing wrong with a spot of peace and quiet each day to help recharge the mind and body. Max was continuing with his story and I strived to pay attention.

"Bill and John were outdoorsmen. They liked to fish and hunt, though as they got older it was mostly fishing."

Who are these guys and why does Max know so much about them? Well, you fool, these are the two soldiers who had come to visit Max and his mother.

"I'm not much for either sport; it seems I never found the time. You, Charles? You hunt or fish?"

I shook my head. "A little fishing when I was younger, but no, not in a while."

"Occasionally I've thought it might be nice to spend more time outdoors, I mean, in the country, the woods, camping and hiking, and fishing."

I could not imagine Maximilian von der Dusenberger hiking in the woods or sleeping in a tent. At least, not unless he had three or four people to tend to him, including a chef and a sommelier.

"In September of 1988 Bill and John took a trip to one of their favorite spots, a river in Idaho. They intended to fish and hike and stay in a cabin owned by a business associate. At the same time their wives went to Los Angeles to visit David and Beth and the grandchildren. After a week at the river Bill and John would go to Los Angeles to meet their wives."

"There's gonna be a bear in the woods, I just bet."

Max glared at me. "You know, Charles, if my wife didn't like you, and if you weren't engaged to my wife's sister…"

"I know, I know. Sorry, please go on, I'll try not to interrupt you."

He took a deep breath and for a moment looked down at the table, as if he was concentrating on where his story went next. The waiter had also brought Max a new drink but Max hadn't touched it. I sipped mine and waited.

***

"Bill, this looks like a great spot."

"Ya think? I was planning on going up the road a few miles to that small lake we found the last time we were here."

"Oh, yeah, I remember, Minnow Lake, it was. Yeah, okay, we'll go there tomorrow. Let's try our luck here. This looks like a nice spot."

"Okay, John, good idea."

The two friends unpacked their gear from the back of the rental pick-up: clothes and food, and most important, their fishing paraphernalia. They hadn't needed to bring as much as when they used to camp out in the open, as the cabin was stocked with cooking utensils and cots that were warmer and more comfortable than sleeping bags. Bill stopped for a moment and looked around him.

"What is it?" asked John.

Bill smiled and slowly shook his head. "I was just admiring the scenery. So busy getting this stuff unloaded I forgot to look around. This is why we're here, isn't it? For the view, the quiet, the smell of the woods."

"Ever the poet! For the fishing, too, don't forget."

"We'll get our share, don't worry. Enough for dinner, anyway. But sometimes I think it doesn't matter. I just love it when get out here, away from the city and the phone and the TV."

"Could be worse; we could be like the kids and live in the smog and traffic of El-A. I don't know how they stand it there."

"Me either. It's the one thing I hate about visiting them now that they're in the big city."

"Which *one* thing? The smog, the freakin' traffic, or the noise?"

"I guess it's our fault; we didn't raise them right, hey John?"

"They've got to make a living their way. You watch, a few years from now they'll drag their tails back to Oregon, tired of the rat race."

"David's got a good practice going there. Couldn't do as well if they'd stayed home."

"Portland's a big enough city for me."

"Yeah, I wouldn't be surprised if they come back some day."

"Forget 'em for now. Let's get to fishing."

The next day Bill and John decided to try their luck at a small lake tucked deep in the woods, unknown to most casual fishermen, called Minnow Lake. The lake was seven miles from their cabin so in acknowledgment of their age they eschewed walking and drove their truck on the barely drivable gravel path that led to the cabin, back onto the dirt road that paralleled the highway, then onto a narrow trail barely wide enough for the vehicle, and reached the shore of the lake as the sun was rising over the hills.

"The girls would give us heck, driving to the lake. I can just hear 'em, 'So you're the guys who love hiking in the woods!' "

"Yeah, I wouldn't mind the hike in, but coming back, it gets dark fast in these woods. I'd hate to get lost out here, especially since it looks like rain later."

"Yeah, well, we don't have to tell 'em."

"Just as long as we catch enough fish for dinner, that's all I care about."

***

"They never made it back to their cabin that evening," Max said in a weary voice, low and barely audible. I knew there wasn't going to be a bear in the woods, but I hadn't the slightest idea what this story was all about or how it related to anything we had talked about earlier in our extended lunch.

"They drowned?" I asked, after waiting for Max to continue.

"No, no," Max answered, his voice rising now. He sat up straight—he'd been leaning forward on his arms as he talked—and

107

noticed his drink, surprised that it was there. He looked at it as if it had materialized magically. Then he raised a finger and a waiter appeared immediately, as if he'd popped up out of the floor.

"It's diluted," he said.

The waiter took the untouched drink and we sat quietly waiting until he returned with a fresh scotch and rocks.

"No," Max said, finally responding to my question. "They crashed."

***

"That was a great day of fishing, John. We have enough for tonight's dinner and tomorrow's."

"Yeah, but I wished we'd left earlier. It's getting dark already and this road is hard to follow."

"It's the only road until we get to the gravel path, isn't it? It'll take us right to the cabin."

"Ah, I don't know…here, I think we turn here; do you remember this?"

"Well, geez, no, I wasn't paying close attention I guess. I know it was a tight squeeze, but I don't remember it being this tight; I think it's to the right; doesn't look like much of a road to the left."

"I don't know, dammit. I need to get out and look."

John got out of the truck and walked ahead, then veered to his left the beam from his flashlight cutting into the blackness.

"Hey, John," called Bill, from the car. "I can hardly see you when you're out of the headlights."

"I think it's this way; follow the beam. This turnoff here, I don't even remember it. Does it look familiar, Bill?"

"Shit, John, I can't see anything that looks familiar."

"You're a big help."

"Get back in the car before you fall off somewhere."

***

"To make a long story short…" Max said.

Please, finally, at last, yes, do.

"The truck went over a cliff, landed in a culvert that was filled with boulders and uprooted trees. Neither man was wearing a seatbelt. Apparently the truck tumbled end over end several times before coming to a stop. They weren't even discovered until a few days later, after the men didn't show up in Los Angeles and their wives began to worry.

"The authorities said it looked like they got lost and took a path that had been closed for years. In fact, the police said they were sure the road had long been overgrown with brush and they were surprised the men were able to see any kind of a road there."

Max looked at me and then took a hearty gulp from his drink. Again I began to feel stupid, because supposedly I should have come to some startling conclusion from Max's epic saga, but I didn't have a clue, except that he was talking about the two American soldiers.

"Who were these men, Max? You are talking about the two soldiers who used to come to see you and your mother, right?"

"Remember earlier I told you about the man I hired to find the two soldiers?"

I nodded. "You mentioned three different men."

"Yes," he said and nodded. "To keep the information scattered amongst them.

"The one who had been an Interpol agent was good at finding people. He found who the two soldiers who visited us were, who helped my mother and I, and who, you know, the one who befriended my mother."

"He became her lover, right, Max? It isn't so hard to say."

"No, you'd think a grown man could say it, but I was a boy then, so when I think of my mother, I still think of myself as I was then, a boy of twelve. And at that time I still was expecting my father to return home."

I nodded; I did understand. I can appreciate that if you lost your mother when you were young, you remembered her the way she was then. I could buy it. After all, I'd been fatherless all my life and there were times when I felt different from other people, less, somehow, because I never experienced what it was like to have had a father.

"I don't know how he did it, but he was able to track them, their lives, all the way to when they crashed in the woods."

"Can you be sure he found the right men?"

"Yes, because by then I had remembered their names, at least their last names as I saw them on their uniforms. And he brought me documentation and pictures."

I thought that finally Max was going to tell me their names, and clueless, as usual, I couldn't figure where this was going yet. Was he going to tell something preposterous, like, one of these guys was my father? Ridiculous! Heck, I wasn't born until 1970, and my mother, she'd been born in 1946. Either of these two men, Bill and John as Max called them, would have been twenty years older than my mother if … not impossible, I guess, but it made no sense.

11

"When was this, Max, that you hired the investigator, as you call him?"

"Oh, I thought I mentioned, it was over ten years ago."

"Ten years! Why then, after all this time, is this an issue?"

"I'll get to that."

God, I thought this was almost over but it seemed this story was going to challenge the *Iliad* for length.

"So obviously by the time my investigator had found out who the two soldiers were, they had died, back in 1988 in the accident in the woods."

"So you couldn't do anything to reward them, if that was your intention."

Max nodded. "But I could for their children, or grandchildren, if I wanted to."

"Their wives…did you contact them?"

"No, I never did, for a reason."

"Being?"

"Patience, Charles."

Damn!

"I had my man investigate their deaths, just to satisfy my curiosity."

"Curiosity about what?"

Max shrugged. "Eh, I had a hunch.

"He was very thorough," Max went on. The accident was almost a week old before the car and the remains were found. The original investigators, the local police, had no reason to suspect foul play of any sort, so they quickly wrote it off as an unfortunate accident; two hunters lost in the woods in pitch black darkness, they went off the road into the ravine, bad luck, end of story."

"And did your man learn anything different, or suspicious, a these years later?'

Max shrugged and was quiet for a moment, thinking.

"He learned that the road the two men took had at one time been marked and barricaded, but no barricade was found at the scene. The report written up at the time—I have no idea how my man got a hold of it—simply mentioned in passing that a barricade had been there at one time but had probably been knocked over or eroded. The police didn't seem to think much of it. Obviously, by the time my investigator looked into it the area was overgrown to th point that it was impossible to say exactly where the men had driver off the road. There was no road anymore."

"Well, maybe the police were right."

Max was silent for awhile, nodding as if agreeing with me. But he wasn't.

"It would appear so at first. But that was before my investigator was able to track Wilhelm Berger to the United States a the time of the accident. Apparently Wilhelm either didn't think it necessary to cover his identity or didn't have the resources to acquir a false identity so he could conceal his movements.

"We, I say, my investigator, tracked him to renting a car in Idaho, a bit more than fifty miles from where the accident occurred. Give the police some credit, the report showed they did check renta cars in the immediate vicinity of the accident, but not out as far as fifty miles. It's too much of a coincidence, I say."

"So do you still have your, ah, *investigato*r, looking for Wilhelm Berger?"

"Not him. As I said I earlier, I didn't want any one person knowing too much about what I was searching for, or what I was learning. By this time I decided my stepbrother wasn't a man I wanted to know, and I didn't want him to know me. Yet, he was my brother so I kept my man on a retainer, to keep me informed about Berger every other month or so. However, I ended that contract years ago and tried to put Wilhelm out of my mind forever."

"How could he not know where you were? Your name is not exactly Smith or Jones, and you are quite well known throughout the country."

"Yes, now I am, but ten years ago I was not particularly famous. My Foundation hadn't been started yet, and Wilhelm may not have known yet that I ever left Europe. Remember, he was in East Berlin for a long time, not a place easy to obtain information we take for granted. And, more important, he likely didn't even know of the existence of a brother until he was grown. He was an infant and an orphan when I fled Berlin, and all he may have known was that his father had died in the war and his mother while giving birth. Quite frankly, he may not have even cared to know about me, at first."

"He got out of East Germany before the fall of the Soviet Union, didn't he?"

Maximilian nodded. "Yes, long before. He apparently lived in the shadows of society, so bribes were a major item in his monthly expenses category."

"And his purpose in finding you was not out of brotherly love, it would appear."

"I'm not sure what goes on in his mind. Like you and I, he basically grew up without a father, except for whatever parental ca. he received at the orphanage. He may have grown up feeling angry and deserted, as I did at times…"

I looked away for a second, remembering my own anger.

"You, too, eh Charles?" Max said, seeing the look on my face. I nodded.

"I think he wanted revenge on somebody, especially the ma. who he felt had abandoned him and his mother. Much like my fath. did to our mother and me. Somehow he managed to learn about the soldiers who befriended his mother—our mother; maybe from an o. neighbor. Whether he did it himself or hired someone as I did, I ha. no idea, but he learned their names and tracked them. But he still didn't know if it was the one or the other, so he eliminated both of them."

"Eliminated! The jargon you use, Max."

"He didn't know which of the soldiers was his father, but he'd learned he had an older brother, me, who had fled from the hospital, or, in his mind, abandoned him. Not that at my age I coul. have cared for him."

"What goes around…"

Max's expression told me he still thought I was somewhat c. a cretin the way I threw out pithy sayings amidst serious discussion. Will I ever grow up, I'm sure he wondered.

"So you've been waiting to hear from him all these years."

"Not really. I had no idea he might be looking for me. He got his revenge on the soldiers, so at that point I concluded it best to leave it be. I had no solid evidence that he committed those murders, though I'm convinced he did, or had it done, and the last thing I wanted to do was expose myself to him."

"But now? The letter means he's found you?"

Max nodded. "He may have been biding his time; who can say? He needed for me to have something of value to blackmail me over. I didn't have a family, and my Foundation didn't exist until a few years ago, so there wasn't much he could embarrass me about. Now, he can threaten Mary Jo and my reputation."

I shook my head and scrunched up my face in confusion. "Max, why didn't he just come openly and ask you for money?"

"Good question. I think the answer is that his own investigating tells him that I know about him, and that I suspect he committed those murders. I can't be sure, but it's the only thing that makes sense. It just took him longer to find me and find out what I know—what he thinks I know—because he probably didn't have the resources to work with. Money talks, as they say, and while my investigations indicate he made a decent living, smuggling drugs and protection rackets, of sorts, he didn't become wealthy; isn't wealthy. He had to do his own searching whenever he had time and without the expert investigators I can afford."

"What kind of work did Wilhelm do when he wasn't trafficking in drugs?"

"Best I could find, a bit of everything, mostly in the construction field. For long stretches there is no record, which could

mean he was involved in black market or other illegal activities. Yo[u]
know the movie, *The Third Man?*"

I nodded; the Orson Welles movie about the black market
selling of diluted penicillin in the days right after the end of World
War Two.

"It's not all fiction, " Max said.

"I believe that whenever Wilhelm had saved some money h[e]
spent time searching for the soldiers, and for me, and of course for
my father, the colonel, who he claims went to Argentina. For all I
know he could have hired some of the same people I did, it's not
inconceivable."

I still had the feeling there was something else coming, or
was I being too suspicious and cynical?

"Max, are you telling me this because you think Mary Grace
could also be in trouble? Just because she's your sister-in-law?"

"Ah, I don't think so, Charles, but one never knows. He has
obviously hired someone to scare Mary Jo, though I'm sure the
almost-accidents are really a message to me. The incidents tell me
that he, Wilhelm, can get at her. A mad rattlesnake doesn't ask if
you're the person who stepped on his den, he strikes at whatever
target is there. But there is a particular reason I'm telling you all
this."

He sighed then and put his head down. He seemed tired
suddenly, older, a Maximilian I'd never seen before.

"After I received the letter I hired a new person, a specialist,
someone who does more than simply search for information,
someone other than who I used before, to find Wilhelm Berger, and
you were right, not just to reason with him, but to eliminate him."

11

"Jesus, Max. You can't take the law into your hands."

"I can't? Don't be naïve, Charles, it's done all the time. Politicians do it, businessmen do it, the police and judges do when they can. Wilhelm is a threat. He's killed at least two men and he threatens my wife, myself, and maybe, you and Mary Grace. I'm positive that if I died with him still running loose, he would be a problem for you and the Marys, and don't tell me you'd go to the police."

"I would."

"And tell them what?"

"It depends what he did," I said, meekly.

He grinned, but it wasn't a 'ha-ha' grin, it was a 'you're so foolish' grin.

"I've beaten around the bush long enough, Charles. I have one more story to tell and then maybe you won't be so self-righteous."

The *Iliad*, the *Odyssey*, and now *Gone With the Wind*.

INTERLUDE: In Flight

The trouble with flying west to east, Los Angeles to Paris, is that if you're on a morning or early afternoon flight (and because my scheduled was forced and hurried I didn't have a choice), most of the flight is during the time of day when people are normally awake. Which makes it difficult to get any sleep, and then, when you arrive in Europe, morning there, it's just about the time you want to hit the sack. That's fine if you have nothing else on the immediate agenda; a short nap and then tough it out until night.

I wouldn't have such luxury. From Paris I had to take a flight to Lyon, and the wait was only an hour and a half, not even enough time to grab a catnap in the lounge. If I let myself fall asleep in the Paris airport I might miss my connection.

I put my head back and closed my eyes and tried to close off the sounds of the airplane: even in business class I could hear passengers talking and coughing behind me, babies squealing and crying, attendants pushing drink carts down the aisles, carts filled with bottles of water, cans of soda, little wine and booze bottles. Even for me, who thinks the five o'clock chime on all clocks should be the clink of ice cubes in a glass, it was too early to start imbibing. I tried the crossword puzzle in the airline magazine, finished it, and read the articles about wonderful places this airline could take me. I even pored through the catalog advertising beautiful items you absolutely had to have to make your next trip more comfortable.

The stewardess brought snacks and I opted for a beer to help them go down. I had today's Los Angeles Times, the USA today, a paperback, and the documents Max had given me to study. I scanned the sports section of the Times. The Dodgers and Angels were muddling, not threatening too seriously to win any old pennant, and fathead Bobby Bonds was tearing up the National League, hitting home runs as if he was playing tee-ball.

I thought about the reports Maximilian had given me. I'd read most of them last night and while waiting in the airport. Rather fascinating, even if it did make me feel like a literary peeping tom. Some of it read like a spy novel.

Wilhelm Berger had led an interesting life, albeit a sometimes harsh and dangerous one. He'd even spent several years in the East German military, some of the time in jail, which is where it seems he made his contacts that propelled him into the drug trade. And a lucrative business it turned out to be for him, even after he got caught. A big part of the mystery in Wilhelm's bio, not the biggest in importance to me, or Maximilian, or my mother, had she known anything abut this yet, but still curious, was how Berger managed to escape East Germany and make his way to the west. I suppose if he was clever enough to find his way across the Iron Curtain, he wasn't going to leave any trail to explain how he did it. And his drug trade contacts likely knew all the secret routes in and out of East Berlin: what checkpoints to avoid, what guards were mostly easily bribed, all the details one needs to know to be successful in one's chosen profession. If the information Max received from his investigator was accurate, Berger must be some tough character if he survived and escaped from an East German prison. He was a person not to be taken for granted.

The trail goes cold for awhile and the next thing we learn is that he's in Bonn, then sometimes Frankfurt, then Barcelona, all ov Europe but clearly avoiding the countries still under Soviet domination, until the fall of the Berlin Wall. After which he expand into new territory: Budapest, Prague, Warsaw, even Moscow and a occasional visit to Berlin. Those trips to Berlin, Max assumes, are when Berger began to piece together the puzzle of his birth, ancestry, and family history.

Really amazing the information that's available if one has t time, the money, and, I guess, the chutzpah to go after it. Most of what I'd read had been obtained, according to Max, via bribes, but still, the information is sitting there, idly waiting for people who ar willing and able to go after it; it's just a function of putting enough money in the right hands.

Something else was bothering me and it had nothing to do with the basic premise of my trip. While the loud voice in my head was screaming, *No! I don't want to find my father*, a troublesome imp was perched on my shoulder saying. *You have an out, young man. You don't really want to marry the girl, do you? Do you love her or are you in love with the cozy nest you've fallen into, a nest layered with the comfort of a secure, very well-paying job, layered with the perks of knowing a rich boss on a first-name basis, and the affection of a great-looking gal who's got everything a guy could a for...*

What more could a guy ask for, is what I repeated to the im He answered something about there being more fish in the sea; I replied I wasn't getting any younger, and he said that was no reaso unless you are deeply in love with the girl. And I insisted I was, or am, I think, and when I realized there was the possibility of a way out, an excuse not manufactured by my usually conniving mind, I began to fantasize how my life would change if Mary Grace and I are forced to end our relationship. Would I quit working for Max? Have to. Give up the good life? The weekends at the ski resort, the essential meetings in Kauai, the cozy get-togethers with Maximilian and Mary Jo, the bar-b-ques and gourmet meals, the late evenings sitting by the fireplace watching a classic movie with Mary Grace cuddled next to me and a glass of Max's fine brandy within reach. Was I more in love with the good life than I was with Mary Grace?

I took out the binder of notes Maximilian's agent had prepared and found where I'd left off. Immediately, though, my mind ran back to the long conversation Max and I had had. I needed to replay it in my head to make sure I understood what he'd told me.

SEVEN: mein Onkel

"Among the things I wanted to learn about my stepbrother was his history with women. Why, you may ask? Partially it was curiosity—you may say nosy— but I wanted to know if I had any other relatives, children of his."

"And what did you discover?"

"I learned that he never married, but not for lack of interest women. He apparently was as interested as any other young man, b for reasons, maybe similar to mine, he just never met someone at th right time and place.

"In particular I learned that he met a girl in 1969, an American who was traveling in Europe with college friends. The gi had apparently decided to visit some places on her own, planning tc meet her friends elsewhere. The exact details I don't have, but the girl met Berger—I should call him Wilhelm, I suppose—in Austria, and they had an affair."

"Hmm, sounds familiar—like the soldier and your mother."

I could tell Max didn't find my comment amusing or relevant. He ignored me and continued. I vowed not to interrupt anymore.

"Again, I can't say for sure about the details, but apparently after a brief dalliance the girl had to leave to link up with her friend so they wouldn't worry about her. She and Wilhelm agreed to meet again later in Salzburg. She showed up, he didn't. She waited a week, visiting all the places she and Wilhelm had gone to during th time of their affair. At least, that is how I envision it. It would make for a real tearjerker of a movie, wouldn't it? A young girl alone in a strange country meets a handsome man and has a carefree, exciting romance, and they promise to meet again. But he doesn't meet her; why?"

Rotten bastard, I thought. Sounds like me. I forgot my promise not to interrupt. "Out of sight, out of mind; it was just a lark for him."

"She gave up, went to meet her friends in London or Rome, and soon after she realized she was pregnant."

"Max, I know you said money can buy all kinds of information, but how could anyone learn all this?"

"I believe by interviewing the friends of the woman who got pregnant. Some story about tracing the father to get money for the woman."

I began to feel uneasy. I caught Max's eyes and thought I knew where this was going. I broke my vow again.

"What was her name, Max? The girl's name?"

He hesitated, then spat out the name as if ashamed to say it and quickly took a chug on his drink.

Gina Hardin, was the name he said.

I looked at him with an anger I knew was misplaced. Or maybe not; if he hadn't been so goddamn nosy he never would have found out and I could have gone on pretending for the rest of my life.

"Gina Hardin, you say? Funny, isn't it, same name as my mother. But my father's name was Hardin, Max. My mother's maiden name was—come to think of it, I guess I don't know it; I never had reason to ask."

"You never wanted to ask, you mean."

"What kid asks his mother her maiden name?"

"True, you wouldn't, but you'd figure it out from your grandparent's name, eventually."

"Well, I didn't have any relatives, Max."

Max sat back in his chair, took a deep breath, and then leaned forward, folding his hands in front of him. For a second he reminded me of a priest, or a therapist.

"Charles, if you want, I'll show you the papers my investigator sent me, it's quite a pile. But here it is, you can't avoid any longer—Wilhelm, my stepbrother, is your father. Your father was not killed in Vietnam, and he, Wilhelm, never saw your mother again after those few days in Austria. He probably didn't even know the girl was pregnant."

"But did he find out?"

Max shuffled his right hand in a back and forth motion. "I'm not positive but I expect by now he has found out."

"And my mother went home, had the baby, me, raised me by herself, never married, and told me my father had died in Vietnam, is that it?"

"You know it's true, Charles, you don't have to ask me. You must have suspected there was more to the story your mother told you."

"I certainly didn't expect to find out your brother was my father! Is that why you hired me?"

"No, no, no." He shook his head. "I learned about you that way, but I also learned you were extremely capable in your job. I would have eventually found a way to tell you, but I wouldn't have

12

hired you for that reason. You should know me better by now, Charles."

I managed a sarcastic grin, knowing that was the truth, at least, the truth as Max knew it. Yet, I sensed a softness he never revealed, other than maybe, *maybe,* to Mary Jo, and that Max hired me first and foremost because he felt a connection to me, maybe even an obligation.

***

For the first few years of my life it seemed normal, just Mom and me, no father. We lived in an apartment building and there were no other kids my age to play with. I had no cousins or other relatives.

(When I was older Mom explained that her father had died in an accident when she was five years old, and she and her mother were estranged for reasons I was too young yet to understand. I keep thinking that one of these days I should sit down with her and have a heart to heart).

When I went to school and met other kids and found out they had both a mother and father I wondered why I didn't have a father. Of course, some of them came from broken homes, but even then, they talked of their father's taking them places on the weekend, such as to a movie, or to play ball. It made me jealous, and then angry, especially when I wanted to do the things I heard the other boys talk about, like playing ball with their fathers.

The cutest girl in first grade was Tammy Willson. She ignored me for the first few weeks of school, but she flirted—if that's the correct description for a six-year Shirley Temple-look-alike who conned all the boys out of their cookies at recess. I never had any cookies because back then we lived on a tight budget, not that I understood then what a budget was.

One spring day I brought Tammy a bouquet of flowers. Really, it was just a bunch of flowers from our yard. I walked up to her and said, "I brought you some flowers, Tammy. I thought you might like them."

She looked at the flowers as if they were poison ivy, and at me as if I was a serf daring to speak to the queen without being spoken to first.

"You're the dumb kid without a father, aren't you?" she said as much an accusation as a question, as if it was my fault, as if not having a father made me bad.

She threw the flowers on the ground and stepped on them and laughed in my face. "Look at these silly flowers the kid brought me, ha!" All the other guys laughed at me.

"You should have brought her a cookie, you do-do", one of the other boys chortled.

I don't know if you can blush at six years of age, but I felt like my face was on fire. I ran inside the school and hid in the bathroom until the teacher found me. Then she called my mother to come and get me because I was being a 'disciplinary problem', like I had an infectious disease, and Mom wasn't happy because she'd had to leave work to come for me.

I got even with Tammy years later, not that I'd been planning anything, when we were in high school. I had been riding around, going nowhere, as teenagers did with their first car, with my buddy Butch. We saw a couple of girls coming out of the theatre. Butch suggested we give them a ride because he had a crush on one of the girls, Macie Jenkins. The other girl was Tammy Willson, who I had managed to ignore from the time of the fiasco in the first grade all the way until now, our senior year in high school. By now her parents were divorced and she lived with her mother.

After we'd driven around in circle for a half-hour Butch and Macie asked to be dropped off at the bowling alley. Tammy didn't object to being left alone with me, so we deposited Butch and Macie and drove on, neither one saying anything for awhile. We stopped at Chris' Drive-In and got sodas and made small talk. She suggested we drive to Shire's Beach, a local hangout near a lake good for swimming and picnics in the daytime, for campfires, drinking beer, and making out in the back seat at night.

I parked twenty yards or so from any of the other cars, windows steamed in most cases. Tammy nuzzled up close to me on the seat. You'd think we'd been an item or something. I wondered if she was trying to make up to me for embarrassing me all those years ago, but I didn't think she even remembered me. Actually I didn't have any problems getting dates in high school, but I seldom went out with anyone more than once or twice. And I had never asked Tammy out. Maybe I was a challenge for her, who also played the field though I knew a bunch of guys had asked her to go steady.

She kissed my ear and I ignored her. She put her hand on my thigh and I tried to ignore her but it was getting difficult. Then she pulled away and said she needed to go to the bathhouse to use the rest room, the tease, but she'd be right back, don't go away, Charlie.

As she was returning, swishing her hips and shaking her golden locks as she walked, a big come hither smile on her face, I started the car.

"Aren't you the kid who was abandoned by her father?" I said, as I drove away, leaving her standing in the sand.

I shake my head now when I think of it. I wish I'd run into Tammy somewhere so I could apologize. But at the time, to an immature high schooler with a chip on his shoulder, it was funny. My buddies thought it was cool, except they said I should have seen how far she'd go before I stranded her.

After mother took me home from school she tried to calm me by explaining that it wasn't my father's fault that he couldn't be here, that he was a hero who fought in a war but unfortunately died. So now I could tell my friends that my father had been a war-hero, and that impressed them.

Inside of me the anger still simmered. I was angry at the people who sent my father to war, at the people who killed him, and at my mother for not keeping any pictures or stories about my father. She said she had gotten angry one day, too, and destroyed everything. I had no reason not to believe her. But sometimes I wondered.

When one of my friend's parents would divorce, I secretly felt glad, that now they, too, would not have a father full time. Then I'd feel bad that I was glad; I probably could have used a good therapist at the time, but most of my thoughts and feelings I kept locked up, and Mom couldn't have afforded to send me to see anyone. I'm lucky I didn't drive myself crazy, but young people are resilient.

As I got older I would act out against my friend's fathers. Smart aleck talk, sassing them, until my mother had to discipline me which only served to make me angrier.

12

My attitude got worse when I started to date. I'd meet a nice girl, and she'd ask me to her house, and I'd meet her parents, and right away I was angry because she had this nice two-parent family, and I only had one. And even then Mom often was gone, working two jobs. I'd come home from school, no Mom. Sometimes it'd be dark before she got home. Then she'd fix us a hot meal and tell me she was sorry I had to wait and everything was fine again until the next day.

How many nice girls I dated two or three times, then dumped them because I was angry, I can't count. Who knows, I might have married one of them had I been nicer, and never have met Max or Mary Grace, and never learned who my real father was.

***

"Uncle Maximilian," I said, barely concealing the glee. "I cannot effing believe it."

"The concept doesn't exactly thrill me, either, Charles."

"And Mary Grace? Did you expect me to marry her so we could be in-laws?"

Now Max laughed, a rare event. "No, Charles, I never thought of it. No more than I thought I would fall in love with Mary Jo; me, at my age, falling for someone who could be my granddaughter? If I wasn't so happy with her I'd be embarrassed."

"Oh, hell, Max, lots of rich old codgers like you marry girls half their age, don't they?"

"Yes, isn't that what they do, trade in the old model for a new one? But I had never been married before."

I nodded. We were managing to avoid the main topic.

"So are you expecting me to do something, Max? Or say 'thank you'? I'm not sure I care at this point in my life that you may have found my father. It's taken me this long to get over being pissed that he wasn't around, so who needs him now?"

He shrugged, as if he'd had nothing to do with it. Like I had brought the problem upon myself.

"You don't want to see him?" Max asked.

I shook my head, but not with much conviction.

"Love him or hate him, it's a normal desire to want to meet your father. No one could blame you."

"Even if only to say, 'Thanks, asshole, for abandoning me'?

Max didn't respond but glared at me with a look that said there was still more to come.

"What, Max? Don't tell you're going to surprise me by having him pop out from behind the curtain, like some old TV show? I don't want that kind of a surprise."

"You think your mother would want to know where he is?"

I shook my head again, not saying no, just saying, I don't know. "Maybe she's known all these years."

"I'm sure she hasn't."

"Why? Did you have your investigator spy on here, too?"

"Don't be angry, Charles. The problem is that Berger moves around and it's difficult to keep up with him. If your mother was in contact with him it would help to keep track of him."

"And?"

"There is no indication that she has been in touch with him. No letters, no money coming in to her, nothing."

"You think he knows where she is?"

He shrugged. "If he was interested enough. She, your mother, might have meant nothing more to him than a fun diversion...sorry, Charles."

"Hey, I understand, I've had several of those fun diversions."

Max's eyebrows shot up, a question there.

"Hey, no, not Mary Grace! She s more than a diversion, Max."

He nodded his approval. Sometimes he made me feel like a kid.

"Anyway, if I recall you weren't exactly ecstatic when I started to date Mary Grace."

"Hmm," he grunted.

"Mom has never said anything that would indicate she's been in touch with...well, anyone from her past. If she's covered up all these years, I don't think she's going to volunteer new information now."

"Will you tell her?"

"I need real proof, Max."

Max took a deep breath, and sighed, the kind that indicated he had to drop a bombshell on me.

"My investigator did search your mother's place. He found a picture, a passport size photo of a young man. He showed it to me. It spawned an image of what Berger might have looked like when he was in his twenties."

"My mother had this picture?"

Max nodded. "Yes. My man brought the picture to show me, then snuck back in and replaced it so your mother would never realize it had been moved."

I shook my head repeatedly. "No, Max, I find that hard to believe. She told me she had no pictures…"

"Charles, nearly everything she told you about your father was a lie."

"Just because it looks like Berger…it could be any young man; it could me my real father, the one who died in Vietnam." My voice began to rise in pitch.

"Was his name Wilhelm?"

"Huh? What do you mean?"

"On the back of the picture was written, 'Gina…all my best hopes for you, W.' "

"W? So what…Williams, Walter…"

"Or Wilhelm."

"But you don't know."

"Charles, my investigator has laid out the details of his research. I'll make all of it available to you."

Now I nodded my head, in acceptance, trying still to wonder if Max was making all this up for some unfathomable reason. Actually he still hadn't dropped the big bombshell on me.

"All the best…not exactly a love note, is it?"

"Charles, there's a problem I need to tell you about, which i why I'm trying to get an idea of how you feel about this new knowledge you have. It's why I started out by misleading you. I needed to know your level of interest in learning the truth about yo father."

I urged him to go on by raising my eyes in a questioning manner.

"I told you I think he needs to be dealt with, or how did I say it, reasoned with. After the letter he sent me I realized that reasoning was not going to work."

"So we're back to 'eliminating' him, are we? You want my blessing?"

" I guess that would make it easier. But you see, I told you I have made contacts with people who work in mysterious ways. People who don't live the kind of lives most of us do. They have no close friends, and if they have lived long enough, no enemies either, at least, that they're aware of. They follow their own rules, they come and go as they please, they change names and identities the way you and I change socks. They are loyal to no one but themselves and their current employer, and then only as long as the employment lasts. They look over their shoulders and flinch at sudden sounds out of habit. Stress is a constant companion."

"Spies and hired assassins, is it, Max?" I was making light of him, but all a person has to do is read the paper to know that such secretive escapades do go on, many of them the product of our own and our allies' intelligence agencies.

"It's not unusual for people who have worked for legitimate agencies to retire but find they know nothing else. They become free-lancers."

I nodded. "Yes, I just read in the paper about a former CIA agent being arrested in some Middle Eastern country on charges of espionage. He claims he's a private citizen on vacation and the CIA disavows him. Who knows what he was up to?"

Max returned the knowing nod, but I don't know if that meant he'd also read the story or simply had nothing to add.

"I wouldn't know how to find such people, or how to hire them, Max, but apparently you do. I guess it's like drugs; if you wa them, you find out where to get them."

"Money talks, Charles. You live to be my age and have as much money as I do and you'll find out. As I said, they play by the own rules. So in this case, the case of Wilhelm Berger, my brother, your father, I have an agent looking for him, with orders to see that he is not a bother to me any more."

"You mean to kill him, don't you Max? Go on, you can say it."

"Don't jump to conclusions, Charles. In my instructions it was explained to Berger that he *will* be killed if he doesn't stay out of my life and stop threatening my family or me. My instructions also included access to an account in Europe for Wilhelm, a one-time payment; I won't succumb to continuous blackmail. I it made eminently clear that if he didn't take my warning seriously he'd write his own epitaph."

"How poetic," I chided. "So when will you know if he's been, ah, reasoned with?"

"I already know he hasn't, so he has to be found again."

"I thought your investi…"

"I ended my relationship with the original investigators I used before so there was no longer any ties between me and them and Berger. Since then, since I received the letter, I started anew. But the new person I hired to take my offer to Berger, and my demands, is unknown to me, as I am unknown to him. He operates a very unusual manner."

"I don't get it, Max. Sounds like a silly way to do business."

"We're not talking ordinary business, Charles. We're talking blackmail, the ruination of my reputation and maybe my Foundation, threats to my wife; this is life and death and you need to take this seriously."

"I do? What have I got to do with it, Max?"

"I received word that my previous agent had found Berger in Frankfurt and delivered the message. I also was notified a few days later that the account I set up for Berger had been accessed, and emptied."

"May I ask how much you sent him?"

"One hundred thousand dollars."

I nodded casually; chump change for Max.

"My agent had instructions to continue to keep tabs on Berger until I called him off. The last message I received was that Berger had gone to get his passport renewed and then had gone to a travel agency to inquire about flights to the United States."

"How long ago was this?" I asked.

"It was after the hundred thousand dollars was withdrawn by Berger, which indicates to me he doesn't take my warning seriously. He must think I'm bluffing."

"Just because he comes to the United States doesn't mean he's coming to hurt you, or the girls. He may be coming to see you, Max."

"Oh sure, after he's threatened and accepted the money. Besides, one other thing occurred since he withdrew the money."

"And that is?"

"The incident on the ski slopes. I don't believe it was an accident."

"Oh, come on Max, you're seeing ghosts where there are none. Berger couldn't have done that."

"It's possible there's no connection, but I don't believe in coincidences. My agent was instructed to tell Berger clearly that he was not to contact me, or anyone in my family, ever again. Now I believe Berger hired someone to scare the girls, and through them, me. It doesn't mean Berger's in this country, yet. In fact, I'm sure he isn't."

"So what are you going to do?"

"Me, nothing, I have already sent my instructions."

I stared at Max for several seconds, waiting. Then I grasped what he meant.

"This time you really do mean to have him killed?"

Max stared at me.

"My agent is authorized to kill him," he said, after several silent seconds that felt like minutes.

"Authorized! Like you have such authority to give? Why are you telling me all this, Max? You could have done this and never told me a thing."

"Yes, well, I've given it a lot of thought recently. I guess I'm getting soft in my old age. Or maybe it's because of the common denominator between us."

"Meaning?" I knew what he meant.

"Growing up without a father. I never found mine, and whether he's a pure bastard or not, I thought I'd give you the chance to know what I've learned about your father."

"And a chance to meet him? If he's still alive?"

"Yes. The problem is that I can't call off the person who is searching for him."

The puzzlement on my face served as my response.

"The way it works is the agent puts an ad in the New York Times and the International Herald Tribune once a week, a coded ad, that lets me know if he has found Berger or not, and if so, what the result was. He has instructions to keep working until he completes the assignment or I call him off, and I simply send whatever money he needs to a bank account in Europe."

"You can't stop him? That's insane!"

"I told you they have their own rules. The person I contact knows me, and he has another go-between, who knows him, but not me. Finally, the agent in the field knows his contact, but does not know me. Layers of buffers so no one knows enough to be a danger to anyone else."

"Your original contact knows you, doesn't he?"

"Yes, but my instructions as to exactly what I want done are sealed so even he doesn't know what they are or who I want found. For all he knows I'm looking for someone to pay off a debt. His contact receives my instructions, but doesn't know I am the one issuing the order. In its own way, it's a beautiful system."

I had to nod and even grinned a show of admiration. "You are right, Max, it is clever. Unless, of course, you want to put out a stop order."

"Technically I could try, by putting a certain ad in the International Herald Tribune. But the agent might not see it for several days if he's following a trail through small villages. Other than that, there is no way to directly contact the field agent."

137

"Newspapers, Max? Have you not heard of e-mail, or faxes

Max stared at me as if I was dumbest klutz on the face of th earth. "Oh, yeah," I said, before he could explain. "Using e-mail or fax could link the person to you, and vice versa, couldn't it?"

His silence was confirmation. For some things, especially illegal ones, old-fashioned techniques worked best.

"I thought you said Berger was in Frankfurt," I said, getting back on script.

"He was, and my agent followed him for the next couple days, which is how he learned Berger was inquiring about flights to the U.S. But Berger must have been aware that he was still being followed because he managed to slip away."

"Hmmm, maybe your agent isn't such a hot-shot."

"Maybe he did become over confident. Apparently Berger had earlier, before my agent found him, made other travel plans. M agent followed him to the airport, but had no way of knowing wher Berger was going. Berger settled in near the gate for a flight to Pari so my agent purchased a ticket on the same flight. At this last moment, just before boarding closed, he jumped up and boarded a flight to Milan. My agent wasn't able to follow, but I believe he ha since traveled to Milan to try to pick up the scent."

"You got all this from a coded message in the New York Times?"

Max shook his head. "No, in this case, because the message was so long, I received a hand written report through my contact."

"Hey, how can you be sure no one along the line reads thes reports?"

Max shrugged and opened and closed his hands, which had been entwined together as he spoke. "You can trust these people, I think. They have an ethic."

"An ethic? They kill people for hire and you say they have an ethic?"

"It's their world, Charles, not mine."

"You seem to have entered it, Max." He looked around the room, as if I hadn't said anything. It was his way of indicating my comebacks were irrelevant, if not insulting.

"So we just sit back and wait to hear that you've had your stepbrother, my father, killed, is that it?"

The gesture of opening his hands wide, then closing them, and the pursing of his mouth was Max's answer, an unusually restrained one for Maximilian von der Dusenberger.

"And if I said, 'Max, I do want to see my father,' where would I start looking?"

"I haven't the foggiest." Then he added, "I suppose Milan, but I suspect he didn't stay there for long."

"You said the letter came from Lyon? Does he live there?"

"He did, but he wouldn't be so foolish as to go back there now that he knows he's being followed. If he had gone to Lyon, the agent would have found him by now."

"Maybe he is here. You said your agent found he was inquiring about flights to the U.S. Maybe he caught a flight in Milan."

Max shook his head. "No. Another inquiry—another bribe—told my agent the only persons with the name Wilhelm

Berger who have entered the country in recent weeks were checked out and they were not our Wilhelm."

"But by now…" I started to say.

Max closed his eyes in disagreement with what I wanted to suggest. It was due to frustration more than anything else.

"Yes, I know what you're thinking. But acquiring and using successfully a false passport is not that easy for amateurs. It require great skill to put one together and it takes time to find someone who can do it for you and it takes a lot of money. And a person nabbed trying to enter another country on a false passport will encounter a great deal of trouble. Does that mean he won't be able to arrange it" I don't know, he's obviously very capable. But I think even if he knows he's being followed, Berger feels safe in coming here on a true passport. Like I said, he doesn't believe I'd have him killed."

Max seldom makes an error, and when he does, it's a doozy I stared at him and he stared back until I changed my gaze to the remaining customers. Have you ever been somewhere, like in a restaurant, as we were, or anywhere at all, and noticed people havir an intense conversation? And have wondered, what could they possibly be talking about? As I looked around, only a few people still in the restaurant, most of them staff, the diners at their tables a involved in their private conversations, a bit of business, or sports, wondered, could any of them, with their wildest stab, the most outrageous guess, imagine the conversation Max and I were having Could any of the other people be having a conversation as bizarre a ours? Now I knew why Max had taken so much time to tell me this story. He was setting the stage for me.

"Max, you're telling me this because you want me to try to find Berger, don't you? Now how would I find him, if your secret agent, James Bond or George Smiley or whoever the hell he is, can't find him? Where would I start to look? I mean, it makes more sense to wait until he comes calling. How much more of the ninety days remains?"

Max shook his head slowly. "Charles, if my investigator is as good as I was led to believe, he will find Berger before then, and he will kill him."

"Well, hell, Max (I was mad now), you set this up, you find him yourself."

"I'm too old to be running around playing spy games."

"You're not too old to be running around with a girl less than half your age..." I was sorry before I dotted the sentence. Max stared me down, then looked away.

"Sorry, Maximilian, I didn't mean anything, I mean I..."

For a moment there Max looked old and tired, a decade older than the energetic, feisty, fighter I've known him to be.

"Max, you're feeling guilty, aren't you?"

His eyes popped up and looked at me as if he'd been caught cheating at cards.

"You set this up, but now you want me to stop you. You've convinced yourself Wilhelm is a threat, but the idea of having your brother, my father, killed, suddenly isn't at arm's length is it? You want someone to stop it, and then if it can't be stopped you can tell yourself that you tried."

Maximilian listened attentively, for a change letting me ramble.

"Can I take it as a complement that since I may become your brother-in-law you've had second thoughts about doing this to my father, even if I never knew him? Is this to maybe make up because your father left you, and, maybe, Max, because you abandoned your infant brother?"

"Are you finished?" he asked.

"Hey, there's no crime in being sentimental, or having seconds thoughts, or feeling compassion."

"Heh, me, have compassion? I've never been accused of that before! Thanks for even suggesting it, Charles."

"I guess there's some good in the worst of us, eh, Max?" I said with a chuckle.

He waved his fingers, shushing me. "There's one other vital thing you should know first, Charles. Something you've wanted to know since I began my tale."

I thought back quickly…but the brain cells weren't functioning too well at this moment.

"Their names, Charles, the names of the two soldiers."

Oh, of course, back to them again; I nodded.

"William Wolfe and John Schneider."

My eyebrows furrowed as if the names were the strangest I've ever heard. I heard what Max said but something wasn't computing. I had to say the names aloud, in a whisper, to be sure, because maybe in a whisper they would lose their power.

"Wolfe," I said, not a question, more of a test of my hearing and memory. Did I hear what I think I heard; did Max say, Wolfe?

"Max," I started, scratching my head and squinting my eyes as confusion rained down on me. "With an 'e' on the end?

"Max, the girls, Mary Grace and Mary Jo, their name is Wolfe."

He just looked at me.

"Of course, it's not an uncommon name."

"No, it isn't. William Wolfe was the soldier who had the affair with my mother. He's Wilhelm Berger's father. His son, David, married a women named Beth Schneider, the daughter of William Wolfe's best friend, John Schneider."

"Schneider was the other soldier," I said, to keep the characters straight in my mind.

"Yes. David Wolfe and Beth Schneider had two daughters, who they named Mary Jo, the first born, and Mary Grace."

Again I heard Max but the internal operating system in my head was running on slow.

"So, so…"

"So the Marys are your cousins, Charles. That's why I was not happy when you and she began to date."

I had quit listening to him. An echo began to reverberate in my brain. 'Does not compute', went the refrain, 'does not compute'.

INTERLUDE: In Flight

I read one more time the letter Max had received. How curious, to receive a letter that in a businesslike way threatens blackmail or even worse, and have it come from, if Max is correct, long lost stepbrother. To top it off, from a man Max had searched for, found, and then decided not to make contact with once he learned what kind of man his stepbrother was.

I used to pretend I received letters from my father, written from Vietnam before he died.

"Dear son," the letters would began…"I hope you are takin good care of your Mom while I have to be away. You need to be th big man of the house until I can get back."

The fact that father had died, according to Mom, when I wa still in diapers didn't enter into my imagination at the time.

And to have something to talk about to contend with the other kids bragging about going to the zoo with their parents, or playing catch with their Dad, I told stories about how my father had killed a hundred of the enemy in Vietnam. And when he was captured it took a dozen bad guys to hold him down, and how he died in a fury of gunshots, him blazing away with a machine gun li Rambo. Some of the kids listened with eyes wide open.

Yes, the big man of the house, at five, six years old. I used t tell my mother that maybe the army made a mistake and Daddy isn dead, and one day he'll come marching home. Until then I'd take care of her. She'd smile and pat me on the head. I think the story sh told me was one she began to believe herself.

The Vietnam War ended before I was old enough to know what it was about, as if I do now. Does anybody? If there was any chance my father had been alive in a prison camp, and would soon be home, those hopes were dashed by the time I was eight or nine years old. So I talked to Mom about getting a new Daddy. It isn't that easy, she'd tell me, and I'd tell her about some kid at school who got a new Daddy. If I remember correctly there was a kid whose father really had died, in an accident, and the mother remarried three months later to the bachelor who lived across the street. I asked Mom if she knew any bachelors, thinking the word meant a man who was waiting to become a daddy. Man, it's a wonder I survived childhood without ending up in the nuthouse.

As I look back now I grew up with an anger eating at me and a chip on my shoulder. Maybe Max and his stepbrother grew up in the same manner. So we're all connected in a way, trying to stumble through a world that has no sympathy for how you were raised or whether you had good parenting, bad parenting, or any parenting.

Max said he didn't remember much about his father, except that he came and went and mostly he remembers that he was in uniform. Max was still a toddler when Hitler began rattling sabers, and as a career soldier Max's father would have been away from home more often than not.

Still and all, as I sit here quite comfortable, actually, now that the noise level has settled down, happy that Max popped for business class seats, (though he could have afforded First Class, the piker) because flying all the way from Los Angeles to Paris in coach is murder, and ponder back in time, I knew, I think I knew, that there was something fishy if not downright false about the story my mother told about my father dying in Vietnam. Even she must have known it would be easy enough for me to check, and maybe she waited for me to do so, even hoped I would, so I'd confront her and she could tell me the truth. I wonder if by now she thinks I'm really stupid for not having confronted her. I had neither the time nor inclination to talk to her before I left for Paris. I hadn't even called tell her I'd be away.

Now here I am, just celebrated my thirty-first birthday and I still don't know the truth and like a kid who's been told that children should be seen and not heard, I'm afraid to walk up to my fifty-five year old mother and say, 'will you finally tell me the truth?'

And what would I tell her if I find Wilhelm Berger and learn that he is my father, my mother's short-time lover of her European dalliance? Anything? Would it be good for her or would it hurt? What if I get to Europe and do find Berger but he's already dead, killed in some accident or found shot to death in the muddy banks of a river, murderer unknown?

I refolded the copy of the letter Max had received and began to look through the other papers, the ones that summarized the history of the man known as Wilhelm Berger, in as much as Max's investigators had discovered.

EIGHT: Cousins

Cousins! Mary Grace and I were cousins! At least, as contended by Max, if his information was correct. It was one thing to learn Max and I might be related; that was kind of comical. But I didn't want to be related to Mary Grace!

Somehow it doesn't sound right. 'Our', grandfather, if Max's info was accurate, someone I never knew, a man who fathered a child in Germany shortly after he end of World War Two, who in turn fathered a child who became me! This same man, then, after the woman he'd impregnated died giving birth, returned to the United States and eventually became grandfather to Mary Jo and Mary Grace.

I even looked up a 'table of consanguinity' and it shows that people who have the same grandfather are first cousins. I didn't like the information the chart gave; I wanted it to be wrong, or Max to be wrong, or something to be wrong. You ought to at least have *known* your grandfather, shouldn't you? And Mary Grace and I didn't have the same grandmother, so doesn't that negate the grandfather aspect? I knew it didn't.

Max promised not to say anything to the Marys while I was away. He figured it wasn't his business any more. (Thanks, Max, after all the trouble you went through to make trouble!) Had he known before he married Mary Jo that his stepbrother was the son of her grandfather, he said he might have acted differently. But his relationship to the Marys wasn't blood, like mine might be.

From being told that my father was actually alive, had not died in Vietnam, and had in fact abandoned my mother, or at least, forgotten about her even if he never knew she'd been carrying his child, to thinking I didn't want it to be him, I didn't want Max's stepbrother to be my father, was making my brain spin. It smacked of a bizarre Shakespearian conundrum, a coincidence far too extraordinary to be true. To go my entire life without knowing a single relative, then to find that I have one, and I'm sleeping with her?

Maybe I needed to examine my emotions. Maybe I wasn't in love with Mary Grace after all, just infatuated. Maybe it'll wear off. Or maybe it's time to do something like I used to do with other women: say or do something so stupid, so obnoxious, that Mary Grace will dump me. I'll quit working for Max (he'll understand) and move somewhere far from the Marys and Max, and even from my mother. What'll I tell her? I'll say, 'Mom, you should have told me the truth long ago.'

Now I had to locate Wilhelm Berger and find out the truth for myself. Weird, but I wasn't thinking so much about saving his life as I was hoping to find out that he wasn't Max's stepbrother. Even if he was my father, I didn't want him to be the son of Mary's grandfather. But what did I tell Mary Grace, if anything, in the mean time? Dare I go to bed with her again, at the risk of creating a creature with three ears, or worse, some debilitating disease or mental retardation? Was it true that could happen if close relatives have a child? I had to avoid Mary Grace until I had more solid information. I wasn't going to take for granted that the information from Max's mysterious agent was gospel. His investigators could be feeding Max what they think he wants. Going to Europe to look for Wilhelm Berger gave me an excuse for a week or so, but what about when I return? What if I can't find out for sure whether or not he's my father; do I say adios to Mary Grace?

It seemed like the original 'mission: impossible'. How do I find a man who doesn't want to be found, and find him before a hired assassin eliminates him? And, in Europe, where I'd be at a disadvantage.

Max did as he had suggested he would try, and as soon as we returned to the office he sent a message through his contact to put an ad in the International Herald Tribune, temporarily calling off the person who was searching for Berger. Later the same day he found a coded message in the New York Times which revealed that the hired assassin had traced Berger to the small town of Chalon du Saone, in the southern part of France, and that Berger had scheduled himself on a river cruise down the Rhone River, beginning in five days. Going on a river cruise did not seem to be the movements of a man imminently planning to blackmail someone. On the other hand, he may be biding his time, waiting for the ninety-day deadline he had given Max to pass. We scoured a map of France and noted that other than Lyon, there weren't any large cities near Chalon du Saone, so it was quite possible the assassin wouldn't find an International Herald Tribune each day.

You should have instructed your man to check the Tribune every day, no exceptions, I told Max. He said the next time he hires a professional assassin he would, ha! ha! The old guy was really developing his sense of humor; about time. Give me another ha! ha!

Even if I could find Berger, how could I stop the assassin from doing the job? Might I get in the way and suffer a similar fate? Max said, no, he was sure the hired assassin was a professional in all ways.

I got a kick out of that, *professional.* I always thought it was funny (funny hmm, not funny, ha! ha!) when in books or films hired killers are spoken of as *professionals,* as if the word blessed their work with legitimacy. On the other hand, all it means is that the person is skilled at their chosen occupation; butcher, baker, candlestick maker, assassin.

How would I recognize the assassin if he's aboard the river cruise ship? Max was no help. He said he hadn't the slightest idea what the assassin would look like, or how he planned to 'do the job' or even if he'd be on the river cruise ship. Maybe he'd be waiting at the end of the cruise, or in one of the towns that the cruise ship docked along the way. For a guy who usually had all the answers, Max was now a fount of ignorance.

However, the news gave us our excuse. Max and I conjured up the scenario wherein I had to leave immediately on urgent business in Paris. Meanwhile I lucked out and found that there had been a cancellation on the river cruise we calculated Berger was going to be on, assuming the information in the message was accurate. So I booked a room—for a single. I barely had time to pack, and no time to discuss my plans with Mary Grace, who was bent out of shape because I made a feeble excuse about having to study contracts and couldn't see her tonight. I didn't actually lie. I did have to go to Paris (that's where I had to go to make connections, and I did have business, and Maximilian does have a small office there. I neglected to mention what type of business, naturally).

You can study contracts on the flight, she'd suggested. You'll have hours. You mean you'd rather read a stack of boring contracts than snuggle up with me?

I dared not say, yes, I would, because I'm afraid of what snuggling would lead to. The easiest thing would have been to explain to her but the explanation was pretty complicated, and I really didn't want to suggest that my long-dead father had actually caused the death of her grandfathers. Besides, if I told her why I was going she'd want to come with me, and I didn't want her getting in the way.

She persisted and eventually, as per Charles' Standard Operating Procedure, words came out of my mouth before my brain could shut them up.

"Don't be so bitchy about it."

"A bitch! You think I'm a bitch?!"

"No, not a bitch, don't be bitchy; there's a difference."

"Oh, really? And you, you are what, a son-of-a bitch?"

"Whatever."

The 'whatever' went over worse than the 'bitchy', because it implied an indifference on my part. Whatever.

I was already en route to Paris as I was reviewing the scene in my head. I'm sure she suspected I wasn't telling her everything but Max backed me up, apologizing to Mary Grace for needing me to leave so suddenly. He agreed not to say anything to the sisters about the real reason for my trip, and when I returned, whatever I found out, we would sit down with the ladies and have a family discussion.

"That is," Max said, "If you want to."

"Fine, make it my decision," I grumbled.

"I think you have more at stake here, Charles, than I do."

"Right now, Max, I wish you'd never told me any of this."

"You may be right, and maybe I'll die regretting I did so. I just know that all my life I've wondered what happened to my father, and why he could never arrange to visit me, and then, when learned about Wilhelm Berger, I thought you had a right to know."

I nodded, admitting with a grudge that he was right. I did have the right, and the need. So did my mother, bless her, even though she lied to me. And what do I do if and when I find him? What do I do about Mary Grace? Once again I engaged in my juvenile fantasy about running away from home and starting a new life somewhere else. I suppose Max would hire one of his internationally sophisticated agents to find me so what'd be the use

The one thing that bugged me, just a twit, was the last thing Mary Grace said on the phone, when I called her from the airport, minutes before boarding. You know, she said, maybe Mary Jo is right for a change. I said nothing because at first I wasn't sure what she meant. She added, please think about it; you'll have plenty of time on your long flight. Sure, I said, grasping what she was referring to; obviously, Mary Jo's strong hints that we should set a date.

Something to dwell on, for sure. In the mean time I figured I can prove this Wilhelm character is not my father, or at least, he can't prove he is, then I could explain to Mary Grace and we'd be fine. If it turns out he is my old man, the sonofabitch, and that he killed the Mary's grandfathers, she likely wouldn't feel too affectionate towards me anyway, so I wouldn't have to worry about setting a wedding date after all. Anyway, I doubt she'd be keen on marrying a cousin.

Max supplied me with photographs he had of the man known as Wilhelm Berger, taken surreptitiously some time in the last few months, somewhere in the world. Max also said he had Berger's fingerprints in his New York office along with a copy of the birth certificate from the German hospital in which he had (supposedly) been born, and where Max's mother had died, and from where Max had fled. It was always easier to meet with people coming from Europe on the East Coast, he said, and he simply never thought to move them from the safe in his New York office.

"If you can find a way to get his fingerprints, we can compare them to be sure he's the same man."

"I don't see what that'll prove. Besides, you seem convinced enough of who he is to order his death. Now you want to check his prints? Maybe I'll just walk up to him with an ink pad and say, 'Excuse me, Pop, would you mind letting me fingerprint you so I can find out if I've been screwing my cousin'."

"Tsk, tsk, such language!"

Max could show a sense of humor at times, but you had to be ready or you'd miss it.

"Charles, the fingerprints I have in my office safe were taken off Wilhelm Berger when he was in East Berlin, and the evidence of my investigators is absolutely certain that this is the man who was born to my mother in the hospital in West Berlin in 1946. The investigator was positive of his trace."

"But how can we prove this is the same man who knew my mother? Who became my father?"

"That's your job, isn't it, Charles? And your problem. If he has tracked down your mother, and knows about you, then I suspect that if you confront him, his reaction will tell you immediately whether he knows you are his son."

"You'd think he'd want to get in touch with me, and her."

Max shrugged and shook his head ever so slightly. The movement revealed wrinkles around his eyes I hadn't noticed before. Looking closer he seemed to have more gray hair than ever. Like the song says, 'I'm older than I once was and younger than I'll ever be,' or words to that effect.

He wasn't ancient, only pushing sixty-eight. But he'd worked hard all through his life, first physically and then mentally, and for the most part, with no one close to share the ups and downs. Until now, with Mary Jo, and instead of being able to kick back and enjoy his old age, he's dealing with a ghost from his childhood. Worse for him than for me; I never figured my father was alive. For Max, he grew up wondering why his father hadn't come for him, and then blamed himself for leaving Germany, making it, he reasoned, impossible for his father to find him. And after all that, he now feels guilty for taking the money from the stranger who, in all likelihood, was working for Max's father, banking Max with money stolen during the war.

"Max, with your resources, and as hard as you searched for information about your brother, why didn't you do the same to try to find out more about your father? I mean, did you give up after you...after the old Nazi hunter died?"

"Good question. I convinced myself that if the old man couldn't find anything about a Colonel von der Dusenberger, then maybe it was true that he died in the war, and was buried in an unknown grave in an unknown field. Deep down I think I came to the point where I didn't want to know, though some day I convinced myself I would finish the search, but not yet, because if I found out the truth, I might not like it."

"Yeah, truth can be harsh sometimes."

"Charles, I need to tell you something."

Now what?

"I try to come across as tough and stern and serious. And in work matters I am. But sometimes I try to portray an image that's not the real me."

His face broke into a wry grin, almost a sheepish grin, as if he'd been caught eating a Twinkie with a glass of his best Scotch.

"The old Jewish Nazi- hunter I told you about?"

I nodded. The one he implied he had *eliminated.*

He shook his head. "I didn't kill him, nor did I have him killed. He was old and dying when I met him. When I was looking for someone to help in my search I heard of this man, who had located several Nazis, but was critically ill and near death. I thought he might be my best bet because he likely wouldn't live much longer. So if I could wrangle some information out of him, and he died soon after, again, I would have cut my ties with anyone who knew what I was doing. And he did die, shortly after I met him, but peaceably and alone in his bed."

"I'm glad to hear that, Max."

"It's funny," Max continued, "funny, that is, in a curious way."

"What's funny, Max?"

"Wilhelm. His father, best I can tell, was a good man. I remember him, you know, coming to visit us, well, to visit mother, mainly. But he played with me, talked to me, and I'm convinced he tried to find my mother after he was out of the army. But Wilhelm doesn't seem to have inherited any of his father's attributes, or our mother's. Instead, as an infant he was shuffled around and the hurt he felt at being abandoned at the hospital, abandoned as he as could best understand it when he learned the story of his birth, then growing up around equally angry boys in the orphanage, then later, getting involved in who knows what kind of illegal activities, all those influences have turned him into a bitter, dangerous person. I dearly wish it were different."

"Did you think of him often in those years after you ran from the hospital?"

"Not at first. I was too young and scared and lonely. He was nothing to me; I never saw him. I was just told my mother was going to have a baby, a nurse gave me something to eat and told me to wait quietly and a little later I was told she had died. Then I ran off. If anything, I felt he was responsible for my mother dying. If she hadn't been pregnant…"

"She might have fallen down the stairs anyway," I interjected.

"Yes, yes," Max said in a strained voice. "And if William Wolfe hadn't…hadn't made my mother pregnant…you can make a kinds of connections and come up with all kinds of fault. At some point you have to take you own responsibility, don't you, Charles? Don't we?"

"Yes, and as adults we realize that, so why are all filled with guilt about things we didn't know about or had no influence over?"

Max looked at me and suggested, "We're human beings?" I could only respond with a mild snicker.

After a moment Max picked up where he was before I'd cut him off.

"Later I wondered about him, obviously a concern that carried over until I was able to have people search for him. I wish I could have just forgotten him totally. I wouldn't have pulled you into this dilemma."

"But Max, you said you first came to know of me through your investigations, didn't you?"

He nodded.

"So, if you hadn't hired me I would never have met Mary Grace, and I thank you for that."

"Will you thank me later, if you feel you must give her up?"

The look on his face was a tired one. He seemed to be aging right before my eyes, years adding up as we spoke. I had no answer to give him that I was sure about so I said nothing.

I finally managed to fall to sleep. The curtains were drawn to separate business class from the helots in coach (among who I'll be on my return trip, for which I had not yet made a reservation), I'd had a generous serving of brandy to calm my nerves, and put in earplugs. I knew I'd be tired when we landed in Paris and every minute of sleep would help.

I cleared customs, retrieved my bag, always a relief to know my underwear has arrived, and high-footed it to the gate for my connection. I got there as they were beginning to board, not even enough time to buy a cup of coffee. Fortunately I was able to quick wrangle a cup when I was on board. My watch said three-thirty (as in a.m.), which means I should be fast asleep in my own—or Mary Grace's—warm bed. But here it was pushing noon and people were beginning to think about lunch.

It was a short fight to Lyon and I used the time to think about what I'd do, or try to do, once I reached Chalon du Saone. First I had to connect with the river cruise company, which should have a representative waiting in Lyon to meet arriving passengers.

Maybe it was just a geographical coincidence that the connection for the river cruise had to go through Lyon, which was where Max owned a home, besides the one in Berlin. If he's familiar with the area, this may be a convenient place for Berger to hang around, waiting for whatever his next step would be. Taking a river cruise might be a vacation; even jerks and professional assassins go on vacation, don't they?

It was now less than thirty days to the deadline indicated in the letter to Max. Plenty of time to take a week's river cruise, then return to Paris or even Lyon, and fly to the States. Likely Berger had already made his reservations, but Max said he had a contact in the State Department who was able to access the information of names that have made international reservations, and no Wilhelm Berger coming into Los Angeles had shown up yet. How anyone did this, I'm not sure, but I am sure it wasn't done legally.

In Lyon we exited the plane by the stairs, no tunnel, and walked into the airport. I noticed a woman holding a sign with my name on it and at first I thought it was the rep from the cruise line. When I approached her she asked if I was Charles Hardin, and when I confirmed my identity she said there was a message for me at the Information Desk.

Oh, oh, now what? When I got the message it was from Max. He said the person he had checking flight reservations had found that a Wilhelm Berger was scheduled to fly from Paris to New York ten days from now, with a return scheduled two days later. Which apparently meant that Berger intended to contact Max soon and instruct him to meet in New York, not Los Angeles. I began to wonder why Berger wanted to meet with Max at all, as opposed to simply demanding that he send money. Brotherly love?

I didn't have much time: time to find him, save him, stop him, *and reason* with him! I guess I wasn't sure exactly what I wanted to happen, but first I had to find Berger, and somehow stop the assassin from killing him. At least I had a picture of Berger. How the hell could I find an assassin when even Max didn't know what he looked like, or even if he'd be close on Berger's trail? And then what, tell Berger to go into hiding? This is nuts, I thought, just as I saw a person standing with a sign identifying the river cruise line.

Those of us who had come in on the plane from Lyon, and others who had arrived minutes before from Frankfurt, had to take a bus to get to Chalon du Saone, where we would meet the river cruise ship. I felt funny on the bus, funny in the sense that I feared I stood out as someone who looked suspiciously like he wasn't on vacation

Look at that man, he obviously is up to something; I hope h doesn't ruin our trip, I imagined everyone thinking. I tried to survey the other passengers, turning my head while attempting harder than needed to pretend I wasn't eyeballing anyone in particular, but agai feeling I was making myself conspicuous. I wanted to see if I recognized anyone who resembled the man in the pictures Max had given me. For all I knew, Wilhelm had been on the plane with me. But I saw no one who resembled him.

Wilhelm Berger—that is, the person born to Ruth von der Dusenberger in the hospital in Berlin in 1946,would be right at fifty five years old now. Other than me, the other passengers looked olde than fiftyish. Typical, older Americans who now have the time and money to travel. And me, traveling solo, a man in his early thirties; had to look suspicious. I mean, this isn't exactly the type of trip a guy goes on looking to meet women.

A guide stepped aboard the bus and greeted us warmly. As the bus pulled out the guide explained that the ride would take nearl an hour and a quarter. She was pleasant, spoke good English, and probably provided worthy information. But within minutes the motion of the bus lulled me into la-la land.

I woke up and for a second I was confused as to where I was I was moving, I was on a bus, or was it a train, and there were other people around. I managed to force my eyes open and soon my brain woke up and I remembered. Outside the scenery was of fields, trees and an occasional structure: farmhouses, barns, fenced pastures inhabited by sheep or cows. My watch told me I'd only slept about forty-five minutes. Still, that should put us near where the Rhone Rover was docked.

From a quick reading of the cruise guidebook I remembered that the ship carried about a hundred and twenty-five or thirty passengers, with a crew of three dozen or so. I figured there shouldn't be so many people that I couldn't spot them all within the weeklong cruise. Probably half were women, and a lot of the men would be older than Berger, so there shouldn't be more than a handful of candidates.

The river came into view. I rubbed my eyes, dug out a handkerchief and blew my nose, and then took a long slug of water from the bottle I'd been given by the tour rep at the airport. I felt reasonably alert.

We were greeted with great enthusiasm by several crewmembers including the captain. I knew it would sound silly so I refrained from asking him whether this was a 'boat' or a 'ship'. Later, in the cruise tour book, I noted the references were to a 'river cruise ship,' so now I know.

I was afraid to nap because it would mess up my sleeping habits. I needed as quickly as possible to get on the local schedule. So as soon as my luggage arrived I took a short shower, first as hot as I could stand, then as cold as I could, donned fresh clothes, and went out to explore the ship—and look for Berger.

It doesn't take long to explore the entire ship. It's a bit longer than a football field and only has three decks, plus the sundeck, or as a landlubber would say, the top of the ship. My stateroom was on the middle deck. Below me the lower deck contained a half dozen guest staterooms, plus a small gym and laundry room. I assumed the rest of the space on the lower deck was for crewmembers, storage, and other departments related to ship functions.

Towards the front of the ship along my deck, a little past th middle of the ship, was the reception area, and a compact gift shop which, when open for business, would sell various souvenirs, such models of the Rhone Rover, magnets, French macaroon cookies, an toiletries for the traveler who forgot to pack toothpaste.

The reception desk was commanded by a pretty girl in a da blue jacket with the name of the ship, 'Rhone Rover,' embroidered on the front, and a cute bow of a lighter shade of blue around her neck. She smiled and said, "Welcome aboard, sir."

The front section of this deck contained the restaurant. I entered and looked around, acting as best I could like a pampered guest who is just being nosy. There was nobody in there except for few crewmembers.

I went up the stairs to the third deck, which contained the snazzier staterooms, a library for passenger use, the main lounge an the bar area. I believe the officer's quarters were up there somewhere, also.

Sure as shootin' the bar was already active with every stool occupied and a dozen or so people standing around with a glass in their hand. Most of the people were white or silver-haired. Come a the way across the Atlantic on an expensive vacation, the first thing some fools look for is the bar. If it wasn't only ten o'clock in the morning back home, I'd join them. To be fair, as I learned later, several of the passengers had been traveling for a week or more in Europe, so for them it was near the cocktail hour.

Again I tried to play the part of a guest who is getting acclimated to the ship, looking a bit lost and confused, to give me an excuse to stare at people's faces, smile at them if they caught me looking, and try to spot someone who looked anything at all like the pictures of Berger. Trouble is, the pictures weren't very clear, and if Berger had changed his hair color, or wore glasses, or made any major change in his appearance, I might not identify him—assuming Max's agent was correct and Berger was on this cruise ship.

Had I been more alert I would have saved myself some worry. In the reception area was a book that listed the passengers on this ship and their stateroom number. It was used for passengers to sign up for various optional tours. Not the best method for privacy, but a simple system that worked for what it was used for. But at this point in time I hadn't seen it yet.

I didn't spot anyone in the lounge that reminded me of Berger so I wandered back upstairs to the library to look for reading material. After browsing for ten minutes I found a paperback that sounded reasonably interesting, (but then, what book goes to press without quips that make it sound like the next '*To Kill a Mockingbird*'), pocketed it, and went back to the lounge, which was more crowded now as couples or groups of passengers began to fill up the couches and the tables situated around the room. A piano player in a striped sport coat was flipping through his music sheets preparing to provide entertainment. If Berger is aboard ship, and unless he plays the hermit, the lounge, or later, the dinning room, appeared to afford the best opportunities to spot him. I went in and sat down away from other passengers, opened the paperback, and pretended to read. A waiter came by and I ordered a scotch and soda.

Didn't I say I needed to adjust to the local time as quickly as possible?

INTERLUDE: An Investigator

The Investigator started from the assumption that William Wolfe and John Schneider had returned to their hometowns after World War Two. That would be the easiest place to start searching.

He had no idea why the tycoon wanted to find these two men, but that was his business.

It turned out not to be as difficult as he thought it would be, seeing as how their names were not exactly unique. Records of GI Bill recipients, college enrollment records, tax returns, marriage and birth records, even tax returns, more than he needed, some available for the asking, some for a mere pittance of a fee, made it simple to follow the lives of the two men.

They both had married within a couple years of returning from Europe. Wolfe and his wife had a son, David, Schneider and his wife a daughter, Beth, born only a month apart. Close friends, indeed, the Investigator considered, even to planning their children!

The children in turn married each other when they were twenty-four years old. Within two years they had two daughters and shortly after they moved to southern California for career purposes. The daughters, Mary Jo and Mary Grace, went into the real estate business after college and at this point in time, early in the year 1997 as the Investigator was finishing his work, the two women still were in the realty business.

Sadly, however, the Investigator also found death records. Wolfe and Schneider had died in 1988 in an accident in the Idaho woods. When he included this in his report he was told to follow up and see what else he could learn about the accident that killed the two men.

He had to pay a clerk a hundred dollars to get access to the old police reports on the accident investigation. It seemed cut and dried, two fishermen out in the dark, unfamiliar with the terrain, went over the side of a road they should never have been on, an abandoned path that had been blocked to vehicles and was overgrown with brush. Somehow they'd missed the main forest road which itself wasn't an impressive route, gone over the side, flipped several times, and without wearing seatbelts, they got thrown around pretty good.

But the Investigator wasn't in this type of business because he accepted everything he read in official reports. Even in this case, where it seemed a simple matter of accidental death, the police had checked recent car rentals to see who else had been in the area and might know anything about what happened.

They questioned several people, hunters and fisherman like the two men who'd died, but none had been in the same area and there was nothing to suspect foul play.

The Investigator went further than the police had gone, deciding to check rental agencies some distance away from the town nearest where the accident happened. His powers of persuasion didn't always work, and at times people refused to cooperate with him and acted suspicious. So he needed to hurry with his work and make himself scarce. But, using his experience at reading people, he found three late night clerks at rental agencies in three different towns who weren't opposed to letting the Investigator pore over old rental agreements for the price of a Ben Franklin. Peanuts to the German tycoon who'd hired him.

The first two pile of records he looked through didn't tell him anything. But near the town of Ketchum, known as the site where the writer Ernest Hemingway had been living when he committed suicide, the Investigator hit pay dirt. At an agency there, more than eighty miles from the site of the accident that had killed Wolfe and Schneider, he found that ten days before the accident had been discovered, a man named William Berger had rented a four-wheel drive vehicle. It was returned four days later, which placed the usage during the time frame that the accident must have happened. William, not Wilhelm, but still…too similar to be a coincidence.

The address given for Berger was in Oregon, and the Investigator quickly determined it to be phony. In a hick town like this a fake driver's license may have passed muster easily. Who this Berger was the Investigator had no idea, but the rental was suspicious to him because of the timing in relation to the accident and the fake address. He included this information in his report to his employer, who thanked him, gave him a generous bonus, and said he would not need his services any more. Too bad; he pays well.

NINE: Finding Berger

The passengers were invited to come to the lounge at seven o'clock the first evening for the official Captain's greeting, and a talk by the cruise director, who would tell us about the ports we would visit, tours that were offered, wonderful historical sites to visit, and the opportunity to imbibe in the delicious French wines. A good chance to learn something and maybe spot Berger.

I got to the lounge early and took a seat towards the middle, vantage point where I could keep an eye on both entrances to the lounge, hoping that I could watch the other passengers enter. As I'd noted earlier, the guests were mostly older folks, but as the lounge filled I did spot a scattering of younger people, my age, mostly couples. One person stood out, literally, because she was very tall, over six feet, a blond lady who looked to be in her mid to late twenties. Other than the handful of kids traveling with their parents she had to be one of the youngest passengers aboard. I didn't see anyone that resembled the picture of Berger and felt a great disappointment. This whole thing might be a waste of time. Already I began to think of how I should leave the ship at one of the towns we stopped, and make my way to the Lyon airport. Would a sudden absence of a passenger spark a problem? Maybe I could feign illness though I don't think seasickness would be believed on a quiet, calm river cruise.

Then I saw him. He entered from the entrance farthest away from where I sat, carrying a glass and mixed in with a group of five or six other people. But as the others found seats this man,

Berger, I was already calling him, took a seat by himself as far from any other passengers as he could, on the other side of the room from me.

When he sat down the head of one person and a lamp on one of the tables partially blocked my view, but I was almost positive it was him and I could feel my heart leap with excitement. I took out the three by five photo of Berger and looked at it, then stared at the man across the room. Yes, yes it was surely him; which probably also means that the potential assassin is aboard.

Now I panned the room looking at all the faces, scrutinizing faces for anyone else who might be eyeing Berger. But a trained killer would be subtler, wouldn't he? And he wouldn't do anything here. Where and when would he strike? At night, would he break into Berger's room, kill him silently and throw him into the river? Would he strangle him or use a silencer? I was not feeling proud that my main thought was talking to this man and finding out who he really is— Max's stepbrother and my father? — before any such violence might occur. I'd warn him, of course, but I had no plans to physically get in the way of an assassin; no hero am I.

The captain was talking and then the cruise director gave a spiel mixing in local humor along with a summary of the planned highlights of the cruise. There was no way I could move across the room to get closer to Berger without disrupting the speakers. And after the talks we were invited to the restaurant for our first dinner aboard. I lost track of Berger in the crowd and when I finally spied him again he had taken a seat in the far corner, at a table for two, though he was by himself. I began to move towards the table when I saw a waiter speak to Berger, who motioned at the setup on the other side of the table. He obviously indicated he wanted to dine alone because the waiter removed the setup. I pirouetted around looking for a vacant chair just as another waiter approached me and suggested I join a group of four people who were seated at a table f six.

So I made small talk with Jack and Eppie, and Frank and Doris. Or maybe it was Jack and Doris and Frank and Eppie. The couples all seemed to look the same, white hair, glasses, hands splattered with age spots; something to look forward to, I suppose. Frank sported a 'Rudolph' nose and was the happy slap-on-the-bac kind of guy, one of my least favorites types. Still, they were amenable enough to pass the time with while we enjoyed dinner. I particularly appreciated the flow of fine French Burgundy, and the food was delicious.

Naturally, as someone traveling alone I stood out and had to answer for that failing. At first they—someone in the foursome, I don't remember who—asked if my wife was ill. I made up a story o the spot about having had a business meeting in Paris, and another one in Marseilles, but with a week's gap, so I found a late cancellation on the Rhone Rover and decided to travel to Marseilles by flowing down the river at a relaxing pace. They bought it and proceeded to tell me all about their jobs before retirement, how they'd made and lost money in the stock market, how much their property values had been increasing, and now they were going to enjoy the golden years, and I should be sure to set up an IRA for myself. I was glad I hadn't said I was in the real estate business. I might have to think of a line I'm in, like lady's lingerie or something.

Every so often I scanned the room still searching for someone who *looked* like an assassin. I imagined a grim, leathery face with beady eyes and a hawk-nose with tiny curly hairs poking out of his nostrils. He'd have on a sport coat but a tiny bulge over his heart would give away the gun he carried. I spotted no one who fit the bill.

I did see one table with two young couples, younger than me, even. There were also two children at the table, two of the few I'd seen on the ship, which might make it a boring week for them. At a table two removed from mine sat the tall blond, sitting with four people who must have been three times her age. Was she taking a trip with her two sets of grandparents, I pondered. Grandparents, something I'd never had in my life. She, the tall blond, and her four tablemates seemed to be enjoying a lively conversation so they either took to each other quickly or were traveling together. It appeared she, the tall blonde, was either accompanying a small group of older people or was traveling alone, a thought that, I must admit, intrigued me. This passing notion was quickly erased by the self-inflicted reminder that I was here on serious business, not to make a move on the only attractive and possibly available female aboard ship.

From where I sat I couldn't see Berger at his small table in the alcove of the dining room, but I might see him when he left the dining room. I wanted to find out what stateroom he was in.

The meal passed pleasantly and for awhile I forgot about Berger. As the room began to thin out I suddenly remembered and twisted my head trying to see into the alcove. Suddenly I saw him, walking towards the exit. I wanted to jump up to follow him but figured that would appear odd so I simply watched Berger leave. He couldn't go far for now, anyway.

A few minutes later I also left along with my dinner companions. One of them asked me if I had signed up for the tour tomorrow morning. I said no, and he told me there was a signup sheet at the reception desk and maybe we'd see you tomorrow. Not sure what I was going to do tomorrow other than try to approach Berger, I went to the reception desk and found the list. I gasped when I realized, here was a list of all the passengers and their stateroom numbers.

No one was paying attention to me so I flipped through the pages, pretending to be looking for my own name. I found my name then, further down the list, there it was: Wilhelm Berger, situated five staterooms down the aisle from me. He *was* on the ship; I'd found him! Hell, he wasn't even trying to hide, using his own name He must feel safe, the fool. I thought of going to him right now, no wasting time, but then changed my mind. I wanted to think this through. Just then the tall blond and the four elderly persons she'd been sitting with came up the stairs from the dining room and congregated around me.

"Oh, pardon me," I said, realizing one of the men wanted to look at the same list I had been studying. I stepped back and bumped into the blond.

"Excuse me, sorry," I mumbled, feeling like a klutz.

"Quite alright", she said, with a smile. "Are you going on a tour tomorrow?" she asked, just to be polite, I assumed.

"Yes, sure, why not?" This was the first time I'd had a close up look at her and it confirmed my initial reaction when I'd seen her from a distance: she was not only taller than me by two or three inches, but she was downright beautiful.

"Should be fun," she said. " I'm already signed up. Goodnight." She abruptly turned and walked away. I watched her go up the steps and into the aisle that led to the staterooms on the top deck, which housed the larger and more expensive staterooms.

I lingered around the reception area until the others had left. Then I went to the list again. Most rooms indicated two people, except, on the middle deck, me, a solo, in stateroom number 222, and Berger, in 232. I scanned the top deck names and for one of the suites, I spotted the name Lisl Meagher. That might be her, the blond. Well, so what?

Not sure how to approach Berger I went back to my room and realized how tired I was. Too tired to think straight. I'd worry about Berger and about how to spot the assassin tomorrow. As I felt myself slipping into sleep I wondered if Berger would wake up dead and how long it would be before he was found.

When we had been bused from the Lyon airport to meet the ship we motored north. Now, the Rhone Rover cruised south so we were back in Lyon, this time with several hours to tour. I wondered if Berger would head home, if he still had a home here.

I slept like an innocent baby lamb and awoke feeling fresh and recovered from jet lag and time zone changes. I would find out later I wasn't quite in tune yet and I would get extremely sleepy by mid-afternoon.

By 7:30 a.m. I was in the dining room ready for a bite of breakfast, surprised that I had such a strong appetite after an ample dinner last night. When I entered the room I saw Berger, sitting in the same place as last night, an alcove in the far corner. So he had survived the night. Clearly he wanted to dine alone and be left alon[e]. That was fine; what I had decided, in my dreams I guess, because when I awoke the plan seemed firmly in my mind, was that I would try to find a chance to talk to him while on tour, maybe edge him away from the group and find a café in which to get acquainted, or, if that didn't work, I would simply knock on his door around seven this evening, before dinner, and insist that I had to urgently speak t[o] him.

I ate alone, slowly consuming a cheese, bell pepper and mushroom omelet, along with toast and two slices of bacon, and coffee. I watched Berger leave the room. The foursome I'd sat with at dinner came in and waved at me just as I was finishing, thank goodness. On the way to my stateroom I passed the reception desk and checked to see if Berger had signed up for any tours; last night had been looking for his name, but didn't note if he'd signed up. If he lived here part-time why would he need to take a tour as part of the cruise? As I had speculated before, I wondered anew if Berger would use the time to return to his home while the ship was docked in Lyon. In fact, maybe this trip was a ruse and he wouldn't come back to the ship. Could it be Berger suspected someone was following him and was trying to throw them off?

A few minutes later, as I stood at the window in my stateroom, looking out at the bank of the river and the trees that lin[e] the street, to my extreme right I saw a man move across the ramp laid out for passengers to exit the ship. The man crossed onto the walkway that wound up to the street level. It was Berger and he wa[s] walking at a hasty pace. I grabbed my room key and my wallet and dashed out. By the time I was on the street he was long gone. I decided I'd forget about the tour I'd signed up for and go out on my own and hope to find Berger.

Lyon is a large city, at the confluence of the Saone and Rhone rivers, the second largest industrial city of France, and third largest city by population, so finding Berger might be a pipedream. With my French limited to 'oui, merci, and escargot', I wasn't going to do well if I needed to ask for directions or help.

I soon became intrigued by the numerous *les traboules*, passages hidden behind the doors of Renaissance facades, which were used as secret pedestrian passages in medieval times. I was also fascinated by a building on which are painted 3D representations of famous people in Lyon's history, pictured as if they were looking out the window or standing on the balcony viewing the outside scene.

Trouble was, once I got caught up in looking at the buildings, produce shops, wine and cheese stores, and the wonderful displays in the bakery windows, I neglected for hours what I was here for. Berger could have walked right past me and I wouldn't have seen him.

I began to tire and looked for a café where I could sit down and get a cup of coffee. I found one easily enough and next to it was a store that sold all kinds of newspapers and magazines. I spotted the International Herald Tribune, the English-language newspaper of Europe much loved by American travelers, and purchased a copy. I had no way to know whether Max's message was in this issue, or how I could find it, but felt I should have a copy in case I needed it later, maybe to show the assassin. With the paper, a *Time* magazine, a cup of coffee and a croissant, I settled down and forgot about Wilhelm Berger.

It was pleasant sitting at a small table on the sidewalk, even with the sounds of a bustling city all around. It began to drizzle but was tucked under an awning so I was able to enjoy the sound and smell of the rain without getting wet. No one bothered me and I ordered a second cup of coffee and read the entire paper. I imagine what an even more pleasant time it would be if Mary Grace were here with me.

Soon I realized I need to do something and remembered what the cruise director had said at the introductory talk he gave last night. He said to use the 'facilities' whenever possible, because finding a rest room in France was like going on a treasure hunt!

I concluded my chances were better of finding my way back to the ship than of finding a restroom by walking aimlessly around Lyon. And coming across Berger was likely even more hopeless. So I hiked back to the ship, (it had stopped raining) and went to my room, did what I needed to do, showered and took a nap. By the time I'd awakened I had missed lunch and was famished.

I dressed and went to the bar where I ordered a drink and pounced on the dish of nuts and pretzels, just what I needed to take the edge off until dinner. The faces around the bar looked suspiciously like the same ones I'd seen yesterday. Reminded me of a guy I once knew who said that his favorite ride at Disneyland was the bar at the Disneyland Grand Hotel.

I noticed a movement next to me and heard a man say 'excuse me' and order a drink. I sidled over an inch or two and turned to look at him. No problem, I replied, and almost dropped my

17

glass when I saw who it was. So now I knew what his voice sounded like. And his drink, scotch and soda, was the same I usually enjoyed.

"Hi," I said. Actually, what I said was "Hi," sounding like I had a frog in my throat, then a clearing of my throat and again, "Hi."

He nodded and said, "Have a good day in town?" His German accent was noticeable, but his English was perfectly understandable.

"Yes. How about you?"

He nodded again. "Oui." Then he laughed. "I try to use the language of the country I'm in, as best I can."

"German?" I asked. Again he nodded.

"I guess if you grow up with several countries around you, you pick up a few words of other languages. In America, we don't have that situation, although in some places it helps to know a few words in Spanish."

"So I've heard," he replied.

It was getting crowded around the bar so I used the excuse to invite him to sit somewhere else. He accepted and we moved to chairs far enough away from the bar so the conversations there wouldn't interfere with ours. Was this my opportunity?

"My name's Charles," I said, and put out my hand. He shook it, we sat down, and he said, "Wilhelm. Glad to meet you.

"You are traveling alone?" Berger asked.

I nodded and then gave him the same story I'd used last night. The better to tell one lie the same way each time then to have to reinvent it when it's needed again.

"You are traveling alone also?"

He gave me tall tale about being a freelance writer who wanted to do a piece on river cruising. He said his wife had died of cancer less than a year ago and he wasn't ready yet to travel with anyone. I gave him my sympathies but added, 'in a pig's eye', to myself.

I kept looking at him to see if I saw myself in his face, twenty-five years from now. Was this how I'd look? I couldn't see i He was rather short, no more than five foot nine, tops, not that I'm a big man, but his body structure didn't resemble mine. His eyes were blue, like mine, but his face was rounder than mine, his hair darker, his nose wider, and his lips thicker. Even is eyebrows were thicker than mine. I told myself he couldn't be my father. I didn't want him to be. I'd survived over three decades without a father and didn't fee I needed one now. I caught myself staring and for I don't know how long, my mind wandered back to my childhood, speculating what it would have been like to have him, (my father?), around when I was growing up.

After an unspoken minute I dared ask, "Any children?"

He shook his head. "Nein. Children never worked for us. You?"

"Not married." I guess my story hadn't made it clear that I wasn't married.

He laughed. "Nowadays that doesn't seem to be preclude having children."

I laughed back and added the tired cliché, "Right, none that know of." Ho, ho, weren't we a couple of fun guys enjoying our sexist jokes.

He offered to buy me a refill and I accepted. While he went to the bar I pondered what I should do. I even wondered if he knew who I was already, and was playing with me.

With my heart beating faster than normal I decided I would ask him straight out, do you know Maximilian von der Dusenberger. Even if he said no, it would get the conversation going in the direction I wanted to take it. Unfortunately, when he came back with the drinks he also came back with a man and a woman who sat down on the sofa next to our chairs.

Berger introduced them as Mr. and Mrs. Conover, Joseph and Mimi, from Denver, people he had met at dinner last night. I knew Berger had dined alone so why the fiction? Mr. Conover was a hefty man, not tall, but thick all around, from his neck to his hands. I'm not good at guessing ages but his wife was a good twenty years younger than he. She was as tall as her husband, pleasant looking, tanned and with an athletic look to her. Robbing the cradle, just like Max.

My mind wandered the rest of the evening as I pondered what I planned to say to Berger, and then thinking about when I'd get a chance again. I noticed the tall blond standing nearby at one point. She nodded to me and I nodded and smiled back. I forced myself to return to the conversation going on around me.

Later, at dinner, I again caught her watching our group (Berger and I and his new friends, Joe and Mimi, from Denver, they said, but they 'looked' European to me, though their English was without accent of any kind, dined together.) Or it could have been my imagination that the only good-looking and, apparently, single woman on the cruise was eyeing me. Maybe she was eyeing Berger looking for a sugar daddy?

My dinner companions invited me to accompany them to the lounge after dinner to listen to the music and have a nightcap. I went with them, but I wasn't interested in their conversation, which was turning more banal by the minute. I'm sure I came off as a snob, but the longer I talked the more I was afraid I'd slip up and something I didn't want to, and give myself away to Berger before I was ready.

I found myself looking for the tall blond, but after scouring the entire lounge, and it isn't too big you can't check out everyone it, I didn't see her. I decided to call it a night and excused myself from the others.

I feel asleep and dreamt of Mary Grace, except that in the dream she had long, blonde hair.

TEN: Confrontations

Before dawn the next morning I went up to the top deck to watch as we traversed one of the fifteen locks we would pass through on our journey down the Rhone. I carried a steaming hot cup of coffee in my hands, using it more to warm me against the chill than to drink. The only daylight was the faint yellow and orange glow that promised the sun would soon rise above the horizon. There was also adequate artificial light from several towers at the lock to see what was happening.

The entire process took about a half-hour. The water level differential going through this lock was forty-two feet. Without the locks, the Rhone can be a wild, dangerous river, we had been told on one of our tours. One of the crew who explained the process to me said because of its power the Rhone is the only river in France considered masculine, 'Le Rhone'. It is still subject to flooding but not nearly as severely as it was prior to the constructing of the locks. Without them the river cruise industry couldn't exist on the Rhone.

We entered a large chamber and at either end gates shut us in. The water level lowered the Rhone Rover until it looked and felt like we were on Wall Street in New York City, in a narrow cavern surrounded by giant concrete structures ascending so high they blot out the sunshine.

The lock, or 'ecluse' as the French say, is very narrow at this point. I could almost reach out and touch the side. I watched as cylindrical hydraulic pumps lowered with us. After twenty minutes or so the cylinders began to rise as did we. By now the sun was up and I was warming and hungry for breakfast so I went to the dining room.

I spent the day staying as close to Berger as I could without bumping into him every few minutes. I watched for him in the morning to see if he went with a tour group and maneuvered my way into the same group. I noticed Blondie was also in this group, though she did not appear to be with anyone in particular. My hope was to get Berger away from the group, maybe when the tour ended, so we could talk. But he stayed tight with the group and usually close to the guide. Maybe he felt safer in a crowd. I could never find the opportunity to speak to him other than a 'hello' and a nod a time or two as we saw each other as the tour progressed through the town.

We were visiting the twin cities of Tournon, an old town built around a massive 10th century castle that had been constructed to provide protection for the town, and Tain-Hermitage, on the left bank of the river at the bottom of the Hermitage Hills. Like most towns in this part of France, the cities were renowned for their wine. I learned that the label on the wine spelled 'Cotes du Rhone', which is the appellation, and that the word 'cote' means hillside. So far, the trip had been educational, though not in the way I had intended.

The guide related the legend of a knight who, weary of fighting, repented and devoted himself to prayer and the cultivation of vines that grew around Hermitage. (Well, if you must repent, best to have some good wine to go with it!).

So I was learning new facts every day but I missed a lot of what the guide said because I was so absorbed in keeping one eye on Berger and the other eye watching for anyone who got close to Berger. The assassin could come around a corner, knife Berger silently, and then take off. Who amongst a tour group of river cruise passengers is going to chase down the killer? But I figured it more likely the assassin was here, on the cruise. Whether he was keeping a close eye on Berger, as I was, walking with the placid group of tourists, or had his plans set for a certain time and place, thus did not need to keep a constant watch on his query, was a question I could not answer. Possibly he had picked up the Herald Tribune in Lyon, as I had, and found a message from Max to back off, but that was another question I couldn't answer.

The tour included a tasting of several famous wines of the region and a visit to a Gothic style 14th century church. At no time did I get an opportunity to speak to Berger. I decided I'd go directly to his room when we returned to the ship. When we did return I saw Berger go straight to the bar where he ordered a beer. As usual, the bar was crowded so I went to my room.

Last night, on an impulse, I had signed up for an afternoon excursion of wine tasting and a visit to a truffle farm. Now, frustrated due to my vain attempts to confront Berger, I decided to put him out of my mind as best I could and do something in the afternoon totally unrelated to my reason for being here, and fie on Maximilian. So I went and I didn't care if Berger was on the tour or not. He wasn't, and neither was my tall blonde acquaintance.

A half-hour bus ride through a pretty countryside of grapevines brought us to the truffle farm. There we listened to an explanation of the history of and the process of growing truffles (told to us in French, by the owner, and translated). We learned that truffles are basically a disease that develops on the roots of the oak trees, but that of the trees planted, only 40%-50% actually developed this disease and produce truffles. The truffles, especially the expensive black winter variety (costing close to a 1000 Euros for a kilo—2.2 lbs.) are highly prized in France and are used in cooking a variety of dishes.

We were led into a woodsy area where we were shown how the owner's dog uses his sense of smell to locate the truffles, which are underground. Pigs used to be employed for this task, but dogs are now the animal of choice because they can be more easily trained to not eat the truffle once they have found it, and as the fields are often far out in the country, it is easier to transport a dog in a pickup truck than it is to carry around a pig. I suspect a dog also provides better companionship.

I was admiring the thicket of oak trees and wandered away from the main group of my fellow tourists and the truffle farmer and his dog. I walked slowly and lightly, feeling a calmness that I hadn' felt in days. Being out in these woods, with leaves cracking under me and the scent of lavender, a plant often used to rejuvenate soil after the oaks trees roots have stopped producing truffles, in the air as if it had been sprayed by Mother Nature, I could almost forget th strange events that had brought me here.

I bent down and picked a few acorns off the ground. I woun up like a pitcher and threw one at an oak tree twenty yards away. I missed, wide right.

I kicked at acorns as I shuffled my feet and then leaned against an oak tree and stood still for a minute, enjoying the scent of the country air and playing with one of the acorns I had picked up. The tour group was a good hundred yards away from me, but I was okay with a moment's seclusion from the group and no one seemed to have noticed I had slipped away. I'd heard enough about truffles and was enjoying being alone. I bent down to pick up another acorn and as I did I heard a zip-like sound above me and the stripping sound of bark being peeled off the tree.

I hesitated for a second, in a stooped position, then stood up and noticed where the oak tree I'd been leaning against sported a clean scar, a six or seven inch gash. I was mesmerized by it and touched the gash, as if feeling it would tell me what had caused it to appear. Just then I heard a 'thwat' and a second gash appeared, an inch from my head. I dove down to the ground, scrunching acorns as I did. I scurried on the ground to another tree, then raised myself into a knelling position. I peaked around the tree and with my peripheral vision caught a movement to my right, two hundred yards away, give or take a first down. It was a man, a person, anyway, bulky in a heavy, dark coat, wearing an equally dark woolen cap, and carrying a rod-like item in has hands. No doubt a rifle. Someone had tried to shoot me! I almost peed in my pants, controlled the reflex, but I did gag from the shock of what had happened. Here I am worried about Berger being assassinated, but it seems he's turned the tables on me! And I'm trying to save the sonofabitch! The person was gone now, out of sight. As he had moved away, from the back view I had, the form reminded me of Berger's friend, Joseph Conover.

I brushed myself off and with frequent looks backward to assure myself the shooter hadn't snuck around to get at me from another angle, I trotted back towards the tour group and eased myself amongst them as they headed back to the main building of the truffle farm.

I couldn't rest on the bus ride back to the ship. Everyone aboard the bus looked suspicious to me. I recognized most everyone by now as people I'd seen around the ship or on tour, but I wasn't sure I could trust any of them. Goddamn Max!

Back on the ship I took a leisurely shower until I felt relaxed then I dried off and lay down on the bed. A nap later I felt resolved and did as earlier planned, and with dry mouth and damp hands went to Berger's room. I knocked repeatedly without getting an answer. went to the bar but he wasn't there. I went to the top deck and saw him talking to one of the crewmembers. While I tried to look casual mindlessly enjoying the view of the river and the countryside (the Rhone Rover was moving again), Berger's acquaintances, Joe and Mimi, came up the stairs and walked over to Berger and began to speak to him. A moment later they passed me, engrossed in their conversation and went below, ignoring me as they passed. I turned look at Conover from the rear, to see if his build resembled the shooter in the forest. I couldn't be sure because the shooter had wo a heavy coat. My suspicion was that Berger knows who I am, and has hired Conover to kill me, or someone else, maybe Max's hired assassin, hasn't gotten the word to back off Berger, and sees me as threat to his assignment.

I remained on the top deck a few more minutes before I wen below, but when I did I could not spot any of the trio. Apparently they'd gone to one of their staterooms. I was getting frustrated and decided it was time for a drink.

The evening didn't offer me any opportunities: Berger dine with Joe and Mimi and after dinner they went to the lounge togethe

The tall blond was again having giggly conversations with the two elderly couples I'd seen her with earlier and I couldn't catch her eye. I went to bed. Maybe all I could hope for now was that I survived the cruise and the hell with Berger. If we both make it, and Berger follows up to present Max with his demands, Max or I can talk to him then. And, not to be too hard-hearted about this, if he doesn't survive before I can talk to him then I won't *know* if he's my father and won't *know* if Mary Grace and I are related. Will *not knowing for certain* be good enough for her? Will I be around to know?

I was afraid the next day would bring more frustration, but now I was worried more for my own safety than I was for Berger's. The shame of the situation was that I was actually enjoying the cruise at those moments when I could forget why I was here and instead focus on the movement of the boat on the river, the scenery, the towns with their medieval history, the quaint streets and shops, the lip-smacking wines, and people-watching.

In the morning I didn't see Berger. I ate a hasty breakfast and since he still hadn't shown in the dining room I went to his room and knocked on the door; no answer. I went to the top deck and looked around, but no Berger. There weren't too many places to hide aboard this ship.

I checked the lounge and the library, even the laundry. I went back to the dining room and there he was, again with Joe and Mimi. I could swear he was avoiding me, which means either I'm getting paranoid or he knows who I am and doesn't want to have a one on one conversation with me.

We were in the town of Viviers, a walled city that has existe
since approximately the 5th century. The previous evening, at our
before dinner presentation by the cruise director, we learned that
Viviers was walled to protect itself from the ravages of the Hundre
Years War and the Black Death plaque. Isolated, it developed a
unique architectural style and some of the buildings, dating from th
15th century, still exist and are in use. I wondered if its walls could
protect me from another assassination attempt.

I reckoned I'd do like yesterday and stay close to Berger an
try to talk to him if I could, but if not, watch for any danger to eithe
of us, not that I had the foggiest idea what I'd do if I suspected the
assassin was ready to strike. Scream like a banshee, was my only
idea.

For over an hour the tour group strolled upon uneven
cobblestone or brick streets that can make walking tiring, viewing
ancient buildings. The streets are narrow and the sidewalks an
afterthought, and there is little automobile traffic, so pedestrians
generally walk in the street unless a car approaches, and then car an
human maneuver to make room for each other.

Some of the buildings are decrepit looking, others alluring
because of the flourishes decorating the facades: busts of men and
women of note in their time, knights on horseback doing battle, and
various creatures, real and imagined. The guide knew her history lik
I know real estate, and gave us a running account of the history of
the city, particular buildings, the people who had lived here, and
events that had occurred, real or legendary.

Berger was in the back of the group, farthest away from the
guide. I sensed a movement behind me and turned to see my man

nonchalantly separate himself from the tour group. I watched as he sauntered along the narrow, rough pavement, feigning a fascination with the architecture. I saw Berger glance over his shoulder at our group, then dart around a produce market on the corner. Our tour guide was leading us in the opposite direction.

I let the group get ahead of me, and then turned to follow Berger. I paused when I noticed the tall blonde heading the way Berger had gone. Now I was puzzled, a far too frequent occurrence lately. I watched as she went around the same corner as Berger had. I let the tour group get farther ahead and then I followed in the steps of Berger and the blonde.

At the corner I stopped and peaked around and saw the two of them ahead, Berger walking at a hurried pace, the blonde slower, pausing now and then to look in the store windows. I glanced back to see where the group was and saw the trailing end pass around a corner fifty yards away.

Wishing I had a London Fog topcoat with a collar I could pull up around my neck, and a fedora hat to help cover my face, the better to make me feel like a spy, I set off following Berger, with Blondie in between us. I still wasn't sure what she was doing. Why did she leave the tour group at the same time as Berger, and march off in the same direction, but at a pace geared not to catch up to him? I crossed the street so that if either of them turned around they wouldn't immediately see me. I wondered if Berger was leading me somewhere, that he wants me to follow him so finally we could talk. But why here? We could talk all we wanted in either one of our staterooms. Maybe his buddy is waiting to take another shot at me?

Eventually we came to the Cathedral of St. Vincent, who is the patron saint of vintners, for what that's worth, where an organ recital was beginning. Was this it; was this why Berger and Blondie left the group, to attend the organ recital? It made no sense because according to the tour guide, we would eventually come here for a recital, but later, an hour or so from now.

Like almost all the churches in these towns in south central France, it was old, built in the 12th century. I watched Berger take a seat towards the front, and Blondie a seat four rows back of him. I tucked myself into the second to the last row off to the left, behind a pillar and in shadows. There was a sprinkling of other people in the church and I got the impression the organist was rehearsing for the tour group's recital. He played several selections, none of which I recognized.

Just as the organist finished the blonde got up and went out. Did she not want Berger to see her? Now I felt stuck; if I left she might see me outside, if I waited for Berger to leave I might lose him. I decided to stay quiet in the shadows by the pillar and watch Berger's next move. A moment later he got up and walked along the transept to one of the small chapels. Another figure appeared, coming out of the shadows from the other side of the nave. He—it looked like a man from the bulk, like the person I'd seen in the woods—stood next to Berger. I assumed they were talking though I was too far away to be sure. Then the figure moved away and walked down the side aisle, still in shadow, and out of my sight. A moment later Berger left the cathedral.

I waited two minutes then went outside and stood in the front of the church trying to do my best interpretation of a bored tourist. I looked left and right, and didn't see either Berger or the blonde. I looked straight ahead down a narrow street that was void of pedestrians.

Thinking I'd lost both of them I started to walk, but then I saw a figure emerge from one of the shops on the street ahead. It was Berger; I didn't think he saw me as he crossed the street and appeared to go into another shop. I scanned my surroundings and didn't see anyone other than a few residents milling around chatting in French.

I walked briskly down the street toward where I'd seen Berger. As I neared the café he came outside and sat at a small table. A waiter followed momentarily and brought Berger a cup of coffee or tea. There was no one else around.

When I was mere paces from the table Berger looked up and saw me. I sat down without an invitation.

"Hello, Berger, we need to talk."

"You are very rude, monsieur. You have not been invited."

"Once the shooting starts the time for politeness is past."

"You're speaking in riddles, Hardin. What do you want?"

"I want to know who you are."

"Since you've obviously been following me you must already have some idea."

"Are you Maximilian's stepbrother?"

A waiter came outside and stood by the table. I looked at him.

"Café," I said.

"I have no reason to deny it."

"He's going to have you killed, Berger. The assassin may even be on this cruise."

Berger picked up a package of cigarettes that was lying on the table. He took a cigarette out, tamped it on the table, taking all the time in the world, reached into three pockets before he found h lighter, lit the cigarette and blew smoke out, fortunately not in my face. At least he was polite, although he didn't offer a cigarette to me, not that I wanted one.

"He wouldn't be so stupid. I can cause him so much trouble

"Not if you're dead." I was trying to be firm and confident, but my insides were jello.

"Nein! Even more so if I'm dead. I think I made that clear t Maximilian in my last communiqué to him. He probably received i since you last spoke to him."

"What communiqué?" I asked.

"I gave him a deadline. You don't need to know it exactly, but it will expire before the end of this month. I informed him that all the records I have regarding Frederick Dressen, Argentinean ambassador, known in his previous life as Colonel Wolfgang von d Dusenberger, all the documents that will show how von der Dusenberger used stolen gold and gems, some of the gold yanked from the teeth of slaughtered Jews, and which allowed him to set u a new identity in South America after World War II, are with a lawyer in New York City. These documents will also reveal that th colonel abandoned his wife to the lusts of American soldiers, and how his money later served to set up his son, Maximilian, in business and eventually fund Maximilian's precious Foundation. I have informed Maximilian that if he doesn't meet my demands all the information will be released to the public. It's also possible something dire might happen to that pretty young wife of his."

"Can't you at least leave the women out of this? What kind of man are you?"

"A greedy one."

" Max will have you killed before your deadline."

"Ha! No, Maximilian understands—I hope he does— that if I do not communicate with my lawyer by a certain date telling him to destroy the records, then they will be released automatically."

"You could be bluffing."

"You don't believe I'm bluffing and neither does Max."

"Why do you need to see him if all you want is money? He's already wired you a hundred thousand, hasn't he?"

"Yes, but that's not enough. He is worth many millions. I'm not being overly demanding, just five million will do me nicely the rest of my life."

"You don't know Max. He'll come after you."

Berger shrugged as if the threat was silly. "That old man? Or you? Ha! Anyway, he'll have no idea where to look for me."

"That's why he hires professionals."

"I have resources, too, young man."

The couple who called themselves the Conovers.

"Have you told Max what you want?"

"Yes, I did, but not where to send it. I'll give him those instructions personally. It will suffice as our family reunion."

"When are you meeting? Where?"

"Not that it's any of your business, but I suppose he'll tell you anyway. In his New York office, next week."

"What day?"

"You're so smart, you figure it out. Why does it matter to you anyway? Who are you and what is your business with me?"

"Let's say that I'm concerned with Max's safety."

"Safety? You don't think I'd hurt him, do you?"

I scoffed, "Oh, no, not the loving stepbrother."

Berger laughed.

"Did you gave Max instructions on where to send the money?"

"You ask too many questions that aren't your business, but no, I'll give those instructions to Max personally at the last minute

"Why? I don't understand why you need to see him at all."

"It's really none of your business." Berger paused and for a moment I saw a vague look in his eyes, almost one of affection. I suppose even the bad guys have emotions.

"Mostly it's a personal thing. I just want to meet him, one time. After all, we are brothers. We may not have the same father, but we do have the same mother."

"Why do you think Max owes you anything?"

He dragged deeply on his cigarette and blew several rings o smoke, each one progressively smaller. Then he stamped the cigarette into the ashtray.

"I didn't know I had an older brother until I myself was in my early teens. And it was much later before I had the time and resources to search for my family's history. The mistake I made wa in assuming he was still in Europe, under an assumed name. I shoul have known he'd gone to America long ago. I should have realized his father had escaped at the end of the war and set him up. When I did learn of the eminent philanthropist Maximilian von der Dusenberger I realized that if he had stayed in Berlin with me, he and I both would have been beneficiaries of his father's wealth. It's only logical, don't you see?"

Actually I did, but I wasn't going to admit it.

"And at least we could have helped each other to deal with growing up without a father. Something I doubt you'd understand."

"Don't be so sure," I sneered.

Berger took a sip of his coffee and waved his hand in the air for the waiter to bring him another one. In the background I saw a flash of blond hair as someone entered a shop up the street from us.

"He went back to Germany to look for your mother," I said.

Berger frowned. "Who went back?"

"Your father, the American soldier. He came back and found out you mother had died giving birth, but he couldn't find any trace of either you or Max."

"Hmm. That I never did learn, only that there were two soldiers, Military Police, who came often to see my mother. One of them impregnated her. I assumed they used her and then went back to their cushy homes in America."

"But you killed them both."

He looked as if he'd been slapped.

"You know too much. Apparently so does Maximilian."

Suddenly I realized I had a big mouth. If Berger had tried to have me killed yesterday, now he had even more of a reason.

I leaned forward putting my face as close to him as I could without standing up.

"Wilhelm, are you my father?"

For the briefest of moments, lest than the flutter of a hummingbird's wing, he seemed to hesitate. But he recovered.

"What? What kind of an absurd question is that? I have no children!"

"Didn't you meet a woman named Gina Hardin in Austria, i 1969? A girl you promised to meet a few weeks later, but you didn show up."

"I don't know what you're talking about! I've known scores of women, yes, even in Austria, but I've never been married."

"Since when does a guy have to be married to get a girl pregnant?"

He chuckled derisively and sipped his coffee. I felt he was stalling, but he also seemed to be adamant that he hadn't known my mother.

"It was a long time ago, Berger, you may have forgotten."

"If you find I'm you father will you call me Wilhelm, or Daddy?"

"This isn't funny, I need to know."

More and more I didn't want him to be my father. I wanted my father to have died in Vietnam in a blaze of glory, bullets flying and bombs blasting. No, I didn't; I wanted him to have come home safe and happy, and to have lived with Mom and me, and played ba with me and taken Mom and me to the beach and on picnics. I didn' want this guy to be my father, but I needed to know for certain.

"Why does it matter to you, at your age?"

"You wouldn't understand."

"Oh, now I wouldn't understand, is it? What if I am, then what? Are we going to have a family reunion? A party? Do you expect me to marry your mother?"

"How do you know she isn't married?"

He looked at me as if he'd been caught. "I…I don't know. I guess I just assumed. Is that why you're here? I thought you were here to do Max's bidding."

"I'm here to try to keep you alive, you idiot, at least temporarily. Max has given you time to live to allow me to find you and ask if you're my father, because it's important to me!"

Now it was Berger who leaned across the table. Now it was him staring me down because he sensed there was something that mattered to me even more than knowing the mere fact of whether or not he was my father. I wanted to hit him, hit him and leave, return to the ship, fly back to Los Angeles, go to Mary Grace and see the wedding date.

"Like all good stories, Berger, there's a woman involved," I said.

ELEVEN: Assassin

"So, you aren't really here to save my life, you're just hopin to learn whether or not I'm your father."

"Yeah, that's about it, when you cut to the chase."

"Then go ahead, for all I care, marry the girl."

"Max's investigators believe you are the man who…met m mother in Austria. I'd rather you aren't."

"How could anyone know that? If I felt it was worth my tin we could do a DNA test, but this is not my problem, young man."

"Who shot at me yesterday? Was it your friend, Joe Conover?"

For a second Berger seemed surprised that I would broach the subject so directly.

"I don't know what you're talking about. I think you're a crazy man, leave me alone."

"I can tell you this for certain, Berger. If anything happens me Maximilian will get you no matter what it costs him." (I didn't know if this was true, but maybe it would give Berger pause.)

He began to rise, as if to leave and as he did I clearly saw, r more than twenty yards behind Berger, the tall blonde. My heart skipped as the fantastic concept occurred to me that she, this young beautiful woman, was the assassin and she was going to do the dee here and now.

"Once I know for sure, one way or the other, I have no reason to watch over you anymore," I said.

Berger leaned over the table. "Watch over me? You can't be serious! I don't need you to watch over me, it is you who should be careful."

The blonde caught my eye. Berger's back was to her and at that moment my worst fear was that she'd shoot him and the bullet would rip through Berger and into me. Shows where my concerns were!

Berger looked away from me, standing now, as if in a huff, distaining me. I looked up at the blonde and she nodded, held my eyes for a second, then turned and on tiptoes walked away. I saw her go into a nearby shop. Berger was still hemming and hawing, laughing at me.

"Berger, how many American women could you have met that you seduced while in Salzburg, then promised to meet again later? Even if you totally forgot her at the time, you'd think now you would recall the incident."

"Even if I did, who can say who got the girl pregnant?"

"Max's investigators are very thorough. They have found specific dates for your movements over the years, the woman's, and when she gave birth, her diary, your file at the construction firm you worked for, a wrinkled old man who knew you…it fits precisely with you being the guy she met. And they found a photograph."

Berger slowly retook his seat. "What kind of photo?"

"Max told me about it. I'll admit I haven't seen it, yet, though I believe my mother still has it. Max said it was the photo of a young man, who looked enough like you would have looked thirty years ago, and it was inscribed with your name." Actually, it'd only been an initial, not a name, but I was looking for a reaction, so a fib was in order.

Berger stared at me, then leaned back in his chair and reached up with his left hand and scratched his eyebrow. He began to slowly shake his head.

"No, no, I don't remember that. Wilhelm is a common name. You have me confused with someone else. It's a coincidence."

In a moment of weakness I began to feel something, maybe pity seasoned with a tinge of sadness for this man, whoever he was. Having never known a father it was difficult for me to suddenly transform years of apathy to love, or even compassion. But still, he was a person who I was beginning to feel a sense of connection with, if only through the convoluted path that leads from a deceased Nazi soldier, to his son, Maximilian, through whom I met Mary Grace.

Connections can be bizarre, but even if this is not the man who met my mother, he gives me the sense of someone who has struggled with an innate meanness in his character, an issue he's never found a way of expelling permanently from his system. So I felt sorry for him. Of course, you can feel sorry for a mad dog, but that doesn't mean you try to pet him.

Again he rose to leave. "Besides, I don't care, I told you already. It matters not to me if I am your father, and it matters not to me if your girlfriend is, is, however you said, related somehow. I'm leaving, and if I see you on the ship I'd prefer you don't speak to me any more. Auf Wiedersehen."

He turned to go then stopped. "By the way, Mr. Hardin, I know people who are expert marksmen. If they want to hit a specific target, they usually do."

This time he did leave, throwing some money on the table as he turned to go. As he walked up the street I wouldn't have been surprised if the assassin took him out now. Well, I warned him. But there was no shot, no muffled sound, and Berger continued along unimpeded.

I sat and watched him walk up the street until he turned a corner and was out of sight. I tossed money on the table and paused as I noticed the two cigarette butts in the ashtray on the table. I took out my handkerchief and with it I picked up the butts and wrapped them. It might be difficult to explain why I had two stinky cigarette butts in my luggage if they are found in customs, but I'd worry about that later.

I walked passed the store I'd seen the blonde go into and looked through the window. I couldn't see anyone. I went inside.

"Bonjour," a feminine voice said. "Bonjour," I repeated, to a lady who stood behind a counter.

The store was small and certainly I'd see customers if any were inside. It was a store selling baby and maternity clothes, something I had no need for, and I doubt the blonde did either. There was a curtained exit at the back of the store with a sign above it that probably meant, 'Employees Only'.

"Pardon," I said, and walked out.

It was after noon already and the sky was getting cloudy and a breeze brought a chill with it. I'd neglected to bring an umbrella and feared I might need it soon. The wind blew harder and I wondered if this was the famous mistral wind that roars through the Rhone valleys at speeds up to thirty miles per hour. These cold, dry winds, activated by high-pressure systems over the Atlantic, are supposed to clear the sky of clouds and allow for a period of brilliar sunshine, I had read. But I'd also read that there was a phenomenon called the mistral noir, which draws in moist air from the northeast.

I pulled the collar of my windbreaker around my neck and began to walk faster, looking for a place to escape the wind and the coming rain. Maybe I should hasten back to the church.

At an intersection with a street named Rue Sibouse I stoppec and looked around the corner. There were numerous shops and cafe lining the street, and a number of people walking while some were beginning to high step it to get inside a shop and out of the weather.

The scene was a pleasant one and made me forget momentarily the stressful conversation I'd just had with Berger. Several shops sported colorful awnings, there were produce and wine marts with displays of their goods for sale, and residents and tourists moving briskly as the rain fell heavier. I turned into the passage and as I neared one of the cafes noticed a few people I recognized from the ship. They were opting for immediate cover rather than trying to get back to the ship. From the posted schedule we knew the Rhone Rover wasn't due to depart until early evening so there was no rush to return.

I nodded to a group of four people who had found a table an were in the process of ordering food and drinks. They invited me to join them and I accepted. I was still wondering what had happened to the blonde, and was my wild idea that she was the assassin possible? Or was she watching me for Berger?

For the next hour or so I was able to forget Berger and Max and blondes and assassins, and enjoyed lunch with people who were really here on vacation. I repeated my same story as I'd told before—meeting in Marseilles at the end of the cruise—which satisfied their curiosity, and they all talked about their travels and where they were going next and it was fine to be with people who didn't seem to have a worry in the world.

By the time we'd finished lunch and two glasses of wine the wind had died down significantly and the rain was nothing more than a harmless drizzle, the kind that can actually be fun to walk in. My lunch companions invited me to join them as they continued to explore Viviers but I declined, saying I was looking for a particular museum.

I roamed the streets, not sure what I was doing or looking for, just killing time. Maybe I should have stayed with the others, for my own safety. I guess what it came down to now was I wanted to find the blonde. It was hard enough to come out and ask Berger if he was my father, so do I ask her straight out, are you a killer?

I strolled the main streets, the Grand Rue and the rue du Chateau, people watching as I went along, and also dared to enter some smaller and less crowded streets. Despite what happened yesterday in the woods I felt a bit safer now since Berger had told me to get a message to Max, plus his jibe about how his friend, Conover, I assume, was just trying to scare me. Okay, he succeeded, but now I think I'm safe, at least until I get a message to Max.

In the main part of town I viewed a 16th century renaissance building decorated with fine carvings, ornamentation you won't see on today's sleek, modern buildings. I enjoyed viewing houses painted in faded pastels, and upon returning to the area around the cathedral, I discovered a view of distant mountains.

I wandered aimlessly, often with my head up looking at the medieval architecture. It was getting dark quickly and I felt a chill a the wind returned. When I scanned my surroundings I realized ther was no one else on this street—no wider than an alley—and I had r sense of direction.

I did not see an intersection nearby in either direction so I continued walking the way I'd been going. All the buildings looked boarded up and whatever shops existed on this street were closed. I wrapped my arms around me as I shivered and then it began to rain hard again.

I walked faster now as I saw the end of the street ahead. At the corner I looked all ways. I was sure that to the right was the river and the cruise ship. Soon I realized the road was leading me uphill and I wasn't sure anymore. There were no shops now, but instead a block wall, remains of the old wall constructed hundreds years ago to protect the town, arose on my right, while to my left buildings had been replaced by the hillside, a high bank of dirt and moss and weeds and bushes.

Now the road sloped downward and the wall on my right loomed higher above me. I thought I smelled the river so I felt encouraged that I was again going in the right direction. The rain came down harder and I broke into a trot. But doesn't it seem that when you run in the rain you get hit by more raindrops than if you just walked?

Above me the sky was a dark gray, ahead of me the road curved and hinted that it would wind downward towards the river, or at least, would get me to a place I might find people. How do I ask in French for the river? Riviere?

Another two or three minutes and the road began to gain height in relation to the wall, or vice versa, and I was eager to get to a point where I could see more of the town and figure out my location in relation to where I needed to go. As I neared a spot where I could peer over the wall I was hit by something that knocked me down and smashed me against the wall. I saw stars, yes, honestly, yellow and red stars and my head hurt and then the stars were gone in a black void and I'm sure I lost consciousness for a few seconds. I was revived as I felt myself being lifted.

Someone, someone very strong, was lifting me. He, or it, maybe the hunchback of Notre Dame, was handling me as easily as I would pick up a bag of oranges. My face and hands scraped against the rough blocks of the wall and I tried to push myself into the big ape that was manhandling me.

My efforts were feeble. He was too strong for me and with no delicacy whatever he dropped me down on the top of the wall, stunning me anew. From this vantage point atop the wall I could see light gray sky in the distance, and a ribbon of darker gray, the river. But immediately below me all I saw was a severe drop off that began as dirt and bushes and boulders which had broken off the wall over the centuries. Farther down the hillside everything melted into darkness. The man began to push me and I grabbed desperately at the edge of the wall. My fingernails split and my fingers bled as I fought for a grip, but I was losing it. I turned my head so at least I'd see who it was that was going to throw me into the ravine like so much garbage. It was Joe Conover. Either Berger had let me think I was safe to get me off guard or Conover was Max's hired assassin and thought I was getting in his way.

I spit into his face and his sneered at me, gritted his teeth and reared back with his arms to give me one final shove. Then I heard two pops, a sound like punching a bag of flour. Conover's eyes opened wide and he stopped in mid-push. Then he tottered backward, stumbling as he grabbed at his throat. A black stream seeped out of his mouth, blood, but in the dark I couldn't see the color. He gagged and fell straight down, his head hitting the pavement with a crack. That alone might have killed him but I think he was dead already from the two shots fired by the tall blond who was standing a few feet away.

"Help me," she said as she walked over to Conover.

I gingerly slipped down off the wall and had to brace myself with one hand as I almost tumbled over.

"What are you going to do?" I wasn't sure if I was next on her hit list.

"Help me lift him over the wall."

"Shouldn't we call the police?"

"Don't be foolish," she said. "Now, lift his shoulders while get his feet." She was commanding; she could have been a combat officer.

We lifted Conover to the top of the wall where I had lain

just seconds before. "Push," she ordered. We did and the assassin, the male one, rolled down into the blackness.

"With luck, he won't be found for weeks", the blond said.

I stood there looking at her, dumbfounded, my face scratched and my hands bloody from clawing at the wall.

She smiled at me as if I were her long-lost lover, her tiny dimples, one on each cheek, giving her the slightest cutesy look, a sweet, girlish appeal. Her long hair swept down ending somewhere towards where it met the curve of her backside. Her legs began way up here and ended way down there.

By now the very tall, very pretty blonde and I had met several times, under more normal circumstances, and had exchanged polite greetings—'Hello, having a good time?' or, 'How are you today?', and that was about all, although more than once I had the feeling the casual sound bites between us were the prelude to a more significant acquaintance. She had smiled those times, too, her mouth wide and full of teeth almost blinding in their brilliance.

On the afternoon of our second day, when the sun appeared on a cloudless day and many of the passengers took to the top deck to tan and warm their old bones— some of them had severely old bones—I saw her stretched out on a lounge chair, wearing a bikini that was probably illegal in several States.

Those old fogies kept finding excuses to walk past her, back and forth, getting their exercise, I guess, the first time in years any of them had decided to take up walking as a hobby. Their wives kept calling them back to sit down or take a nap. I only stepped on my tongue once, so I thought I was doing pretty well in containing my admiration for Miss Longlegs.

Now I was quite surprised to meet her along the deserted streets of the village of Viviers at a time when most of the cruise ship's passengers were back on board, cleaning up, or having a drink, relaxing and unwinding from a day of traversing the streets of Viviers.

Besides being taller than me she was standing up hill and looked down with a grin that was a combination of Mona Lisa's and Cruella Deville's

"So what are you doing here, Mr. Hardin?" she asked, pleasantly. (She knew my name?!)

My eyes were level with her breasts; if she took another step forward I was afraid she'd poke me in the eyes.

"I, ah, was just admiring...the view," I said, as I looked up her. Her smiled widened. She stepped forward and I stepped back, stumbling on the uneven pavement of bricks laid decades ago. I caught my balance by bracing one hand against the wall.

"You should go home, Mr. Hardin," the lady said, "before you get hurt."

Her right hand emerged slowly from the pocket of the thick woolen sweater she was wearing, a striking off-white and soft tan combination, and when it was out of the pocket it held the gun she had just used. I assumed it was still loaded, and warm from its recent workout.

From somewhere I coughed up a dose of courage; or maybe it was stupidity or that I was frozen in fear and didn't know whether to run or kneel and ask for mercy.

"I'm here to stop you," I said, as firmly as I could, though I'm sure it came out as stuttering gibberish.

"I don't know what you're talking about," she said, rather warmly, considering.

"I think you do," I replied, in my best thriller-novel confidence, new found since she hadn't yet shot me, although the gun was still in her hand.

I must not have come off as scared as I felt, because as if she'd read my thoughts she smiled and put the gun in her pocket.

"You're the person hired by…hired to take care of Berger, aren't you?"

"Why don't we go back to the ship and talk this over, in my room, along with a drink?" There was a question mark at the end of her sentence but it had the essence of an order, not a suggestion. Besides, I was here to stop her so if talking it over a drink would do the job, why not? Anyway, if she had just saved my life, she wasn't likely to take it, right?

"I saved your life; some say that makes a person responsible for the one they saved. What do you think?"

I managed a grin but didn't say anything.

She seemed to know the way so I followed her lead. We walked slowly, like two tourists tired from a long day of sightseeing, as if nothing unusual had occurred. I was eager to get far away from where we'd disposed of Conover but not particularly eager to return to the ship with my face and hands scratched and bloody. I ran my handkerchief over my face.

"Do I look presentable?" I asked

"It'll do until you can clean up. Keep your head down and your hands in your pockets when we arrive at the ship."

When we reached level ground we emerged into a street of stores and traffic and people. I turned to look at her. She smiled at me, a look that conveyed either treachery or amusement. The light was dim, as these medieval streets had been modernized with only the minimum lighting needed to avoid walking into a wall as one explored the beguiling passageways. But the shadowy light did nothing to detract from her marvelous good looks. How could this person be a killer? Why not, I suppose was the answer; why does a hired killer have to be ugly? James Bond wasn't ugly. The femme fatales in all those preposterous spy movies aren't ugly.

Speaking of James, what would he do? First of all, whether she intended to kill him or help him, he'd make love to her, that was a given. Too bad this wasn't a spy novel and I the hero. Yet, why did she suggest—order—us to go back to the ship? If she wanted to off me she could do it in one of these narrow alleys and no one would find me until morning, after the cruise ship was miles down the river. Or she could have let Conover do it.

Possibly it was because she has no stake in killing me; no reason and no money involved. She was here to kill Wilhelm Berger not me. Maybe she wanted to talk to me to assure herself who I was and why I was here. Maybe she was thrown off by the mere fact that I'd found her. Or maybe she wanted to frolic with me before putting me out of her way—permanently.

Walking with her now, she at least two inches taller than me, I wondered if I could take her if I felt my life was threatened. She was a few years younger than me, I calculated, but certainly I was stronger than her though she might know some fancy judo moves and could flip me off the balcony into the river. Frankly, that might not be so horrible. The river wasn't very wide or very deep, and I could swim well enough, if she hadn't broken my neck first.

It was fully dark by the time we reached the dock where our ship was waiting. I checked my watch—we were only minutes away from our scheduled departure time. We were probably the last arrivals, except possibly for Berger. Maybe she simply didn't have time to deal with me in town because she wanted to get back to the ship. And Berger? I assumed he was still in Viviers, but it had been hours since we talked at the café and he could have gone straight back to the ship after he left me. And of course I was pretty sure Mr. Conover wasn't going to join anybody for dinner tonight. I wonder if his wife will worry. I wonder if she is his wife, or *was*.

I turned to my savior as we reached the walkway that led down to the river's edge and to the Rhone Rover. "Are you letting him go? He's here, isn't he, in Viviers?"

She made a moue that seemed to indicate unconcern. Then she shrugged her shoulders as if she had no idea what I was talking about, but her gestures were not convincing. Come to think of it, maybe she had done away with Berger this afternoon, and that's why I never saw him again.

Then as we crossed the gangplank and entered the reception area I saw him. Berger was aboard! Blondie saw him too, I'm sure, but she acted indifferent, as if she had no idea who he was. I caught his eye and he seemed surprise, even shocked, to see me.

She nudged me towards the stairs that led to the top deck, the one that housed the larger rooms including the suites. As we arrived at the door of her suite she stepped ahead of me and pulled out her key—I had feared the gun. She was sailing in style, all by herself in one of the suites. Crime must be paying her well.

She unlocked the door and pushed it open. "After you," I said. She smiled and went in. I followed like the curious cat.

INTERLUDE: Wilhelm

The boy stood before the desk of the orphanage director, who frowned at the boy and shook his head. He berated him for fighting again, the third time this month, the director reminded the boy.

I know the other boys can be cruel, and you have to defend yourself, Wilhelm, the director said. I understand the problem, but it seems every week you are in another fight. Do you know why the boys tease you, he asked. The boy shook his head.

It's because there are stories that even your mother, God rest her soul, didn't know who your father was, but that it might have been either one of two American soldiers who came to visit your mother. Some say they even killed your…your mother's husband, who was a colonel in the army. Others say the colonel fled to South America. And, since you are slightly smaller than the other boys your age, and because they, like you, are often angry that they have to live here, without parents, you are an easy target. I realize this doesn't necessarily make it better for you, but I thought you should know.

The director also mentioned that at age sixteen Wilhelm could leave the orphanage voluntarily, and at age eighteen he would inherit a trust fund set up for him and his brother, should his brother ever reappear.

Wilhelm had heard whispered rumors but this was the first definite news Wilhelm had received concerning a brother. The director told him the story of how Wilhelm's brother had run off in a panic from the hospital when he learned that his mother was dead. So now the boy knew that his father, his mother, and his brother had all abandoned him. The fact that it may not have been their intention did not make it easier for young Wilhelm to understand.

The years passed and as Wilhelm and the other boys his age, including the ones who had harassed him, grew older, the fights seemed silly and a waste of time. Most of the boys were eager to leave when they were old enough, but often at sixteen didn't have another place to go to live. Wilhelm stayed until he was eighteen, then, with his inheritance he had a place to live and some money to spend.

The first thing he did with his money was to hire a lawyer to sue the United States Army to learn who his father was, and to learn what happened to his mother's husband, Colonel Wolfgang von der Dusenberger. The case didn't get far, as Wilhelm had no idea of the names of the soldiers who used to visit his mother. But the lawyer managed to get hold of the case file into the investigation of Colonel von der Dusenberger.

This colonel was of only minor importance to the Allies as their emphasis was to bring to justice the Nazis responsible for the most heinous of deeds, so not much concern had been given to locating the colonel, once initial efforts had been unsuccessful. However, the files indicated that preliminary investigations had been done by the Military Police, and a report prepared by Lieutenant William Wolfe and Sergeant John Schneider. The lawyer suggested Wilhelm take his case further by accusing the two American soldiers of taking his mother by force and suing them. The lawyer had learned from the files that both of the MPs had been taken off the case in January of 1946 and had returned to the United States and mustered out of the army. The file even listed their leave destination, as they were first given thirty days leave before their discharge was completed.

At that point Wilhelm thanked the lawyer and said he did not wish to pursue the issue any longer.

At this juncture in Wilhelm's life, just over eighteen and needing to work, searching for his father, and/or searching for the man who he thought of as the one who *should* have been his father, was not feasible. However he did find that there were Nazi hunters who were only too glad to track down Nazis who had escaped at war's end and hadn't been accounted for. The colonel, Wolfgang von der Dusenberger, was not a high priority at first, as the focus was on higher-ranking persons and those who were directly involved with the death camps.

But Wilhelm stayed in contact with one such eager hunter who sent him periodic bits of information on supposed sightings of former German military and administration personnel spotted all over the world, usually in South America. All too often there was not enough manpower to track down every little clue.

In 1978, Wilhelm paid a small fortune to a guard at the East German prison he was locked in, to abet his escape. Wilhelm devoted the next two years to tracking down every clue, no matter how slight, regarding possible sightings of Colonel von der Dusenberger.

His hunt took him to Switzerland, Austria, Poland, Russia, and a handful of South American countries. By the time he had the data that he was sure positively identified the colonel, now known as Frederick Dressen, the man had died. He could not gather any specific information regarding what had happened to the Ambassador's estate, other than that most of it had been left to a son in the United States, and some to his aide, a Mr. Heinz Zimmerman. Wilhelm was informed that Zimmerman had disappeared after the Ambassador's funeral, and had left no forwarding address.

Wilhelm hadn't forgotten the information he'd learned concerning the American soldiers who had questioned his mother about the whereabouts of Colonel von der Dusenberger. He'd learned the identities of the two men, one of whom was his father, who had abandoned him and his mother, her to her death, he to a life of struggling to make ends meet, and where they were living shortly after the war had ended. He knew what he wanted done next would cost him a great deal of money, which is why he'd had to wait so long.

Almost fifteen years had passed so it took time and work, and yes, lots of money, for Wilhelm to find someone who could go to the United States and pick up the trail. And to complete the job.

Through associations Wilhelm had made over the years as he drifted from legitimate work to drug dealing, life in East Berlin, and various illegal activities, he met a man named Johan Kantor. At least, that was what the man called himself. He would use various names over the years, sometimes Conover, sometimes Durand, and others, depending on what nationality he was posing as or where he was working. He knew English like a native, and enough French and

Italian to get by. He and Wilhelm Berger would develop a long-term relationship.

The man Wilhelm hired, Kantor, was no fool. He certainly didn't use his own name when he traveled, and he didn't use his own name when he rented a car in a small town in Idaho. But he did his job and was paid handsomely.

It was late in the year 1996 that Wilhelm noticed an a feature article in *Time* magazine about an American real estate magnate and philanthropist with a very German-sounding name.

The name Maximilian von der Dusenberger cannot be a common one, Wilhelm Berger reasoned. He read the entire story, which gave a brief biography of the man, who claimed his father had been killed on the Russian front in World War Two and that his mother had died from a fall in their home, a fall due to rickety stairs weakened by Allied bombing. She was a victim of the war, von der Dusenberger claimed.

There was little said about Maximilian's childhood other than to mention that after his mother died he roamed the streets and found work helping to rebuild the cities. Maximilian claimed his memory of his childhood was clouded due to the hardship of those days after the end of the war, and the trauma of his parent's deaths. He did mention that through the generosity of a group of philanthropic Americans who desire to remain nameless, he was able to get an education and eventually immigrated to the United States.

TWELVE: Bosum Buddies

Her suite was considerably larger than my stateroom, with just enough space for people to move around without bumping into each other, and sliding doors that led to a roomy balcony. A bucket of iced champagne was placed near the bed; she must have ordered earlier in the day to be delivered to her room in the early evening, a if it was the most common thing to do.

"You need such a large room for yourself?"

"I like to pamper myself. Besides, I'm not alone now."

I scanned the room and noticed a copy of the International Herald Tribune on the table. I reached over and picked it up.

"Do you read this regularly?"

"Of course."

"And you found a message from…"

"Later. You need a shower. Help yourself, my bathroom is larger than yours and everything you need is in there."

"I need a change of clothes. I'll go back to my room and clean up and join you later."

She reached toward me and began to unbutton my shirt. "Relax, Mr. Hardin. Give me your key and I'll go get clothes for yo while you take a shower. You do look a sight and you shouldn't walk around the ship looking like you've been scuffling in the dirt. And you can't expect me to share a glass of champagne with someone who has bloody hands and a dirty face."

21

Why did she want to go to my room? Was she looking for something? I couldn't imagine what it was. I had no real valuables, just some cash, which was locked in the safe. Was she afraid if I went to my room I wouldn't return to hers?

I gave in rather easily, thinking a hot shower in her swanky bathroom might be a pleasant luxury after my near meeting with St. Peter. Besides, we did need to talk so I had no intention of trying to avoid her. I gave her my key and sat down in a chair and began to take off my shoes.

"By the way, what should I call you, Lisl?"

"That's one of my names, but my friends call me Anna," she said.

I nodded. "I'm Charles, but you already know that."

"Enjoy your shower, Charles," she said, and smiled and walked out of the suite.

I finished undressing in the bathroom, dumping my damp and dirty clothes on the floor. Everything I'd been wearing was ruined, or if not, I'd didn't want to wear again. I turned on the water and stepped in.

The hot water poured down on my head for a full minute before I dosed my hair with a generous dollop of lavender shampoo. Rubbing the shampoo into my hair was also good for cleaning my fingers and nails, which were filthy and bloody and sore from grasping at the wall.

I let the shampoo set in my scalp for a luxurious minute then turned to face the shower to let the water run on my forehead and down my face. It felt good and cleansing. I didn't hear the door open and shuddered for a split second when I felt the hands on my back. Then I smelled her scent and relaxed and let Anna's soft hand scrub my back. I didn't think an assassin could be so gentle.

"We need to dress quickly or we'll be late for dinner," Anna said, as she rose from the bed. I glanced at the clock and saw that it was after seven. "Yes," I agreed. "I am starved. We'll miss the tour director's chatter this evening."

"Would you rather have spent the last hour in the lounge?" Anna asked.

I smiled and gave no other answer.

I began to dress while Anna went into the bathroom. A few minutes later she was out, and ten minutes later she was dressed and ready to go. She had tied her hair back into a long ponytail.

"I'm sorry I don't have time to make myself look more presentable. You don't mind, do you?"

"You look delectable," I said. I immediately felt guilty because once I had told Mary Grace the same thing.

"We haven't had a chance to talk yet," I said as we walked down the hallway towards the dining room.

"We have plenty of time," Anna said.

"We do?"

"The ship will be sailing all night long. You have somewhere else to go? You have a good book to read?"

I shook my head. When we entered the dining room it was almost full. I looked for Berger and saw him with Mimi Conover. They were seated at a table with several others but had their heads close to each other in conversation. Berger saw Anna and I and stopped talking. Mimi eyed us, too. She wasn't smiling but neither did she look like she was distraught over a missing husband. I nodded and winked at Berger. I had no way of knowing if Berger thought I was simply having dinner with a new friend or rather Anna was the person hired by Max. If he suspected Max had someone following him, he probably wasn't expecting a woman.

"Over there, for two," I heard Anna say to a waiter. He led us to a table at the far end of the room, out of sight of Berger and with a tiny bit of privacy so we could converse.

Anna took the seat that gave her a view of the dining room while I had my back to most of the room. A habit, I suppose, for a professional assassin. The word stuck in my craw; I had just made love to a professional killer. I tried to convince myself she wasn't a killer; she had just happened upon Conover as he tried to kill me. And she just happened to have a gun.

"I don't want to talk business now," she said.

"Fine, but I do need to get a message to…your employer, my friend, about what Berger told me this afternoon."

"You seem to think you know something."

"Would I mention what is otherwise an inane idea to a stranger?"

"Maybe if she had saved your life?"

"Ah, yes, we have become rather intimate rather quickly, haven't we," I replied, my face aglow. She smiled back and I was taken again by how lovely she was, especially when she allowed a smile.

"Pretend for a moment I can get a message to your friend, what would I say?"

221

I gave her the gist of my conversation with Berger, and told Anna to assume he could be dangerous, but that I would try to be with Max when he met Berger.

"He wants five million dollars."

Anna was impressed by the amount. "Hmm, this man is ve wealthy, isn't he?"

"Yes, and he's actually my employer, too, Anna, and a friend."

I neglected mentioning that he's was supposed to become n brother-in-law in the near future, but since I hadn't been able to get definitive answer from Berger about his relationship with my mother, my future with Mary Grace was definitely on hold. But none of that was any of her business.

"It's *Anna*, rhymes with wanna, not *Anna* as in banana," Anna instructed. "You need to pronounce it correctly."

A waiter came by and took our drink orders and we proceeded to examine the menu. As usual, the offerings made me salivate. Anna and I ordered similar meals, the 'La salade Nicoise' start, then I had the 'Provencale cream of garlic soup' while she opted for the 'minestrone de legumes.' We both chose the 'Le filet mignon de veau flambé au cognac' for the entrée. Oh, Mary Grace will carry on if she finds out how I've been eating. On the other hand, gourmet dining in France without her is the least of my offenses.

Anna and I made small talk over dinner: do you travel mucl Oh, yes, and where else have you found that is special? How was th weather there? What else do you enjoy, hobbies, sports, basketball? Of course I played basketball, how did you guess? A wild stab. It g a little silly and we found ourselves giggling. I wondered if Berger was laughing tonight.

Over dessert I asked, "So how does a girl like you get into a business like yours?"

"What business is that?" she responded, between bites of crème Brule. (I was stuffed and passed on dessert, though I was contemplating a cognac). She let the spoon slide slowly out of her mouth as she looked at me coolly, as innocent as a newborn baby.

I looked around to be sure no one was near the table, then leaned forward and said, "Aren't you the person hired to kill Berger?"

She squinted her eyes in disbelief. "What an incredible suggestion!"

Any person who was accused of something so ludicrous would be far more aghast than Anna was.

"Well, you've been following him, and what you did today…"

"I just happened along, and this man was trying to throw you over the wall. Would you rather I had just watched?"

"Of course not, and thanks, by the way. In all the commotion I don't think I ever thanked you."

"I thought you did, in my room a little while ago."

"Okay. But the way you handled yourself, and you carry a gun. I don't think this was the first time you…"

Anna interrupted, "Let's go back to my room and finish the champagne."

"I think I've had my fill of champagne. Let me order a cognac to take with me."

We went to Anna's suite where she poured herself a glass of champagne while she kicked off her shoes at the same time, first one, then the other, without spilling a drop, as if she did that exact same trick every day. I sat down on the bed with my back up against a couple of pillows.

"Anna, I was told by Ma..."

"Quiet! Don't say any names. I don't want to know who sent you here."

"The same person who hired you. But he said you worked through a middle man so the only way he could contact you was through coded newspaper ads, and he wasn't sure if you would get a message in time."

"In time for what?"

"In time to stop you from killing Berger."

"You're silly, Charles. I was never hired to kill anyone. It's not what I do, despite what happened today."

"It's kind of a long, convoluted story, Anna."

"I don't want to hear it, Charles. I mean it, that's not the kind of talk I meant we'd have."

"What did you mean?"

She turned away and looked out the windows at the passing river. It was dark and there wasn't much to see. She was silent for a moment and I waited while she sipped champagne. She put the glass down.

"I don't know. You tell me lies about yourself and I'll tell you lies about myself."

"Why lies?"

"Because after a few days on this ship we'll never see each other again, so what difference will it make?"

She had a point.

I nodded towards the paper that still set on the table. "So you did get a message recently?"

"Yes, several days ago."

"And you won't tell me what it said?"

"Why should I?"

"How can you be sure I'm not the person who hired you in the first place?"

She turned suddenly and looked at me in surprise, as if the idea was utterly ridiculous.

"If you were, you'd know the message."

"*How* can you know, Anna?"

"Because the message my employer sent told me to expect you, and to watch out for you."

"Watch out for me?"

"Yes, Charles, watch out for you. How am I doing?"

I had to laugh. "I think you've gone beyond the call of duty."

She picked up her glass of champagne and we clinked glasses, then put our drinks down.

"And, how do you say, to stick with you."

"Stick with me, eh? For how long?"

"Until we get to New York."

"What? Are you serious?"

"He pays well, this friend of yours, so I will follow his orders."

"But did he also tell you to leave Berger alone, because I needed to get information from him?"

"I told you before Charles, I wasn't hired to kill Berger. I was hired to follow him and to report his movements."

"Then why did…why did my friend tell me he'd hired someone to kill Berger, and I needed to hurry to Europe and find him before you did?"

She shrugged. "How do I know? Maybe he wanted to give you a sense of urgency. Why would he hire me to kill him and then tell you to go find him? How do you think he, and you, found out Berger would be on this cruise? I sent that information. And if I'd wanted to kill Berger I could have done it a dozen different times in a dozen different towns. It's not what I do."

"Damn him! I think you're right. If he hadn't told me Berger's life was in danger I might not have come looking for him."

"And he has something vital you need to get from him?" she asked. She sat down on the bed now and put a hand on my leg and began to rub it.

"Yes, I need to…"

Anna touched my lips with a finger. "Shh, I don't want to know your secret."

"If you don't want me to talk about anything about me, then you have to tell me about yourself."

"Later." She leaned closer to me. "Now, just kiss me."

So I did. For king, and country.

When I awoke it felt like I was alone. Had I gone back to my own room? I rose up on my side and saw her standing outside, on the balcony. There was almost no light, other than the reflection from the lights on the top deck of the ship. She was a dark, shapely silhouette.

As I watched her the clouds moved on and the three-quarter moon shone down on the river, and beams of light lit her face and upper half of her torso. I got out of bed and went out to the balcony. Anna smiled and took my hand.

"It's so quiet, and peaceful. I could live this moment over and over."

"You make me wonder if you've had many peaceful moments in your life, Anna."

She didn't answer, but just stood there looking out at the river. Silvery rays of moonlight lit the water in streaks and on the shore, a half mile away, an occasional spot of light could be seen, the porch light of a farm house or the street light in a tiny village. Anna took my hand and we went back inside. I lay down on the bed and she sat on the edge.

"Are you going to distract me again, Charles?"

"No, Anna, I'm too sleepy; sorry,

She laughed. "Good, I was only teasing."

"Can't you tell me anything?" I asked.

"I can tell you that tomorrow we should take the tour to the old Roman aqueduct. It's a marvelous sight to see. I guarantee you will love it."

I laughed. "This is amazing; two o'clock in the morning, on the Rhone River, a beautiful moon the only light, lying in bed with a beautiful woman who saved my life a few hours ago, talking to her about a Roman aqueduct. Who'd believe it?"

227

"No one has to."

Neither of us said anything for a long time, waiting for the other.

"Tell me your story, Anna," I said

A deep sigh prefaced her nudging near to me.

"My father is Israeli and my mother is Syrian."

"Hmm, an unusual combination"

"Yes. He, my father, was Mossad…you know them?"

I nodded—the Israeli secret service, efficient, sometimes brutal. "Was?'

"My mother was found be a spy for Syria. She was put in prison—is still in prison. My father was forced to resign."

"Was he a spy too?"

"No. He would have been executed if he had been. But because his wife was a spy and he never knew it he was labeled incompetent."

"So what did he do?" I asked, when she failed to say any more.

"He became a free-lancer."

"You mean, like a mercenary?"

"I guess you could call it that. He tried to work for what he identified as worthwhile, moral causes. I'm sure he believes he always does the right thing, but…"

"And you? You followed him?"

Anna moved into the bed now, sliding against me until our bodies were tightly meshed with each other. She held me tight. I wondered when she had last experienced any physical comfort. Wh me?

"Yes, and no. Even when I was a little girl he taught me how to defend myself. He knew that in his profession he'd made enemies who wouldn't reject the idea of attacking his family. Later he taught me his talents, his tricks, his investigative ways. But he didn't want me to become what he had become, a hired assassin. Ironically, after he was thrown out of Mossad, they would hire him back for jobs they didn't want to be associated with. He said he only took on terrorists, people who were known to have killed Jews."

"But..."

"But, sometimes I think he became... too extravagant; maybe that's not the right word...too confident in his own judgment. He warned me not to become like him. I don't believe he was bad...is bad...just angry and afraid."

"And what did you become?"

"I'm nothing more than a detective. And a not very good one."

"Oh? And I suppose you speak seven languages, have a photographic memory, and are intimate with prominent people on five continents."

Anna frowned. "Why would you think that? One travels in Europe often enough you pick up a working vocabulary in several languages, yes, enough to get a room and order a meal. But I don't know anyone famous and half the time I can't remember what phony name I'm using unless I look at the phony passport I'm carrying."

"I was sort of joking."

She was quiet for a moment, then said, "Too often something unexpected happens."

"Something like Conover?"

She nodded against my chest.

"Did you know him?"

"I thought I recognized him from a description, but I had never met him. The name doesn't sound right."

"What do you think he was after? Me, specifically?"

Again I could feel her shake her head, her hair brushing my chest. "Why ask me? I told you, I don't need to know who or what or why."

"But you are relying on people you don't even know to make judgments about people you don't know."

"That's why I don't take on assignments that require…what you said."

"Assassinations?"

"Yes. I won't do that. I didn't think this job would involve anything like what happened today."

"Does it bother you? Killing someone?"

"Yes; you must believe me, today was not normal."

"Once would be enough for me. I had a dream once, in which I and another fellow killed someone. It wasn't clear who we killed, or why, or how, but we did, and we got away with it. And in my dream the torment I felt, the guilt, was almost a physical pain. When I awoke, in a sweat, I swear it took me twenty minutes before I was convinced that it had all been a dream and nothing more."

"I know", Anna said. "Even when it's someone who was doing what he was doing to you, it feels bad."

"Is that why you couldn't sleep tonight?"

She snuggled up even closer to me, so close we could have been one body. For such a hard-nosed lady she felt as soft as a cloud

I stroked her hair and saw that she had closed her eyes and was asleep.

The next day was the nicest of the trip. I forgot about Berger, I forgot about Max, I forgot why I had come here. I simply enjoyed a day of being with Anna, touring Avignon at our own pace, until we took an afternoon tour. Trouble is, Anna is on a working trip, and so she slipped up, as we found out later, and I abetted her by dominating her time and taking her from her work. But that's for later

We toured the Papal Palace, which has walls seventeen feet thick in places and sits high atop a giant rock; it was virtually impregnable in its time. The walk up is a bit of a climb but the view and the tour of the Palace is worth the effort.

We also walked through the Les Halles covered market. Everything gastronomical is sold here—bread, wine, fruit, cheese, candy, vegetables, pastries, and seafood of all sorts (we saw fish here we'd never seen before, and they didn't look too appetizing to us!).

At a small café with red and yellow awnings, on a street so narrow two couples going opposite directions could barely pass each other without bumping shoulders, but which Anna said she knew had excellent food, we dined on a tender white fish that Anna promised wouldn't be as ugly as the ones we had just seen, perfectly sautéed vegetables, and a creamy chocolate pudding that melted in my mouth.

In the afternoon we took a tour to see the Pont du Gard (the bridge on the river Gard), a UNESCO World Heritage site. The Romans built this tri-level bridge as an aqueduct nearly 2000 years ago. It was designed to carry water over the Gardon valley to the city of Nimes. It was built without mortar—the massive stones fitting so tightly together mortar wasn't necessary—by up to 1,000 workers toiling for three years. Our guide said that technically the aqueduct could still function as designed, but the cost of maintenance on such an old structure would make it financial unfeasible.

Later we wandered the streets of the village of Uzes, a home to scads of art galleries and stores selling ceramics and painted furniture. I could not remember when I'd last had such a pleasant, carefree day. I could barely recall what it was I did for a living back in the States. Talk about the irresponsible world traveler. And we didn't see Berger or the Conover woman all day, not even in the dining room or lounge that evening. It should have been a warning.

When I awoke again it was due to voices and banging noises. Being a bit stressed lately from things like being shot at and having brute try to throw me over a cliff, my heart skipped a bit and for a moment I had this panicky feeling that Berger was breaking into the room. There was knocking on the door. I glanced at the clock and it showed 5:15. The knocking hadn't awakened Anna.

I went to the door and asked, "Who is it?"

"It is Senior Officer LeMay. I need to check that everyone is alright."

"We're fine."

"Please open the door, monsieur."

"Just a second. Let me put some clothes on."

I grabbed a robe from the bathroom and pulled the sheet up to Anna's shoulders. I opened the door as Senior Officer LeMay was knocking again.

"This is your stateroom, monsieur?"

It quickly occurred to me that lying would make no sense. "No, it belongs to the lady who is still in bed and sleeping."

"I need to verify that she is here, monsieur."

I opened the door wider and let him step in. He looked at the bed and saw Anna, still asleep, or at least acting as if she were.

"What's going on?"

"And your stateroom is…? LeMay asked.

"It's 222, why?"

"And is anybody in that stateroom now?" the officer asked.

"There better not be," I answered. "Now what the hell is this about? Is it against the rules to visit the stateroom of another passenger?" Some visit, all night.

"No, of course not, monsieur, but three passengers are missing and we are trying to account for everyone."

"Three?" I was expecting only one. "What happened?"

"We don't know. Please, I need to confirm your names."

"I'm Charles Hardin, of 222, and she's An…, Lisl Meagher, of this suite. And as you can see, I don't have an ID on me right now. Come back later if you want to see our passports."

"Thank you, that won't be necessary," he said and he left, but not before turning one more time and looking towards the bed, and smiling at me with his eyes.

Anna still slept—so much for the alert secret agent who sleeps with one eye open. I dressed quietly, scribbled a note and left it on the bed in case she awoke before I returned.

The hallway was crowded with passengers. Some were up and about and getting ready to leave the ship as the Rhone Rover was already docked at its final stop, and all passengers would be departing soon for wherever was next on their agenda. Some were going home, a few to Paris, some to Marseilles. Others who had a more leisurely transportation schedule were unhappy about being rousted and curious as to why. Some asked me what happened as I passed, as if I should know, but I shook my head and mumbled, 'dunno'. I went to a nook near the lounge where coffee was always available. Several people were already there. I poured myself a cup

"Anybody know what's going on?" I said.

"It seems they can't account for three people," said a guy I' seen around but hadn't talked to before.

"I was awake early because we have to get the first bus out here for Marseilles, so we can make our flight connections."

I nodded.

"The way I got it from one of the crew is that people who needed to leave early, as soon as we dock, like my wife and I, were supposed to have their luggage out already, to be put on the bus soon as it got here.

"So apparently there is a couple and a single guy who hadn' put their luggage out and when a crew member knocked on their door, no one answered. They pounded trying to wake them up. I heard it and thought there was something bad happening."

I sipped my coffee and nodded knowingly. I think I already knew the story. Berger and the Conover woman—who more and more I doubted was Mrs. Anybody—had not come back last night, and of course Conover himself would never be returning. I had noticed that the process for exiting and returning to the ship was a little lax as far as verifying that everyone was aboard. The ship left at a specified time, and everyone was expected to be aboard.

"I guess they were in a hurry and got off in the middle of the night."

"It's still the middle of the night," said one guy who looked like he hadn't made it to sleep at all last night. "Bunch of us stayed up late, talking and drinking; last night of the cruise and all."

"Wouldn't someone have seen them?"

"Maybe they never came back to the ship yesterday."

I shook my head. "Dunno," I said. I refilled my coffee cup, and in a second cup I filled it half and half with coffee and hot chocolate, the way Anna liked it.

Back in the suite Anna was awake. I handed her the cup of coffee and chocolate. She took a sip.

"Hmm, delicious. Thank you. I read your note, so what's happened?"

I told her what I'd heard, that it must be Berger and the Conover pair they were looking for.

"Let's just hope Conover's body isn't found before we get out of the country; they might detain everybody who was on this cruise."

"But why now, here, when we are so close to the end of the cruise?" I said.

Anna chewed on that for a moment. "For one, I doubt the Conovers were using their real names, and two, I suspect Berger wi have a forged passport for his trip to the Untied States."

"You think? Max was convinced that Berger didn't have the wherewithal to come up with a fake passport."

"I just thought of it," Anna said, "because of that man, Conover. My father mentioned a man like him. The name wasn't Conover, it was something German, but the description fits him. Ar he was said to travel with a younger woman posing as his wife. Fro what I recall, he was said to be an extremely dangerous man, and an excellent forger."

"I still don't get the why of it."

"Berger must want to get to New York before us, so we aren't there when he meets your friend."

"Maybe because he intends to kill Max after the money is transferred. Oh, I'm sorry, you said no names."

"No harm. I don't know, but that's a possibility. I think it's too late for me to change our travel plans. He will only have a few hours lead on us. I have transportation arranged for us. What time is it?"

We both looked at the clock. "Assuming they let us leave, w should get dressed and get going. I blundered yesterday, not keepin a closer eye on Berger. I hope it doesn't cause harm to anyone."

With that said, Anna got up and went to the bathroom. "I need to shower and wash my hair. It may take me a while, so if you want to go to breakfast…"

"No, I'll wait for you. Do you need…"

"No, we haven't got time, but thank you for offering."

INTERLUDE: Anna

Anna was fifteen when her mother was taken away. Her father said there was a trial, but when Anna saw her mother again she was in jail, already convicted of spying against the state of Israel.

Anna could not understand. Her mother managed a clothing store; she wasn't a spy. But even her father seemed to take the charges as a given. He didn't fight, he didn't cry, he just walked around as if he didn't know what to do with himself.

When she visited her mother, Anna was told not to worry, that everything would be alright. To do her studies and behave.

"I'm not a child anymore, mother," Anna replied. "I'm almost sixteen years old. You can tell me what happened."

Her mother merely shook her head slowly and began to sob. I made mistakes, she told Anna. I thought I was doing the right thing and later when I tried to get out of it, they wouldn't let me. Who wouldn't, Anna asked, almost screaming. It doesn't matter anymore, her mother answered as her voice broke and she began to weep uncontrollably.

Once a week Anna would visit her mother and always ask, when will you be coming home. Her father's work took him from home most of the time, so Anna lived with an aunt, an elderly aunt who didn't talk any more than absolutely necessary and treated Anna as an imposition on her hospitality. Her father said he had to change jobs because of what Anna's mother had done.

Anna was seventeen years old before her father sat her down one afternoon, shortly before her graduation from the 12th grade.

She would have her eighteenth birthday in a few weeks and then she would began her mandatory two years of service in the Israeli Defense Forces.

The father was a tall man but his daughter could already look him in the eyes, having continued to grow long after her female friends had stopped. Hence the need to sit her down so he could feel he had an iota of authority by looking down at her.

"Anna, your mother will not be home for a long time. Espionage is a serious offense. I'm sorry, I thought you understood, but you always ask when she will come home."

Anna avoided looking at her father, wanting the conversation to go away.

"Anna, do you understand me?" her father asked with a hint of firmness. "You're not a child anymore."

"I haven't been since mother went to prison. I know she won't be coming home any time soon. I always knew. I kept asking because I hoped that if I did I could make it happen, make them reduce her sentence."

"No, her crime is too serious."

She began to weep and her father reached down and put his hands on her shoulders and gently raised her up. They hugged until the weeping ceased.

"I'll be okay. I want to be like you."

"What to do you mean, Anna?"

"I want to do the kind of work you do. Secretive work. Isn't that what you do, ever since you quit the Mossad?"

"I didn't quit, Anna. They made me quit."

"Why? I thought you still worked for them, but you just had to travel more."

"No, they made me quit, as a punishment for not knowing what you mother was doing. So now I'm…sort of a free-lancer, if you will. I do much the same work, sometimes for Mossad—which you cannot tell anyone—but, yes, I have to travel, all over Europe, the Middle East, sometimes Africa."

"Can you teach me what you do?"

Her father looked at Anna as if he hadn't seen her in ages, for the first time seeing her as an adult, a woman now, no longer a child, and then began to shake his head. But he wasn't saying 'no'. He turned from her and walked around the room while Anna waited for him to say something.

He stood by a window, his back to her, his head turned slightly so she could hear him.

"I don't want you to do what I do. It involves…things I don't want you to have to be a part of."

"Why? Do you kill people?"

Now he turned and faced her, and walked back to where she still stood. He looked at her and reached a hand to cup her face. He smiled and she responded in kind.

"You are the one light left in my life, Anna. I don't want it to ever go out."

"You haven't answered me."

"Yes, I have done so. You are old enough to understand that we, as nation, as a people, have many enemies. We don't need to discuss the why or the how. Some of those enemies, there's no other way to deal with them except by…raw justice. I can't say I always like my work, but I do know I don't want you to do it. You have two years in the IDF, and then you will go to a university."

"I understand that, of course I will. Unless I want to stay in the military."

"Hmm. I wouldn't object if you chose to. Listen, I'll tell you what, in the next weeks I will give you a primer on the work I do. Not the guts of it, Anna, but in a way you may right…"

"Right, how, father?"

"Because of the work I have done, both in the Mossad and since, I have made enemies, too, personal ones. They wouldn't blink at taking out their hatred of me on you. So you need to be able to handle yourself. You'll learn some of that in the next two years in the IDF, but I can teach you more."

"I can't wait!"

Anna volunteered for an extra year in the Israeli Defense Forces and used the extra year to study especially hard in methods self-defense and counter espionage. She then went to Tel Aviv University where she studied Mathematics and Literature. But instead of taking a job after graduation she went to live with her father in Paris.

Even then her father traveled frequently but when he was home he tutored Anna in the fine points of detective work, everything except the fine art of assassination. She did learn how to handle firearms and how to protect herself, and the father and daughter arranged for numerous ways to contact each other secretly or ways to warn of potential danger.

Anna had never experienced any of the dangers her father worried about, but she knew the possibility existed. Two of her friends from the IDF had died and rumor had it they had been working for Mossad, attempting to infiltrate a terrorist group.

Anna's father would have preferred Anna get a quiet, safe job, but he was proud of his daughter and knew she had a stubborn streak she had inherited from him, along with his height. And, it was fun to have her with him when he was in Paris, or when they could return to Israel for a few weeks of home rest. He never let her go with him on missions he thought might be dangerous, so when he said no to Anna, she worried constantly until he returned, and until he did he sent her daily messages.

Finally, her persistence won out and Anna's father connected his daughter with a man who could arrange certain jobs for her. Her father had insisted that his friend only find jobs that did not involve actions that would be considered criminal, such as robberies, or worse.

Still, he also insisted that Anna arm herself and keep in contact on a regular basis. Daily, if you can, he scolded. Do this for a time, get it out of your system, then find a nice young man to marry and give me a soccer team of grandchildren.

The tall young woman smiled at her father and said, I may have to start going to basketball games to find a man tall enough to marry me.

THIRTEEN: Stepbrothers

"I didn't expect you today, Wilhelm. Your message said you'd be here tomorrow."

"When you'd have your bodyguard with you?" asked Wilhelm Berger.

"Bodyguard? Why, brother, am I in danger from you?"

Wilhelm smiled. "It should be me who is worried. I understand you hired someone to kill me."

Max shrugged his hands. "I thought of it. I have had you followed for a long time."

"You had me followed but didn't want to meet me?"

"I didn't care for the man I learned you'd become."

Maximilian von der Dusenberger and Wilhelm Berger were sitting comfortably in Maximilian's grand office on the 78th floor, high above the busy streets of New York City. The cacophony of the streets was as far away as the moon. Berlin of the 1940s was as far away as another universe.

Maximilian spent about a quarter of his working days here, the rest of his time on the West Coast. It was early afternoon, and most of the people who worked on the floor were at lunch, at one of the restaurants or cafeterias either in the massive building or out enjoying the pleasant, late summer weather.

"Maximilian, you could put a nice size swimming pool in this office," Wilhelm had said, thinking he was being clever.

"You're not the first person to suggest that," Maximilian had replied.

Maximilian sat behind his desk with his elbows on the desktop and the fingers of one hand intertwined with those of the other hand. An untouched cup of coffee set next to his left elbow. He'd had his two cups of morning coffee long ago, and usually enjoyed a cup after lunch. But the desire for the coffee evaporated when Wilhelm walked in. In the top draw on the right side of his oak desk was a loaded pistol, the safety off. Maximilian knew that was dangerous, and he hadn't meant to take the safety off until tomorrow, Tuesday, the day Wilhelm's message said he would arrive. But when Maximilian got to his office early this morning, on a hunch he'd checked to see that the gun was loaded and ready to use, in case Wilhelm showed up a day early and Maximilian needed it. There was no telling what crazy stunt Wilhelm might pull. So Maximilian wasn't really surprised when the stepbrother he'd never met before was announced by security. At first he considered telling the security officer to accompany Wilhelm, but then decided to allow his visitor the benefit of the doubt.

"You, of course, the great Maximilian von der Dusenberger, the great philanthropist, have been an angel all your life."

Maximilian looked at Wilhelm, who sat on the other side of the desk in a beautiful maroon leather chair. The chair cracked pleasantly as he adjusted his body to a cozy fit.

"Wonderful furniture, Max. Must have cost a fortune."

"I don't want to banter with you, Wilhelm. Let's take care of our business."

"Is that all this is to you? Business? No handshake or hug for your long-lost brother?"

Maximilian said nothing, just glared at Wilhelm.

"Yes, with all your millions I suppose spending five of those millions isn't a big deal, is it?"

"You know, Wilhelm, I don't mind giving you enough money to take care of yourself for the rest of your life. I just wish you had come to me peaceably. Not threaten me, not threaten my wife. You put my wife in danger and it's difficult for me to forgive and forget."

"Ho! Forgive and forget? You are the one who ran out on our mother. Who ran out on me. Who then took all of the money from the father who had also run away. You all left me behind, and you talk about forgiving and forgetting? You have nerve, Maximilian. Anyway, the... threats were to get your attention, Max. They weren't as serious as they sounded."

Max sighed, leaned back in his chair. He reached for the coffee and took a sip, an action to stall, to give him time to ease his temper. It was cold.

"Wilhelm, I was twelve years old. I didn't even know you'd been born. At the hospital they told me my mother had died, and asked where my father was. Well, he'd long since been assumed to have died, and I was scared. I thought they...someone would come for me and take me away from my home...and I didn't know what to do. Yes, I panicked, an orphaned twelve year old. For that you hold grudge all these years?"

"I became an orphan, too, Max. But I didn't have a wealthy benefactor to take care of me."

"I believe you inherited the house and there was some money, too."

"A pittance."

"If you hadn't engaged in certain activities maybe things would have gone better for you. As it is, you still seem to have done well enough. You never married, did you?"

"It's funny, but I was thinking that now that I'll be financially secure, it might be time to marry. I have a lady friend, she's with me here, in New York, who is amiable to the idea."

"Good for you, Wilhelm."

"I need to be sure I'll be safe from you, Maximilian, after we complete our arrangements."

"You give me or destroy all the material you have about my father, original and all copies, and promise not to say anything about it to anyone, ever, and you have my word I won't take any action against you."

"What about this Hardin fellow you sent looking for me?"

"Charles? He means you no harm. Didn't he tell you what he's trying to learn?"

"Yes, some nonsense about me being his father."

"Are you?"

Wilhelm opened his mouth to speak, then stopped, and looked off to the side, for a moment taking in the pictures on the walls but not really seeing them.

"We are getting off track here, but…I told him, no, that I wasn't, and that I didn't care anyway if I was or not. Which is not totally true. I was surprised by his question and did not know what he was talking about.

"But, Maximilian, I'm not as horrible a person as you might think. I do have feelings. If I have a son, I would like to know him, even if we couldn't be friends, just like I wanted to know you. He started me thinking and I do recall a trip I made to Austria, when I was working construction. I did meet a girl there, a very nice American girl.

"We had fun, a fling, an affair that obviously meant more to her than to me. I may have said things I didn't mean, things that at the time sounded right. If I said I'd meet her again I either forgot, or lied, who knows after all these years. So the truth is, I simply don't know. He's taller than me, but that's not unusual, and there does seem to be a slight resemblance around the eyes..." he tailed off.

" I really don't remember what his mother looked like."

"It's an important issue for him."

"Yes, and as I said, I would welcome the idea of a son, but I can't help him. He needs to work this out with his mother."

"And the woman he's engaged to."

"Engaged? Really? From what I noticed on the river cruise the engagement is as one-sided as was the affair I had with his mother in Austria."

"What do you mean?"

Wilhelm shook his head. He stood up and moved about the office, to the window on the west side which provided, on clear day as this one, with a view that tourists paid to see from the Empire State Building and other skyscrapers in the city.

"I thought you sent him...to rough me up, is that the slang? Convince me to leave you alone, and maybe kill me?"

"I didn't send anyone to harm you, Wilhelm, at least, not *yet*. I hired someone to follow you, yes, and to watch over Hardin. I don't even know who he is."

"You don't?" A thin leer developed on Wilhelm's face as he remembered the sight of Hardin and the tall blonde lady when they came into dinner, the evening Conover had disappeared.

"What, Wilhelm?"

Wilhelm turned to face Maximilian. "This man, Hardin, he also accused me of killing two Americans, including my own father."

"There appears to be some evidence of that."

"What evidence? You have something?"

Maximilian shook his head. "No, certainly nothing substantial. I had an investigator look into the accident these men died in. He found that you... correction, he found that a man named William Berger had rented a car a few days before the accident, in a town nearby."

"I see. I have a friend...correction, I had a friend, who worked for me. It was years ago, this accident. I sent him to find the American soldiers. I wanted to know which one was my father."

"To blackmail him?" said Maximilian.

Wilhelm paused, but ignored the jibe because it cut close to the bone.

"He swore to me there was an accident before he had an opportunity to talk to the men. I believed him."

Maximilian grunted.

"I think we've all made mistakes. The friend I mentioned; he disappeared while on the river cruise. I think he took his job of protecting me too seriously and I, ah, didn't communicate my wishes to him as clearly as I should have."

"You seem to have excuses for everything, Wilhelm."

A shrug of his shoulders was all the response from Wilhelm.

"Yes, Wilhelm, we've all made mistakes...many mistakes for many years."

"Enough, Maximilian, I didn't come here to engage in gossip."

"Alright then, what do we do?"

Wilhelm pulled a notebook out of his pocket. "Here's the phone number, the account code and the password. You call, make the transfer. Then I will call, and change my password. And in case you have any tricks planned, I will immediately transfer the funds to several other banks other than this one."

"What about the materials you have; the papers?"

"I have everything here." Wilhelm pointed to a brief case he'd brought with him and which set on the floor next to the maroon chair.

"I'd like to see them."

"So suspicious, dear brother. I suppose caution pays in your line of work, doesn't it?"

"And yours?"

"Actually, I don't have a line of work anymore, Maximilian, and I don't intend to."

Wilhelm opened the brief case and handed Maximilian an accordion folder. Maximilian opened it and began to browse through the papers. There were reports going back decades tracing the history of former Nazis who had escaped to South America, reports on those who'd been found and jailed or executed, on those who'd never been found, including Colonel von der Dusenberger, pictures, newspaper articles, and finally, fingerprints and DNA analysis. The latter, while not yet fully accepted as proof positive of a person's identity, was becoming more accurate and accepted as such. There was also a computer disc.

"The disc?" Maximilian said, holding up.

"Nothing more than a summary of the hard copies," Wilhelm said.

"You're sure this is all? What about copies?"

"I swear, Maximilian, I will destroy the copies once I return to Europe and the money is safely transferred to new accounts."

Maximilian sighed deeply and leaned back in his chair. "You drive a hard bargain, Wilhelm. I suppose I have to trust you, don't I?"

"What would I have to gain by releasing the material?"

"You might come back in a two or three years and ask me for more money."

"Would you like me to put in writing that I'll never ask for another cent?" Wilhelm said, almost laughing as he said it.

Maximilian grunted. "That would be a real lock-tight legal agreement, wouldn't it?

Wilhelm walked up to Maximilian's desk, put both hands flat down on the edge and leaned forward towards Maximilian.

"Maximilian, I realize this might not mean much, but I swear I'll do as I said. I know we can never be friends, and we aren't going to walk out of here chuckling and talking about the weather on our way to lunch at Delmonico's; the chances for that have long passed.

I simply want a share of what I think belongs to me, and I'll go away forever and leave you alone. You can disagree whether I should get any of the money, you can think what you want of me, but I'll uphold my part of the bargain."

As sincere as Wilhelm sounded, for a few seconds as Maximilian stared at his stepbrother he considered reneging on the deal. He'd let Wilhelm release the information that disclosed that Maximilian's father had been a Nazi, had escaped with stolen gold and gems, had become an ambassador in Argentina, and had funded Maximilian's education and seeded his business ventures. At my age, Maximilian said in his mind, why do I care? Isn't it better that the truth comes out?

If I hadn't married Mary Jo, if she wasn't a part of my life now, and the one who will carry on the work of the Foundation when I'm gone, I'd tell Wilhelm to go to hell.

Maximilian picked up the notebook Wilhelm had given him, looked at the numbers, and picked up the phone.

While Maximilian was on the phone Wilhelm paced around the room inspecting the pictures on the walls and the various decorative items and books on the shelves that filled one wall. He wasn't particularly interested in their beauty or value, but it gave him a temporary feeling of superiority, to pose as nonchalant while Maximilian divested himself of a portion of his fortune. An amount significant to Wilhelm but in the big picture not so to Maximilian, other than as a thorn in his finger, an irritant to be blackmailed.

"It's done," Maximilian said.

"Wonderful!" said Wilhelm as he clapped his hands together. "May I now use your phone?"

Maximilian rose from his desk. "I'll leave you alone," he said. He walked out of his office to the reception area where he found that his secretary had returned from lunch.

"Good afternoon, sir. I saw you had someone in there so I didn't bother you."

"That's fine. He needs to make a private call. Do I have much on the schedule today?"

"You said you wanted to personally pick up someone at the airport this afternoon, otherwise, it's clear the rest of the day."

"And tomorrow?"

"At ten in the morning you have a meeting with the Realty Board President, and lunch at twelve-thirty with the mayor."

Maximilian nodded. He was feeling a bit like a whipped puppy. As he had told Wilhelm, he wouldn't have minded giving him money if he'd just asked for it. Maybe I did abandon his baby brother. Not when he fled the hospital; he was a boy, in panic. But later, years later, maybe I should have searched him out, gone to him and brought him to the United States, and given him a job. It's possible I did fail in my duty.

Maximilian knew he would go to his death wondering if he was doing the right thing. He'd wrestle with the issues of his pride and the truth, with family ties and practicality, and probably never come to a soothing answer.

Tired of waiting Maximilian returned to his office to see Wilhelm sitting quietly with a thin grin on his face. He nodded towards the materials Maximilian had taken out of the briefcase.

"All yours."

Maximilian pressed a button on the phone console on his desk. "Yes, sir?"

"Mrs. Zarlington, please bring in the portable shredder."

"Oh, sir, I can shred something, if you'd like."

"No, I want to do this myself."

"Right away, sir."

Maximilian sat down, glanced at Wilhelm, and then looked away, fighting the aura of depression that was overcoming him like the first hint of a headache that you know won't go away no matter how hard you try to ignore it.

"You know, Wilhelm, had my father not escaped, or fled, he would have been either killed or captured. No Military Police would have come to the house looking for him, and you would never have been born."

Wilhelm motioned with his hands to say, 'so what?'

"Ifs, ands, buts, Maximilian. I *was* born, to the same mother as you, but only you benefited from your father's money. Who knows, maybe he would have been imprisoned for awhile and then released, and I would have been born later."

"Had he not fled, or been captured, then there wouldn't have been much money."

"A point for you, Maximilian but still it's an 'if' or a 'but'."

"Had father and mother had another child, it could never have been exactly you, you fool."

"Let's not end our meeting being angry, Maximilian."

Mrs. Zarlington entered carrying the portable shredder.

"Set it over the basket, and thank you."

The secretary did so and looked first from her boss and then to the other man. She instantly knew this was a meeting the better she knew nothing about, now or ever. She walked softly out of the room and closed the door.

Maximilian proceeded to shred all the papers and the computer disc. He even checked all the side pockets of Wilhelm's briefcase but found nothing more.

When Maximilian looked up he saw Wilhelm writing in a notebook. The pen he was using looked oddly familiar.

"What is that?" Maximilian said in an irritated tone.

"What is what?" said Wilhelm, not looking up.

"That pen, where did you get it?" Maximilian walked around the desk to where Wilhelm was standing. He reached for the pen.

Wilhelm pulled back. "What are doing?"

"Let me see that pen," Maximilian said, his voice developing a menacing tone that startled Wilhelm. Wilhelm held up the pen for Maximilian to see.

Maximilian looked at but did not touch it at first. The pen was an old-fashioned fountain pen, solid black with thin gold trim. There was writing on one side, a few words in German. Maximilian's German was rusty but he knew the words referred to the *Third Reich.* He'd seen the pen many years ago.

"Where did you get this?" he asked.

"It was in a desk in the house. It must have set in there for years. Even then I don't think I came across it until I'd been in the house for several months. What of it?"

Maximilian grabbed the pen from Wilhelm, although he had to tug as Wilhelm resisted, not giving up the pen willingly.

"This was a gift to my father. *My* father, not yours! It was given to him after the fall of France, for his leadership in combat. I was given to him personally by General Heinz Guderian. Even I, a lad at the time, knew this was special. It is not yours to keep."

Wilhelm reached for the pen and Maximilian gripped it tighter in one hand and pulled it to his chest and raised his other hand to ward off Wilhelm.

"It became mine with the house, Maximilian! The house, the furniture, it became mine. What of it, it's just a pen!"

"No! It's something of my father's! I have nothing else of his!"

"No? Only how many millions of dollars?"

Wilhelm again stretched out for the hand that held the pen and Maximilian struck Wilhelm, knocking the younger man off balance causing him to go to the floor on his knees. Wilhelm grunted more in surprise than in pain. He rose on one knee and stared at Maximilian, who stood above him, still clutching the pen to his chest.

Wilhelm appraised the situation, not wanting to get into a fight; he was too old for that. But Maximilian was older. Wilhelm slowly rose to his feet. He straightened his jacket and brushed a hair in his hair. Then he lunged.

Maximilian was caught off guard and took Wilhelm's charge hard on his chest. Wilhelm pushed forward like a football guard leading the blocking for the running back. His charge ended only when he'd pushed Maximilian against the wall.

"Oof!" exclaimed the older man. Wilhelm grasped at the hand that held the pen but Maximilian had a death's grip on it. He pushed Wilhelm in the face with his free hand.

The two men grappled, neither giving way, both beginning o breathe hard. Finally Wilhelm stepped back, stumbling, almost falling over again before he caught his balance.

"This...is foolish... keep the goddamn pen!"

Maximilian stayed close against the wall, the pen still held close to his chest as if it was more valuable than all his millions, all his buildings, his homes, his cars. Maximilian was reluctant to ease his guard lest Wilhelm was feigning resignation.

The two men stood there facing each other like gunmen of the Old West waiting for the other to draw his gun first. Then he remembered. Maximilian took a small, easy step toward his side of the desk, eyeing Wilhelm carefully. He took three quick steps and opened the drawer that contained the gun. He reached into the drawer and pulled out the weapon and pointed it at Wilhelm.

Just then Mrs. Zarlington rushed in. "I thought I heard noises...is everything alright? Oh my God!" She stared wide-eyed at the gun.

"Mr. von der Dusenberger? Are you alright? Should I get someone?" She stared from one man to the other, but gave her most vicious glare to Wilhelm, sure that he was the aggressor despite the fact that it was her employer who held the gun.

"No, no, everything's fine here...isn't it, Wilhelm?"

Wilhelm nodded and said "Yes, yes, it is fine."

Maximilian set the gun back in the drawer and closed it. "We're fine, Mrs. Zarlington, thank you."

"Call me, sir, if you need anything," the secretary said as she departed, closing the door only after she gave Wilhelm one more knife-cold stare.

"I think our business is over, Wilhelm," Maximilian said, his voice panting slightly. "I remind you about the copies."

Wilhelm took a moment to reply, stepping slowly back to the leather chair he had been sitting in earlier,

"I can either destroy them myself or send them to you to do the deed, whatever you prefer."

"How about I send someone to verify?"

"As you wish. I am returning tonight. You have my Berlin address, so send your man, or woman, as it were, there anytime within the next two weeks. After that, I expect to be gone."

"Where will you go?"

Wilhelm's sly smile said it better than words: you can't possibly expect me to tell you. "Au revoir, Maximilian."

"Forgive me if I don't shake your hand," Maximilian said.

Wilhelm stood, the two men glared at each other for a second, and then Wilhelm spun sharply and walked out of the office. Alone again, Maximilian examined the pen and his eyes blurred from an old memory that was stuck deep in a place he hadn't accessed his entire adult life. He stuck the pen into his pocket and slammed a fist into the palm of the other hand.

***

The first thing I said to Max when we spotted him waiting by the luggage carrier, his mouth agape, was: "If you were a younger man, I'd punch you in the nose. But then you'd probably fire me."

Max shrugged and permitted a smirk to etch his face.

The next thing I said was, "Has Berger arrived yet?"

Max looked at me and then at the tall woman standing next to me. He had obviously seen her walking with me and knew we were together. His mouth remained half-opened. It wasn't often one saw Maximilian von der Dusenberger at a loss for words.

"Maximilian, this is Anna. This is your man in Europe."

"My word," Max said, almost too low to hear.

"I'm sorry, sir, for fouling up. I let Berger get away from me. I shouldn't have let that happen."

"It was my fault," I offered.

"No, I shouldn't have been distracted from my work."

Max found his voice. He waved a hand at both of us to be quiet. "No, no, it's fine. Things went well."

"He didn't threaten you?" I asked.

"Not really, no. We had a little…discussion. Anna, you are the person I've been sending coded messages to, you, not a man?"

"Yes, sir. Normally I do a better job, but…"

"You did fine, really. I gave you extra orders, to look after Charles, so I understand if it became difficult to keep track of everything."

Anna and I glanced at each other, hoping the guilt on our faces wasn't evident to Max.

"I need to use the restroom." It gave me a chance to step away before Max caught me blushing, and allow time for he and Anna to discuss details of her assignment. When I returned they were laughing, so I guess employer and employee were okay with each other. I hoped she hadn't told him how precisely she had guarded me.

"Anna told me about your close calls. Knowing that, I said she will get a bonus. Had I known earlier, in fact, I might have been harsher with Wilhelm, though I'm not sure how, exactly."

We were driving from the airport, Max doing the honors. It occurred to me that I doubt if Max often drove himself.

"Do you even have a driver's license, Max?"

He looked at me askance. "Of course. I'm just not sure if it's up to date."

"Wonderful. Be careful. Don't you usually have a driver?"

"Yes, but I didn't want anyone to see who I was meeting."

"So what now?" I asked. "Is Berger still here? Did he say anything about the conversation he and I had?"

"He said he was leaving later today. I don't know where he right now. Yes, we did converse a bit about the business you had with him. He basically said he'd told you all he knew, and he couldn't help you anymore. I think he's a pathological liar, so I can be sure of anything he told me."

"That was my impression, too," I added.

"He said you needed to talk to your mother."

I nodded, agreeing with something I'd known since forever

"Does she know?" Max asked, his head turning a fraction to indicate Anna, in the back seat.

"No, sir," Anna chimed in. "I'm not aware of what business Charles had with Berger. I told him I didn't want to know."

"Hmm. Better."

She wasn't dumb. Anna knew I didn't come to Europe to kill Berger, and I wasn't involved in the money issue, so what else was there, except, a woman?

"Max, you didn't really intend to have Berger killed, did you?"

Again Max's eyes shifted, pointing to Anna.

"Sir, I never received such orders. I don't do that kind of work and wouldn't have taken the assignment."

"Sorry, Charles," Max said. "No, I'm not sorry. I told you that because I felt it was vital for you to talk to Berger as soon as possible, not even to wait for him to come to see me because I couldn't be sure what tack he would take. After I got his letter I figured he would either make good on his threat if I didn't comply, or, if I did pay him off, he would quickly disappear, and you wouldn't get a chance to meet him and talk to him. I wanted you to feel it was urgent."

I looked back at Anna. "It's what you said."

"Anna, this much I can say; there was, is, a possibility that Wilhelm Berger is my father. He isn't sure, and doesn't seem to care. I was trying to find out."

"I reasoned it was something like that," she said.

"So what do you think? Do he and I look anything alike? Do you think we could be related?"

She stalled, either not having a gut feeling, or trying to decide which was the most diplomatic answer to give me.

"Your eyes, Charles. Your eyes look the same. I noticed that immediately."

"Oh," was all the response I could give. "I guess it's difficult to see your own eyes in someone else. I looked at his face, and his build, and I didn't see much similarity."

"Does it matter anymore?" Anna asked.

I nodded. "Yes, I think so."

Max looked at me sharply, as if surprised that my answer wasn't more definitive. At that instant I think he realized Anna and I had become more involved than we were letting on.

Was I involved with Anna? Or was I like Wilhelm, enjoying a brief fling with a beautiful woman just because the opportunity had arisen? Did I use the excuse that Mary Grace and I may be finished to ease into a temporary but fun relationship that would end as Anna had said, '…a few days from now we'll never see each other again, so what difference will it make?' Did a brush or two with death make me want to grasp at life in the unique way a man and a woman can to prove to themselves that they are still alive?

"I've reserved two rooms for you," Max said. It must have been a minute since anyone had said anything. The way he said it seemed to imply, why did I get two rooms if the two of you only need one? I felt I'd disappointed him.

Then he added something he could have kept for later, when Anna wasn't in hearing distance, "I didn't come alone."

I didn't say anything. Thanks, Max.

"I…wasn't given much of a choice, and anyway, I thought it might be a good idea."

"At the time, I'm sure it seemed like a good idea, Max."

No sense hiding it anymore. "Where is she staying?"

"Same hotel, her own room."

At least Max choose to let Mary Grace and I arrange the sleeping situation on our own.

I heard Anna clear her throat. She hadn't said anything in several minutes and I knew she was only letting me know she understood.

"Do you know who I am, Anna?" Max asked, thoroughly changing the subject.

"No, sir, other than 'Max'."

"I'm of some minor fame, at least in this country."

"Sir, I'm just a small town girl from Israel. I've never even been to Disneyland."

We all laughed. "Anna, you come to southern California, any time, and Mary Jo and I—that's my wife, Mary Jo—will take you. Any time at all."

"Thank you, sir. I appreciate the offer. By the way, is there anything else you want me to do?"

"Yes, one thing has come up. I'd like you to try to find out where Berger goes, where he is setting up his new home. He said he'd be in Berlin for two more weeks, but I don't believe him. I don't know if it's possible for you to do, but if you could spend a little time on it, just so I can keep tabs on him, I'll pay you well."

"You've been very generous already, sir. I'll see what I can do."

"I'd as soon never have contact with him again, but I'd like to know where he is. Also, someone else is taking care to assure he has no more copies of certain documents that he and I have agreed should be destroyed. However, if you have any inkling that he has other copies, maybe with a lawyer or in a bank vault, do what you can to see that they are destroyed also."

"That might be difficult."

Max nodded. "Yes, it's just a precaution. Don't specifically go to any trouble, it's just something to be aware of."

"Yes, I understand."

I understood, too. That means Anna is going to be sneaking around trying to find Berger and, if she finds his new residence, verify that he has no more incriminating papers or files.

"I'll explain tomorrow exactly what you to look for. I hope I'm not rushing you, Anna, but I need you to do this quickly, before Berger clears out for parts unknown and his trail is lost."

"I'll do my best, sir."

"Good. Let's forget about work for awhile. I've made dinner reservations at the hotel for all of us."

Great, we'll all have dinner. I can hardly wait.

FOURTEEN: In New York

As we entered the hotel Max whispered to me, "She's in 1410."

The rooms were reserved in Max's name, but Anna and I had to sign in for ourselves. Anna signed in as Lisl Meagher. She was in 711 and I in 715.

"Make sure the rooms and any extras stay charged to my account," Max said to the clerk.

"Very good, sir."

"Let's all meet in the Skylounge, say, in forty-five minutes? We'll have a drink and then go to dinner. I think we all need to relax."

It wasn't a question so neither Anna nor I responded. We took the elevator to the seventh floor.

"So what will you do, Charles?"

"About what, Mary Grace, Berger, you? "I don't know. I probably can't make a decision until I get back to California and talk to my mother."

"I wish I could talk to my mother."

"Can't you visit?"

"Yes, but it makes us both sad, and there isn't much to say anymore."

"I'm sorry. Anna."

We rode up the rest of the way without speaking. Outside my room we stopped. Anna offered me one of the two keys cards to her room. "In case you want to talk later."

I looked at her, not sure what she was offering, but took the card.

"I know you can't offer me one of yours; I understand."

She didn't, really. Mary Grace was not going to share my room tonight, but it wasn't a subject for us to talk about standing in the hallway.

"Do you read the New York Times everyday, Charles?" Anna asked.

I nodded. "Almost everyday. Do you read the International Herald Tribune everyday?"

"Whenever I can get a copy. It's how my father and I communicate. With our coded messages. He and I both travel so much it's seldom we see each other anymore. I could teach you my code. It's not too hard to learn."

"Yes, I'd like that. Will we have time?"

"You'll have to make the time."

"Should I call for you in a half-hour?"

"No, I'll meet you there. I'm sure someone else will need to be escorted."

She turned away and walked to her room and I entered mine. The phone was ringing.

"Hello."

"Charles! It's me, how good to hear you voice."

"Yours too, MG. How've you been?"

"I've been fine. Maximilian explained how busy you've been and that you couldn't contact me for over a week. I don't believe him but at least he's loyal in covering for you. I hope the work went well. I've missed you so much. Shall I come to your room now?"

"Max wants us to meet in the Skylounge soon."

"Yes, he told me. I'll come to your room and we'll go from there. What's your room? Oh, I do have some bad news."

"What's that?"

"I'll tell when I see you; be there in a few minutes."

"I'm in 715."

She sounded cheery, but what was with the bad news? Did she find out we may be cousins and was calling off our pseudo-engagement?

"I guess it's just as well that Maximilian got us rooms so far apart."

I waited for the rest of it.

"Dear, I'm sorry, I'm sure you're as eager as I am, but it's, you know, the bad time of the month for me…think you can wait a couple of days?"

"Oh, I see, well, that is bad news," I said with a grin that I hoped didn't express my relief. "Well…I mean, I understand."

"I could stay with you anyway, but it might be too great a temptation."

"Yeah, and to tell the truth…jet lag and all, I'll probably hit the sack real early." Clearly she and I have to talk soon, like yesterday.

When we arrived at the lounge Max and Anna were already there. Max stood up and made introductions.

"Anna, this is Mary Grace, my sister-in-law and employee."

I was glad he didn't add, and Charles' fiancé.

"And Mary Grace, this is Anna, my, ah, European consultant."

"Oh, I see. Nice to meet you," Mary Grace said as the women shook hands.

The 'oh' from Mary Grace could have meant a number of things. Like, 'oh', as in, 'I didn't realize you had a European consultant, Max'; or, as in, 'Is she why you didn't bring Mary Jo with you on this trip, Max?'; or as in, 'Why didn't I know we were meeting with a European consultant?'; or, 'Was she by chance working with Charles in Europe this past week?', or, 'She's far too young and too good-looking to be your consultant, Max, and Charles!'

"So…" started Mary Grace after she'd sat down. "I trust the work in Europe went okay," she added, looking from Anna, to me, and to Max.

"Yes, yes, the preliminary report is that things went quite well, right Charles?"

"Yes, they did. There were a minor hiccup or two and unexpected occurrences, but otherwise, fine."

"We'll go over everything tomorrow morning, is that okay, Charles?"

"Sure, Maximilian." Max usually doesn't ask.

It was already obvious from Mary Grace's lack of comment when she came to my room that Max hadn't said anything to her about Berger or about my real reason for going to Europe, but I had thought by now he'd want to clue her in. I suppose with Anna here now wasn't the time. So we ordered drinks, made small talk, went to dinner, by which time it was difficult to keep my mind on conversation because I felt that Mary Grace was getting suspicious. Either that or it was my guilt flashing on my face like red lights at a railroad crossing.

I did hear: "Anna has to fly back tomorrow, Charles. She has one more task to finish up for me."

"Oh, yes, that's right." I said. I knew immediately my 'oh' spelled disappointment as clearly as if I'd been holding a big sign like a limo driver trying to catch the eye of someone coming out of the terminal. I didn't mean it to sound as if her leaving mattered to me; actually, it's better Anna had to leave soon. What would I do with both she and Mary Grace around at the same time?

If I hadn't then glanced at Mary Grace as if I was checking to see if she'd heard me, I might have gotten away with it. The look in her eyes was a much bigger 'OH' than what had slipped out of my mouth.

Instantly I figured things couldn't get worse so I said, "I'll drive you to the airport, Anna."

"Thank you, Charles, that would be convenient."

"I'm sure the airport has a shuttle," offered Mary Grace.

"It's the least I can do for Anna, after the help she was to me."

Mary Grace didn't say anything, which was worse than another 'oh.'

For the next several minutes Max and Anna talked but I wasn't paying attention and I tried to feign interest in scanning the restaurant patrons while Mary Grace turned into an icicle. Shortly thereafter Anna rose to leave.

"Excuse me, everyone, but I am tired and am going to sleep early. I hope I see everyone tomorrow before I go. Max, you and I need a to go over what you need me to do yet, right?"

"Yes, how about breakfast at eight? We can go over everything then."

"That's fine. Mary Grace, it was lovely meeting you. I hope to see you again."

"Yes. Have a good flight home."

She left and after another minute or two of silence Max also announced his departure. "I'll leave you two alone," he said.

Chicken, I mouthed to him.

"Tell me Maximilian is not having an affair with her," said Mary Grace, as soon as Max was out of hearing distance.

"Of course not." Maybe I'd lucked out, her thinking that about Max, and not about me.

"Is she really his European consultant, Charles? What kind of consultant?"

"It's a real long story, something that might be better told when we have more time and I'm not tired, but briefly, Anna was hired to follow someone in Europe, someone Maximilian thinks is his stepbrother."

"What? I didn't know he had a brother of any sort."

"I don't think anyone did. He's known for a number of years but something came up and he needed someone to talk to this fellow. Max didn't even know Anna was the person he hired. He went through a middleman, I guess you'd call it, and assumed it was a man."

"Sounds more like hiring a detective who snoops on wayward husbands."

Saying anything to clarify Anna's line of work would have done no good, and I wasn't sure how to explain her line of work anyway.

"So what was your part in this?"

"Well, Anna's job was more of keeping tabs on this guy, but she had no knowledge of the, ah, business that Max needed to conduct with him. Money's involved, of course. So I had to meet him, but that's the long story. Let's plan on lunch tomorrow and I'll tell you everything, promise."

Hopefully my nose wasn't growing.

I started to rise, but Mary Grace stopped me.

"So tell me one other thing first so we can get it out of the way.

"What?"

"Did you know it was Anna you were meeting in Europe?"

"Not her, no. I was supposed to meet Max's consultant, as he calls her, yes, but I, and Max, assumed it was going to be a man."

"Did she stay at the same hotel as you?"

"Ah, yeah."

"Why did you offer to take her to the airport tomorrow? And can I come with you?"

"She literally saved my life, MG," I said, trying to steer the conversation in another direction.

"Really?" she said with derision.

"It's part of the long story."

"You're changing the subject."

"When we have time tomorrow I'll tell you the whole story. But I owe her and want to be able to thank her. Plus, we have a bit of unfinished business to go over tomorrow."

"I see."

"Meaning?"

"Meaning, I don't see."

"Mary Grace, just because she's…"

"A knock out?" Mary Grace finished for me.

"Okay, she's hard not to notice. Look, let's stop this now." I didn't want this conversation to drag on anymore, before I said something I'd regret.

We rose at the same time and walked to the elevator, neither speaking. This wasn't how I wanted it to go. I rode up with her to the fourteenth floor and walked her to her room. We stopped at the door and Mary Grace hesitated before she scanned the keycard.

"MG, Anna is a detective, and like I said, even Max didn't realize the person he hired was going to be a woman. She was also there to guard me because Max thought I might be in danger. And she did save my life. I'll see you in the morning."

She didn't say anything. She opened the door, and then she turned and gave me a sisterly kiss on the lips. She went into her room and the door closed. Maybe I should say, a kissin' cousin kiss. I stood there for a few seconds, thinking she might open the door and ask me to come in. She didn't, I left, and rode the elevator down to the seventh floor. In my room I took off my shoes and lay down on the bed.

Next thing I knew I was waking up, the light by the bed still on. The clock showed 11:30 so I'd only slept an hour. I went to the bathroom and splashed cold water in my face. Then I checked that I had the keycards to both my room and Anna's with me and went out to learn about secret codes.

I borrowed Max's rental car to take Anna to the airport, knowing it would earn the wrath of Mary Grace. I reasoned that it was quite possible I would never see Anna again, and even if my mini-affair with her was a blip in the seasons of my life, the memory was one that would stay forever. It's like the blizzard you experienced forty years ago; you may never again get caught up in such a magnificent storm, and the adventure may have lasted for a time that is equal to one one-hundredth of your life span, but you never forget it.

Between the time we spent talking during the night, when she taught me her communication code, and the ride this morning, I had explained to Anna that my sole purpose in going on the river cruise was to find Berger and determine if he was my father. I told her about Max's investigations. I wanted to tell her everything, I thought I did, but something held me back, so I didn't go into the significance of the possible blood relationship between Mary Grace and myself.

We also exchanged e-mail addresses but Anna said when she is traveling, especially in small towns, she doesn't always have access, hence the difficulty in connecting with Max.

"Is this really important to you now, after so many years of thinking your father was dead even before you were born?"

I nodded my head like one of those baseball bobble head dolls before I answered. Still, I was lying because the truth is that the most important reason was to determine whether there was a blood relationship between Mary Grace and I, and for a reason that I couldn't quite wrest out of my conscious, I wasn't ready to tell Ann about that.

"Isn't it important to you that you are cut off from your mother?" I said.

"That's not fair."

"Maybe not, but it must hurt. Yet, you at least knew your mother while you were growing up. I never knew a father. I have no idea what a father is."

"Is that why you've never married?"

She had me there.

She persisted. "Is that why your haven't married her? Because you are afraid of being a father? Or because eventually you will leave her?"

Goddamn but it's irritating when someone can read you so well, especially deep into your psyche.

"You can be damn nosey, Anna."

"You don't know me well enough to say that."

Normally, the pattern in my life has been that if a conversation gets to this point I'd say something to the effect of, 'buzz off.' Instead, I said, "I'd like to know you better, Anna."

"What I don't understand is how will you find out for sure. Do you want me to ask him?"

I looked at her strangely as I maneuvered the car through the hundreds of taxis clogging the roads. Driving in New York is not sane, but I was doing it only to have time with Anna, without havin to whisper in the back seat of a cab. I'd forgotten that she was still working for Max.

"You mean Berger? Why would he tell you?"

"Maybe I could scare him. He must have determined that his friend didn't abandon him. He might assume I actually am a trained assassin."

"Speaking of which, Anna, one more time; tell me straight…"

"I never killed anyone before last week, in Viviers. I swear."

"I believe you, and I'm glad."

"In fact, after I verify that Berger hasn't any more copies of the papers I am going to quit this work and find something …more legitimate."

"Like?"

"I have a degree in Mathematics. I could teach in an Israeli school."

"A teacher, eh?"

"I could, but teaching sounds boring, and it doesn't pay well in Israel."

"There's nothing wrong with being a legitimate detective, is there?"

"Maybe not, but I didn't do such a good job. I lost track of Berger, his man tried to kill you twice, and he reached Maximilian before I was there to provide protection."

"Fortunately, he didn't need it."

"That's not the point."

I could get you a job with Max's Foundation, I didn't say. I could, but why set temptation in front of me?

"I understand," I said. "Will you write to me? You wrote down my e-mail address, didn't you? And my home address?"

"Yes, yes, I have it. But I won't contact you if you are going to marry your girlfriend. Why bother?"

A deep breath. I turned in obedience to the sign noting the direction to the airport parking lot. "Why bother, indeed," I said, softly.

We parked and I got her luggage out off the backseat and carried it for her. We hadn't spoken the last five minutes.

"You never answered my question?"

"Which one?"

"How will you find out about Berger, and do you want me to ask him?"

We walked several paces, crossed at a pedestrian crosswalk, and into the terminal before I answered with a question.

"When will you be in Lyon?"

"I'm going to Berlin first, but probably before you are back home in California."

"Why would you do that, talk to Berger?"

"Because there's something you're not telling me."

"That's not a very good reason."

"No, but your eyes tell me I'm right."

"Okay, but don't do anything…dangerous, or that could cause trouble. And the same with what ever you have to do to verify that Berger hasn't retained any of the information he's suppose to destroy."

"I will be careful, Charles, you can be sure."

She'd responded with a softness in her voice as if she was giving me a guarantee, as if she felt she had to promise to be careful because I had asked her to, not for any reason of her own.

"In the mean time, I…" I almost told her I needed to talk to Mary Grace, to tell her about the possibility of our being cousins…I still saw no purpose in mentioning that to Anna, until it was necessary, if ever.

"When I get home, I need to talk to my mother more about what she remembers, to help me figure this out."

"You mean about who your father is? A woman will know."

"What do you mean?" I asked.

"Your mother says your father died in Vietnam, right?"

I nodded. "Yeah."

"But you say Maximilian's investigations indicate this man Berger is your father. You don't think your mother knows this?"

"How would she know?"

Anna grunted her disdain. "You are a fool. I don't even have children and I understand that a woman would know. You are so naïve, Charles."

What an odd situation. First, a girl I only met a few days ago knows intimacies my near-fiancé doesn't yet know, and second, a man my age has to go to his mother to discuss an issue which may determine whether I can marry a girl I'm…supposed to be in love with. And why does my brain now say, 'supposed to be', instead of, 'am in love with'?

I stopped walking and looked at Anna, up at her, something that still seemed awkward. I might have to start wearing inserts in my shoes to make me taller.

"Anna…is it really Anna? And your last name, you haven't told me."

"Yes, it's Anna. I use aliases, like Lisl Meagher, so I am no easily identified as related to my father, because of the business he in. After I finish my assignment for Maximilian I will be staying at my father's apartment in Paris. Will you send me a message telling me what happens?"

"Of course. I have to practice what you taught me."

"If you like. I will be going to my father's apartment in Pari to stay so you can e-mail me there. That'll be simpler."

"But not as much fun. I want to practice being a secret agent."

"You're silly," she said, but pleasantly.

"You must write first and tell me what you learn from your mother, and I'll tell you if I find out anything from Berger. And the maybe, I'll tell you my last name and my address in Europe."

"Why can't you tell me now?"

She shook her head to indicate I was an idiot. "Mary Grace in love with you. You were in love with her, too, before you came Europe. Now you aren't sure, because you met me. If you marry he we will never see each other again, so you don't need to know my name. You are using this issue about the man Berger to stall your relationship with Mary Grace. As I said before, there's something you're not telling me, and until you are completely honest with me, we can go nowhere."

She checked in while I waited aside, a bit stunned. There wasn't much time and not much more to say, and too much more to say. We found a corner away from foot traffic and said good-bye with a kiss that sent sparks down my spine. We must have been an odd couple to anyone who saw us, with the woman bending to kiss the man. But I didn't care.

Driving back in traffic so hectic it made me wish I'd left the car and taken a cab back, I promised I would try *not* to think about Anna for the next few days and see if the infatuation, if that's what it was, wore off.

So what do I tell Mary Grace? One, I could tell her nothing, that is, leave out the part about Berger and make up some story about why I went to Europe. Forget Berger, and marry Mary Grace and live happily ever after. Max wouldn't sell me out.

Or, tell her why I went and that I was convinced Berger wasn't my father and we were okay. Marry her and live happily ever after. Leave out the part about how her grandfathers died in Idaho.

Three, tell her the whole story, honestly (other than certain details about Anna, obviously), and go talk to my mother. Also, wait to see what, if anything, Anna finds out if she talks to Berger. When it comes down to it, if Mary Grace and I are cousins, it's over. I'll have to leave the firm, go away, forget Mary Grace and forget the cozy foursome she and I had enjoyed with her sister and Max.

My brain was drained. It wanted to be with Anna, seeing her board the plane, seeing her take a seat, settling in, but I shook it off. I turned on the radio and listened to whatever came on. I slammed on the brakes as the car in front of me suddenly stopped. It was almost noon and I told Mary Grace I'd meet her at 12:30 for lunch. Despite having been shot at and thrown against an eight hundred year old stonewall, cruising down the Rhone sounded quite attractive right now.

INTERLUDE: GINA

When giggling among themselves Gina and the other girls a
talked about the chance they'd have a sizzling romance in Europe,
maybe with a debonair Frenchman or a bold Italian. But realistically
they didn't expect anything of the sort, and when they arrived in
London they huddled together like newborn chicks and it was
museums and art galleries, shows and restaurants that drew their
interests.

Mainly the girls intended to visit London and Paris, Florence
and Rome. They didn't expect to have time for much more. Maybe
some side trips, like to Versailles, or Stratford-on Avon or Chartres,
if there was time. Gina wanted to go to Salzburg to the birthplace of
Mozart. Julie agreed to go with her because no one else wanted to
go.

Miraculously, just what they had laughed off as only a
fantasy did happen, and soon Gina was spending her afternoons and
evenings with the handsome and worldly German, Wilhelm Berger.
To be honest, Gina admitted to herself, he wasn't dashing and awe-
inspiring in his looks, somewhat crude, even, but he was fun and
generous and knew his way around the city. Julie hung around the
first few days, but when Gina began to spend her nights at
Wilhelm's hotel, Julie decided to leave and catch up with the others
Gina promised to meet them all in Paris in ten days.

It was a whirlwind adventure. Wilhelm had to go to work
very early so Gina got into the bad habit of sleeping late. She'd

spend the late morning walking about the town and shopping for gifts and souvenirs. She visited the Hagenauer House, where Mozart was born in 1756, which now houses a museum, and the Marionette Museum, and various other tourist sites. By a little past two in the afternoon Wilhelm was done working and they would go to a café, usually sitting outdoors in the perfect late summer weather, and pass an hour or more talking about each other's lives. Gina's favorite café was the Café Tomaselli, established in 1703 and where Mozart himself would go to drink coffee. Gina did most of the talking, as Wilhelm always managed to avoid giving out much personal information.

Soon they were spending the rest of the afternoon in Wilhelm's hotel room, and then would go out in the evening, to a Mozart concert, or an art show, then a late dinner and maybe another concert or a walk through a park or a enjoy a late-night cordial or dessert wine in one of the city squares. No cars were allowed in the squares and the sound of people leisurely strolling over the red brick pavement provided a pleasant background for friends and lovers who didn't want to let the night end. Eventually they would return to Wilhelm's hotel. Gina couldn't understand how her new beau could party so long and hard, sleep three or four hours, and be up before dawn to go back to his construction job. I'll sleep when I'm dead, he would say.

Gina reluctantly left Wilhelm to meet up with her friends, lest they worry about her. When she returned to Salzburg two weeks later Wilhelm was nowhere to be found. He did not meet her, as planned, at the café where they had first met, nor any of the other cafes or city squares where they had wiled away the hours. He was not at the hotel, and when she visited the construction site where he'd been working, she was told the job was complete and the workers had all gone back to Germany.

Gina had a picture of Wilhelm and showed it at the hotel. Yes, he was here, with you, madam, but he checked out over a week ago. I believe he returned to Berlin. She briefly contemplated going to Berlin but realized the foolishness of chasing a man who had probably already forgotten her name.

She went to Rome to meet up with her friends, now on the last days of the trip. There she told them that after two days together she realized that the background and cultural differences were beyond reconciling, so she and Wilhelm had accepted that their summer had been fun, and say adieu, and nothing more. Already Gina was feeling different in a way she could not describe but which she sensed was unique. She thought she had been careful, but what if Wilhelm had gotten her pregnant?

Gina was clearly carrying long before she managed to finish the semester. She only needed two more classes to graduate but had to defer to have her baby. She did not want to say she became pregnant by a stranger in a foreign land, who had no interest in her, so first she hinted and then, after word came that Charlie had died in Vietnam, claimed that he was the father, their one night together, just before the European trip. Everyone knew Charlie had been sweet on Gina, so it wasn't hard to believe.

The next several years were difficult. Gina had no relatives to help her with the baby, so she had to pay for daily baby sitters while she went to work. Several of her college friends adored the baby and helped as much as they could so Gina could work a part time job two or three evenings a week. Sometimes she felt she hardly knew her son, they had so little time together.

And of course the boy had no father figure to do the things males did together: play ball, go fishing, fly a kite. As Gina's friends married they soon became involved more and more with their own families and Gina and young Charles began to feel alone in the world. Kids teased Charles because he had no father, or teased him that his mother had dozens of boyfriends, and that's why she was seldom home. This was definitely untrue. Gina didn't even go on a date for five or six years after Charles was born, and even those occasions were rare. It wasn't that she didn't like men, she was just always tired. A date would take her to the movies, and she'd fall asleep.

But through perseverance they managed, and Gina finished her degree requirements and got a job as a legal assistant, which paid her enough money so she could began to save for a house and for Charles' education. She could quit working her part time job and have more time with her son. By then, however, Charles was older and going out with his high school friends to ball games or movies. He dated, Gina knew, but rarely did he date anyone more than once or twice.

So still alone, Gina began to drink in the evenings while she watched television. She'd been out of the regular dating circle for so long she didn't even know where to meet eligible men. Sometimes she'd think about Wilhelm, her one real romance, and sometimes she'd think about Charlie, the poor boy who died without making love to the girl he chased after so fervently. Or had he? At times, usually when she had had too much to drink and her brain was fuzzy, she'd think back to the night with Charlie and wonder, did we or didn't we make love? Surely I would have remembered, but maybe my mind has tucked it away because we were drunk and it was no way to lose one's virginity. Maybe Charlie is Charles' father. Sometimes she'd fall asleep in her chair in front of the television and awaken when her son came home, or the clock struck twelve times.

More than once she tried to tell Charles that his father was a German she'd only known a short while. But the lie she'd built was too strong to knock down. She waited for Charles to ask more about his father, thinking then she would tell him, but as he got older he never asked anymore.

Three good things happened a few years later. Gina was able to buy a small house, Charles graduated from college, and Gina met a man named Tom, who she began to date regularly. When they became intimate, she said, it was like falling off a bike. What? Tom asked; never mind, Gina replied.

She tempered her drinking, shifting to wine instead of hard liquor, and began to enjoy a social life for the first time in two decades. The relationship did not lead to marriage; after living independently for so long she couldn't bring herself to commit. Her friend Tom was okay with that for several years, but eventually a job took him away. He asked Gina to marry him and move with him, but no, she was too ensconced in her life patterns to make a major change. She had friends at work, mostly divorcées, with whom she could go to movies or concerts, and after Tom she dated casually, not eliminating the possibility of marriage, but accepting that she no longer felt the need.

Gina's life wasn't particularly exciting, but it was a calm, relaxed one, and now that she had managed to raise Charles to the point where he was on his own, she was at peace with the way her life had gone. If the days were often mundane, she felt a serenity in her cozy home, a satisfying job, a small circle of cherished friends, and a son who despite the chip he still carried on his shoulder, the result, she surmised, of never having had male bonding with a father, was a good man, with a good job, and who maybe, she prayed, would one day make her a grandmother.

Since most days rolled over from one to another without much differentiation, two days did stand out for Gina, two eerie days that she had never been able to reconcile in her mind.

Gina came home one Friday evening, after having stopped with some co-workers for pizza and beer, to her dark house, looking forward to a long, hot bath, and then a couple hours of sitting quietly with a good book and listening to soft classical music.

When she came into the house, through the back entrance that opened to the kitchen, something was odd. There was a scent, or an aura, a movement in the air. At first she thought, gas? —but no, definitely not gas.

When a person lives alone for a long time, and seldom has visitors, the slightest change may be noted and seems to be as consequential as if someone had come in and moved all the furniture around or painted the walls. It doesn't smell right, the temperature isn't right, the air isn't as fresh…something is awry.

Gina feared someone was in the house. But why, she had nothing of value. Even if a burglar had broken in he would not have found anything worth stealing and would have left. So maybe that was it; someone had been in the house. Not Charles; he would not cause a disturbance that would knock Gina's senses off balance. A stranger.

She flicked on the light switch, and then walked slowly into the next room and turned on a lamp. Nothing seemed to have been disturbed. She stood at the end of the hallway that led to the two bedrooms and the bathroom. Gina never thought of herself as particularly brave, but she also didn't frighten easily. She lifted one leg and took off her shoe, then the other one. She crept back into the kitchen and took a knife out of the butcher's block.

Gina walked slowly down the hallway in her stocking feet. The first door was to the bedroom Charles used if he stayed over, and which otherwise Gina used for sewing, ironing, or storing things she didn't know what to do with. Holding the butcher knife in front of her she turned the knob on the door slowly, then pushed the door open quickly, involuntarily stepping back as she did. Nothing happened. She reached inside the room to turn on the light and looked in; normal.

She did the same with the bathroom door, and then walked to the end of the hall where her bedroom was situated. This door was open, as she had left it. Again she reached around the doorframe to switch on the light. Again, everything looked normal, but the sense of disturbance was stronger here than anywhere else. Someone, she was sure, had been in here.

There was little to check. She had a jewelry box but it only contained cheap costume items, trinkets and earrings. She could never afford expensive jewelry and the most valuable piece she owned was the watch she wore, a gift from Tom. Perplexed, Gina stood in the room and surveyed it from corner to corner, up and down. She went into the closet, too small, which is why some of her clothes were now in the closet in the other bedroom. She even checked the drawer where she kept her underwear, thinking some weirdo broke in to get his kicks playing with panties and bras. Before she opened the drawer she knew that if they were disturbed she'd burn every item. But nothing was out of place. She could call the police, but they'd probably laugh at her for saying she had a bad feeling, when nothing was missing, nothing was moved.

Gina finally relaxed, but her evening was spoiled. She didn't feel like lounging in the tub and she didn't feel like washing her hair. She called Charles, but he didn't answer. She went back into the kitchen and opened a bottle of wine, then went into the living room and turned on the television. She didn't even feel like reading or listening to music. When she began to get sleepy she didn't want to go into her bedroom, so she pulled an afghan around her and fell asleep in the chair, the television playing a black and white 1940s movie.

In the morning the sun shone brightly and Gina was refreshed and felt a tad silly about the previous night. The sense of disturbance had dissipated and she wondered if she had imagined something that hadn't been there. Why though, it's not as if I'd been drinking hard liquor?

Saturday was a fine day. She had errands to run, to the grocery store, the cleaners, the bank. In the afternoon she treated herself to a movie and lunch. She came home late afternoon when the sun was low and a faint breeze left a chill as it passed.

When Gina entered it was the same as the previous night. Now she was scared. Anybody here, she called out. Charles? She called her son from the kitchen telephone extension. This time he answered. Were you here, Charles? No, Mom, why do you ask? I don't know, something feels funny, like someone has been in here. Wait outside, I'll be right there.

Charles lived a half hour away and Gina did not want to stand outside her own house for half hour feeling foolish. She did as she had the night before, except she walked quickly and loudly down the hallway, carrying the knife in front of her.

She went directly to her bedroom and again scanned the room, looking at every item there, from the pictures on the wall to the tacky model of the Eiffel Tower she had purchased in Europe on her one and only visit across the Atlantic. Then she went to her jewelry box. Last night she had opened it and saw that the few pieces she owned were still there, as she expected. Nothing very valuable. This time she looked closer. Again, nothing unusual.

She pulled up the top section knowing what she would see underneath. It was the picture Wilhelm had given her with his less than romantic note written on the back. She'd never shown the picture to anyone. It was there, but it'd been moved. It should have set in the middle of the box, but it had been moved. Okay, I could have moved it slightly just now, couldn't I?

Why the next thought occurred to her she could never explain. She went into the closet and got down on her knees to reach into the far corner. There set a shoebox. She hadn't looked inside in years, but she knew the top lid should fit on tightly. But it was slightly askew. She stretched for the box and pulled it to her. Still kneeling on the floor Gina opened the box. Inside she pulled out a small book, the word 'Travel Notes' stamped on the cover. Not much of a travel record, Gina mused. My weeks in Europe in 1969. She'd never added anything more.

She opened the book and began to read. She read about visits to the British Museum; to see 'The Mousetrap', the original 'the butler did it' play, which then had been playing daily for over fifteen years, and by now, over thirty-five years; to the Louvre and Versailles. Gina then skipped ahead, to Austria. There she read about visits to the coffee shops of Salzburg, to the Wasserspiele Hellbrunn Park and Fountains, where she and Wilhelm got wet, like most of the visitors, and to the Mirabell Palace and Gardens, where the von Trapp children had sung 'Do-Re-Mi' in *The Sound of Music.*

Gina shivered as she read her words, words gushing about her romance with Wilhelm, how delightful he was, how urbane and even tender, a term Gina now realized was an exaggeration on her part. Not that he was callous, but he wasn't sophisticated, as she remembered back, and he had displayed a tendency towards a temper. Some of what she read sounded silly in the shadow of thirty plus years. Still, it was fun to read the words of a naïve, young, eager girl, the girl that she had been then.

And why—who—how, would someone have disturbed these items, the photograph and the diary? Had it been Wilhelm, after all these years, wanting to reconnect, or find out about his son? Did he know he had a son? Or I'm I wrong in seeing something that's only in my imagination?

She heard a car and realized it was Charles. He didn't want him to see the book. She put it back into the box, shut it tightly and shoved it into the corner where it would lay again, undisturbed until sometime when she had the yen to look again. Probably should destroy it so Charles doesn't come across it later, after I'm gone.

Gina convinced Charles her imagination was running wild, and after he left she began to clean the house. She scrubbed walls, she moved furniture and vacuumed everywhere, got on a step stool and dusted the corner of the ceilings, even took all her clothes out of her closet and cleaned there with especial vigor.

After a few weeks the memory dimmed and she never thought about the incident since then until the day Charles and Mary Grace came to see her, shortly after Charles returned from his own trip to Europe, on business for Maximilian.

FIFTEEN: Family Ties

"Oh, Charles, this is insane. We can't possibly be cousins!"

"Shh! We don't need everyone on the plane to hear us."

"They won't, there's hardly anyone around us."

We were flying first class, courtesy of Maximilian. Except for fighting the traffic to get to the airport, standing in line to check in, standing in a longer lines so you can take off your shoes, belt, sweater, jacket, empty your pockets of everything including lint, running back to get your belt after you left it on the conveyor, than waiting again for the plane to show up, first class almost made flying worthwhile.

"Why can't we be?"

"It's just...aren't there some rules about that?"

"About being cousins? It's very easy."

"Don't try to be cute. I mean, what we've done. You know, more than a little kissin'."

"That's the point, MG. If we're first cousins we shouldn't..."

"Even if we love each other? And we didn't know we were related?"

"MG, I'm not even sure the law would allow us to marry."

"So, we can just live together."

"You don't mean that, do you?"

"I can't believe you're that old-fashioned, Charles."

"I don't mean the part about living together. I mean ignoring our...our kinship. It's supposed to be dangerous to have children when you're so closely related."

"Hmm. Yes, I know. I guess we'd have to forego children."

"What would your sister say?"

"We don't have to tell her, do we?"

"Max will know. You can't expect him to keep a secret from his wife."

"It's not like we're *full* cousins; we don't have the same grandmother."

I didn't reply.

I heard a impatient sigh come from Mary Grace, never a good sign. "I'm just trying to think of our options. Are you eager to get out of it, dear?"

"What? Get out of what?"

"Marrying me."

"Geez, MG, I'm sorry, right now, I don't know what to think. Believe me, one of the options I considered was not telling you anything about Berger. Just forget it and pretend I never heard of him. But I can't forget him. And if I didn't tell you, and we had children, and they were, somehow, what, tainted, deformed…uh, I'd never forgive myself."

The stewardess appeared with meals so we shut up and began to pick at our food. I don't think either one of us was interested but was something to do other than continue the conversation. We could go round and round until we landed in Los Angeles, and continue the argument until southern California had solved its traffic problem, and nothing would be settled. I had to talk to my mother, pin her down as to exactly what she knows, or remembers.

I'd called her, told her I was in New York on business and wanted to see her as soon as I got back. I told her I was bringing

Mary Grace with me and she offered to fix dinner. I readily agreed because the conversation we were going to have wasn't fit to be spewed out in public. I think Mom thought Mary Grace and I were going to announce a wedding date and I felt bad that I hadn't discouraged her of that assumption.

"Mary Grace, it's so good to see you! It's been weeks." The women hugged and I thought Mary Grace gave Mom an extra special squeeze.

"Been busy, Gina, so has Charles."

"What were you doing in New York, Charles? Something for Maximilian?"

"More than New York, Mom. I was in Europe, too."

"Oh, really? I didn't know that." Her response was shaded with a tinge of caution, or so I interpreted.

I had finally explained to Mary Grace about the river cruise, about talking to Berger, about the man taking a shot at me at the truffle farm, about almost being tossed over the wall in Viviers and being saved by Anna, and finally, I had to hem and haw and lie when Mary Grace persisted in asking more about Anna. I saw no good coming from admitting what had happened. It would hurt her and for no good purpose.

"Where in Europe? Did you go too, Mary Grace?"

"No, Gina, I didn't go, and I'm still a little peeved."

"It was business."

"All of it?" Mary Grace asked.

I rolled my eyes and shook my head. We'd been over this and now she was bringing it up again to get my mother on her side.

"A river cruise?" mother exclaimed, after I returned with a bottle of wine and an opener. "And you didn't take Mary Grace?"

I went back to the kitchen for glasses. "And you didn't take your mother?" I could hear her calling out.

"Oh, man, this sucks," I mumbled.

I spent the next fifteen minutes steering the conversation away from my trip. I didn't want to spoil dinner. I was stalling. Mary Grace kept giving me the eye but at least she acknowledged that it was best to enjoy dinner first before I accused my mother of misleading me all my life.

Dinner done, the table cleaned, the dishes in the washer, one more glass of wine poured, and we sat down, sighs all around.

"I hope you enjoyed it," Gina said. "I don't get to cook for anyone very often."

"No friends coming over?" I asked.

"Yes, but no one special," Mom said.

"Not since Tom?"

Mom ignored my comment and said, with smiles and glee, "Now, Charles, tell me why you're really here."

"It's not what you think, Mom."

It took several fumbled starts but finally I began to tell the story of Max's search for his stepbrother and how it led to him believing he and I were related. I gave the edited version. I left out the part about the deaths of Mary Grace's grandfathers and almost everything about Anna (except Mary Grace kept interrupting to mention how tall, blonde, and lovely she was). Even then it took me forty minutes to tell.

"How can this be?" Mom asked. "It's not possible, is it?"

Her denial wasn't convincing. She leaned back in her chair and her mind went somewhere. Her eyes averted me, averted anything, everything that was real, as they focused on a faraway past.

"Mom?"

"Gina?" Mary Grace said.

"Oh? Yes, hmm, I ah, was thinking of something."

"Like what, Mom? Like the man you met in Austria, the year before I was born?"

I thought she would be thunderstruck but instead she was calm and even smiled wryly, as if she'd been caught with her hand in the cookie jar an hour before dinner.

"Charles, when said you'd been to Europe, not just New York, I felt this ripple in my stomach. Something, maybe a little ESP there, but I wondered if you'd finally made the connection."

"Gina, do you understand what this might mean for Charles and me?"

Now she was confused. "No, I guess I'm not getting everything. Go back, Charles, and tell me how this came about."

"I may need another drink."

I let Mary Grace explain while I went to get Mom a glass of water, but before she could finish both women were crying.

"Oh, my," Gina whimpered.

"Mom, I...I know this isn't something a son should ask his mother about but, are you sure the man in Austria, Wilhelm, is my father?"

Her head bobbed around as if she couldn't decide to nod 'yes' or shake, 'no'. "Who else?" she said, so soft we hardly heard her.

I went to Mary Grace and held her. Instead of her settling down now all three of us were tearing up.

"Excuse me for a minute," Mary Grace said. She wiped her nose with a tissue and then went into the bathroom.

"Where did all this about my father dying in Vietnam come from?"

"You're right, Charles, this isn't a topic we should be talking about now; we—I, should have talked about it years ago."

I waited, not wanting to push her to where she changed her mind and waved off the issue. But she couldn't any more; neither Mary Grace nor I could let this go.

A sniffle, a sip of water, and she began.

"In the summer of 1969, a few weeks before school would start again, a group of us who had become friends in college decided to go to Europe. Sort of our way of sowing wild oats, if you will."

"I thought only guys did that."

"Oh, we weren't planning any wild times, mostly museums and art galleries, a play in London and the Louvre, of course. There was this guy I knew in college, Charlie. He had dropped out, but he still came around. He was infatuated with me, I guess, and I did go out with him, but he was a teenage boy, so you know what he wanted."

I blushed, "You don't have to give me all the details, Mom."

Mary Grace had returned and she sat down next to Gina and gave her a hug. Gina patted Mary Grace on the hand.

"Charlie must have known what was going to happen when he dropped out of college, and sure enough, he was drafted. People nowadays forget that men used to be drafted into the Army, Charles."

"Yeah, Mom, we've got it soft these days."

"Don't be sassy, you all have it too easy. Anyway, Charlie tried again with me, just before I went to Europe, but we'd been drinking a lot and soon his advances became comical. I felt sorry for him.

"The next day he called me, all apologetic. He wanted to see me one more time. But I couldn't. The other girls and I were packing and were going to spend the night at a motel near the airport, so we wouldn't have to rush frantically in the morning.

"I never saw Charlie again."

"Vietnam?"

Gina nodded.

"So he wasn't my father?"

Mom shook her head. "No, not unless he could wish me pregnant."

"So that's where the story comes from? You made it up based on Charlie?" I tried hard to keep my anger down and my voice calm. I knew I wasn't doing a good job by the look Mary Grace gave me.

"When we were in Europe all the girls wanted to see London and Paris, Florence, Rome, Versailles if there was time. I wanted to gad around a bit, see some other places. I figured I might never get this chance again. I was quite the tomboy growing up, so I tended to do things that guys liked to do.

"My friends were insistent I couldn't go on my own so a girl named Julie, who I wasn't particularly close to, agreed to go with me. We took off and promised to meet everyone in Paris in two weeks. We went to Munich and then to Salzburg. I wanted to see the birthplace of Mozart and there was still time to catch a few performances of the summer Music Festival."

"I remember you used to listen to classical music on the radio. I thought it was boring then."

"So one sunny morning Julie and I are sitting at a table outside a café, having coffee, when this nice young man starts talking to us. I think he tried German and French and when we looked at him in confusion he tried English. Julie was frantically paging through her English-German dictionary but the man wasn't paying any attention to her. For some reason he was attracted to me. He knew enough English to start a conversation. He wasn't extremely handsome, but he was pleasant, and I think I was in a susceptible mood."

"And you're sure his name was Wilhelm Berger?"

Mom looked at me first as if I was a dunce, then with sadness. "Of course I'm sure, Charles. As you said, I don't need to give you all the details, but in no time at all I was in love."

Gina looked down at her hands and her eyes began to tear up

"At least, I thought I was. Probably not really; I hardly knew him, but we had fun and I guess I was ready. If Charlie hadn't gotten drunk, I would have been ready for him.

"Julie wasn't happy with me because I wanted to spend all my time with Wilhelm. The afternoons and evenings anyway. He worked from early in the morning until mid-afternoon. I don't know where he got his energy because for the two weeks I was with him we were always up very late."

Gina stopped and her eyes flitted toward Charles. She blushed.

"Julie tired of being the extra wheel and left to meet the others and I promised I'd follow in a week. The week went by like a blip and I told Wilhelm I'd come back to see him before returning to the States, even if I was late for the start of school. Wilhelm promised to meet me, at the café where we'd first met, but he wasn't there when I returned. I went to all the places we had visited, the cafes and shops, and of course his hotel. I didn't want to believe he'd forgotten me so quickly but after a few days I woke up and realized it had been a fling for him, no more, and why should it have been more? I was the one being foolish. So I went home."

"And found out you were pregnant," Mary Grace said. Mom nodded.

"And felt foolish telling people it was a man you barely knew."

Mom shrugged, started to say something, but instead just nodded again.

"I hid it for awhile and when I couldn't anymore I hinted that it had been Charlie, because he was the only guy I'd dated recently, and everybody knew he was sweet on me, so it was believable. I had no idea what I was going to say when Charlie heard. I imagined he would be the gentleman and marry me anyway and be a father to the child."

"But Charlie never came home, did he?" Mary Grace added.

Mom shook her head. "Poor dear. He got killed ten days after arriving in Vietnam. And everybody cried for me and I went along with my story and pretty soon it became real. And I didn't have any pictures of him, Charles. I'm sorry. The longer I held onto the story the more real it became. I figured someday you'd come to me and ask for the real story, but you didn't. Why didn't you?"

"I think because I knew it wasn't true and I feared there might be a story you would find embarrassing to tell me."

"Yes, and you were right."

"No, no I wasn't. There's nothing embarrassing about your story."

"How can you be sure this is the same man who is Max's stepbrother?"

I thought I'd covered that but I went over it again. For all our sakes I needed to, but like a train coming into the tunnel with no place to hide from it, we all saw the headlight bearing down on us.

"We'll go to Germany and see him," Gina said.

"Huh? What, Mom?"

"You heard me. This is important…can there be anything more important to you and Mary Grace now, than knowing the truth?"

"I…" I didn't want to seem eager to accept what appeared to be the truth, but I felt by now I knew what the truth was.

"Yes," chimed in Mary Grace. "We'll go see him and find out for sure."

"Even after all these years I think I'd recognize him," Gina said.

"You said he didn't look like you, Charles. Isn't that enough?" Mary Grace asked, forgetting, deliberately, I'm sure, that Anna had said she thought there was a resemblance.

I shrugged with my hands. "Maybe; it's not easy to see yourself in another person. I was looking at him with an eye to see what I wanted to see—or not want to see. The problem is he told Max he would be moving somewhere new, neither Berlin nor Lyon. I don't know how much time we have. Max's agent is supposed to see him and I asked, ah… the agent to talk to him, see if he'd say anything more than what he told me. I should hear soon."

A scowl from Mary Grace.

"I have pictures. The…agent Max hired took some."

I avoided looking at Mary Grace; the mere mention of Max's agent—Anna—was a topic neither of us wanted to bring to the surface.

Like a magician pulling an endless scarf out of his pocket, I reached into the pocket of my jacket, which I'd hung on the back of chair, and pulled out the pictures of Wilhelm Berger that Anna had given me.

"Oh, you brought the pictures," Mary Grace said, the 'oh' sounding like an accusation, as if I would have destroyed the pictures had I really loved her. I handed them to Mom.

She looked at them without speaking for a good half-minute, from one to the other. I wondered what struggles were going on in her mind. I know she was rooting for Mary Grace and I to be happy together, to get married, maybe give her a grandchild or two. But at the same time, I think deep down she was wondering if it was possible to see Wilhelm again. I'm sure she was totally ignorant of what Wilhelm's life had been like, and I hadn't filled in all the gory details. Which I would if she insisted she wanted to see him. But if tried to stop her, I'm sure Mary Grace would have assumed I was trying to escape from her.

"Hmm. Well, it's hard to tell. The pictures aren't very clear.

I think she was fibbing, or at least, not seeing what she didn want to see.

"It's a worth a try, isn't it, Charles?" Mary Grace said. She sounded desperate and I felt like a heel.

"What? To try to find him?"

She nodded.

I felt sure it'd be too late by the time we got to Europe, but I couldn't say so.

"Yes, of course. We need to go immediately."

"Even if…the agent says Berger is your father, you can't just accept that, can you? The agent might have selfish reasons for doin so."

So there it was. Mom wasn't quite getting everything Mary Grace and I said, but her face indicated she sensed a tug-or-war going on. I think it was then that I made my decision, and it didn't matter if we found Berger or not, though I would do everything possible to find him if Mary Grace persisted.

There wasn't much to say as I drove Mary Grace home, but she kept gabbing anyway. She was all excited about going to Europ and confronting Berger. I think she knew she was spitting into the wind but needed to continue yakking to keep her hopes up. Yes, I agreed, I would take care of tickets in the morning and get us on the first possible flight.

But I knew—I really knew, it was a waste of time. Wilhelm Berger was my father, Mary Grace was my cousin, and Berger would be long gone anyway.

I dropped Mary Grace off, went home, and found a message from Max. He said Anna had called him and that she would call again at his office tomorrow morning at eleven and she wanted to talk to me.

About? I asked. She didn't say, Max replied, but she said she had confirmed as best as possible that Berger had no more documents related to the identity of Max's father, and that he had disappeared.

I told him about my evening and that Mary Grace and Gina want to go to Europe to meet Berger. It's hopeless, I believe, Max said. Anna had reported that Berger had sold the houses in Berlin and Lyon and she doesn't know where he went.

In the morning Mary Grace called early to remind me about the plane tickets. I had already checked the schedule and found that the earliest we could get a flight was late afternoon, but I didn't book it. I went to Max's office and waited for Anna's call. In the mean time Max filled me in on what she already told him.

"Anna caught up with him in Berlin. She followed him to a bank where he went into the safe deposit area. She then followed him to his house and he gave her what he swore was the last remaining set of the papers and she destroyed them. Berger insisted there were no more copies. Of course, he told me the same thing when we met in New York. He's not a trustworthy man. Anna said it was fairly easy to get back into the house later, when Berger was gone, and search it. She did not find anything else along the lines I had briefed her on. She talked to him, about things she will tell you.

"Anna continued to keep an eye on Berger and followed him to Lyon. When she realized where he was going she got ahead of him and searched that house, too. Again, she found nothing so I feel confident the issue is done with. She also confirmed that Berger had sold both of the houses."

"Where did he go then?"

"She saw a woman pick him up in a car."

"The Conover woman?"

"I believe Anna said that was the name the woman had used on the river cruise."

"And where did they go? Did she follow them?"

"She tried. They drove out of the city, headed, it seemed, towards Paris. They stopped at a restaurant on the outskirts of Lyon. Anna waited outside, lest they spot her if she went inside. She waited two hours. Their car never moved and finally she decided to go into the restaurant. They were nowhere to be found."

I chuckled.

"Funny, you think?" said Max.

"No, Max, but Anna said she was going to give up the detective game. She said she didn't think she was good enough at it.

"I don't think she was following him for me anymore, Charles, but for you."

The phone rang.

"Anna?"

"Yes…how are you?"

"Fine. I hear you talked to Berger."

"Yes. He didn't seem as unfriendly to me as you had indicated he was when you spoke to him."

"I'm sure a pretty face helped to ease the venom in his tongue."

"Maybe. He told me about your dilemma."

"Ah, so now you know."

"Yes. I'm sorry for you, Charles."

"Don't be sorry. It's better that I know…that we know."

"What will you do now?"

"What exactly did he tell you?"

"That he knows you're his son."

"Is he positive?"

"He said it wasn't too difficult to determine. He came to the United States about ten years ago. Gina Hardin still lived in the same area as the address she had given Wilhelm when she knew him in Austria, so it was fairly easy to find her. He never contacted her, he says, but he followed her, and made inquiries. He learned about you."

"He wasn't interested in meeting with her, my mother, or me?"

"No, he said it was unfortunate what had happened, but that he wasn't in love with your mother and never expected her to return to Austria. He said it appeared that both she and you had made good lives for yourself and he saw no reason to inject himself at this point, after all the years that had passed."

"Hmm. Probably the best thing. So he moved on?"

"Maximilian told you I lost him again. It's a good thing I'm done working for him, before he fires me."

"You did fine."

"So what will you do…no, never mind, it's not my place to ask."

"What would you like me to do?"

"That's not fair, Charles. You have to decide this for yourself."

The decision had been made; it'd been made last night. No, it had simmered since way back when Max first spoke to me in the restaurant about Wilhelm Berger. Certainly it never dawned on me that I might be related to Max, and/or Mary Grace and Mary Jo, but knew as soon as he became so mysterious in his presentation it was leading up to something momentous.

That Max's investigations would lead to my father was one thing, that they would lead to Anna was another. If Berger wasn't my father Anna would still be an element I would not be able to disregard. It would make it a lot more difficult to explain to Mary Grace, is all.

"Where are you?" I asked.

"At my father's apartment in Paris."

"Will you stay there?"

"Yes, until I hear from you, or don't hear."

"I'll send you my flight information as soon as I get scheduled."

Off to the side I could see Max's head rise up, his eyebrows arched and his tongue running across his lips, stifling a comment.

"Altmann," Anna said.

"What?"

"My last name."

"Nice to meet you, Anna Altmann."

"Nice to meet you, Charles Oliver Hardin."

"I'll call when I have flight details."

Anna gave me her phone number, and a moment later we hung up, endearments hanging in the wind and stuck somewhere in the wires or cables or satellite beacons or whatever it is that sends voices across the seas and through thousands of miles of air. I stood by Max's desk looking down at the telephone. Max sat on the couch, leaning forward, his hands placed on his knees.

"Well," he said as he patted his knees. "Why am I not surprised?"

"Aren't you?"

"No. I also wouldn't be surprised if you come back in a year or so, crawling back to Mary Grace. But I guess it's something you have to do, isn't it?"

"I guess so. You mad at me?"

He didn't say anything but after a few seconds he shook his head. "No, but I feel for Mary Grace. I know she can be…well, I'm married to her sister. Neither one is perfect, but then, are we, Charles?"

"Far from it."

"Will you talk to Mary Grace before you leave? Don't be a bastard, Charles."

I nodded. "Yes, no more running out without saying goodbye. I think she knows it's over. She understands and this idea of going to Europe to confront Berger, it's my mother reliving a fantasy. I'll set Mom straight and have her come to Europe to meet Anna in a few weeks."

"It doesn't seem fair to Mary Grace, Charles."

"No, it isn't Max, it sure isn't."

"You know I have an office in Paris, Charles."

"Thanks, Max, I'll let you know."

"An early lunch?" Max asked.

"How about I meet you later? I need to call Mary Grace now."

***

CAST OF CHARACTERS

Charles Oliver Hardin—vice president of market research in a real estate firm owned by Maximilian von der Dusenberger

Gina Hardin—Charles' mother

Maximilian von der Dusenberger—wealthy real estate magnate

Wolfgang von der Dusenberger—Colonel in German Army during WWII; Maximilian's father.

Ruth von der Dusenberger—Wolfgang's wife and Maximilian's mother

Wilhelm Berger—Maximilian's stepbrother

Mary Grace Wolfe— Charles' girl friend and sister to Mary Jo

Mary Jo Wolfe—Max's wife, Mary Grace's sister

Anna (Lisl Meager)—European detective hired by Maximilian to track down Wilhelm Berger

Joseph & Mimi Conover—acquaintances of Wilhelm Berger

Lt. William Wolfe—American soldier who befriends Ruth at end of WWII; grandfather of the Wolfe sisters

Sgt. John Schneider—friend of Lt. Wolfe

About the Author:

E. R. (Gene) Wytrykus retired after over three decades as an auditor, and took up creative writing as a retirement hobby. He has self-published, through Wheat Field Publications, a book of short stories, a combination of fiction and non-fiction, entitled "*By The Short Hairs*", and several novels: "*The King of Coins*", which used Gene's interest in numismatics and an incident during his years as an auditor, to form the basis of this story of international intrigue; "*The Money Run*", which used Gene's job with the Army in Vietnam in the late 60s as the basis for this mystery (Gene has also written a screenplay adaptation of "The Money Run"); "*A Stone to Roll*", a story of three people who are drawn into each other's lives at a time when all are going through personal crises; "*A Road of Your Own*", the sequel; "*The Girls of His Dreams*", the time-travel mystery of a grieving man whose dreams back in time present him with the possibility of saving his fiancé, who was killed in a bizarre robbery; "*The 9th Inning*", a dramatic novella focused on the last batter in a championship baseball game, (the book also includes three short stories); and "*Family Ties*", in which two friends of different generations find that their searches for their fathers may tie them closer together than they had anticipated. Gene lives in Lincoln, CA. with his wife who is a published author in the field of bariatrics and dietary issues.

www.ingramcontent.com/pod-product-compliance
Lightning Source LLC
Chambersburg PA
CBHW020341180626
46812CB00001B/291